*Also
by Ellie Alexander*

Sticks and Scones

Ellie Alexander

St. Martin's Paperbacks

This is a work of fiction. All of the characters, organizations, and events portrayed in this novel are either products of the author's imagination or are used fictitiously.

First published in the United States by St. Martin's Paperbacks, an imprint of St. Martin's Publishing Group.

STICKS AND SCONES

Copyright © 2024 by Katherine Dyer-Seeley.
Excerpt from *Killing Me Souffle* copyright © 2024 by Katherine Dyer-Seeley.

Town map by Rhys Davies.

For information, address St. Martin's Publishing Group, 120 Broadway, New York, NY 10271.

www.stmartins.com

ISBN: 978-1-250-32619-5

Our books may be purchased in bulk for promotional, educational, or business use. Please contact your local bookseller or the Macmillan Corporate and Premium Sales Department at 1-800-221-7945, ext. 5442, or by email at MacmillanSpecialMarkets@macmillan.com.

Printed in the United States of America

St. Martin's Paperbacks edition / September 2024

10 9 8 7 6 5 4 3 2 1

To Ashland, you have my heart.

Acknowledgments

Many thanks to my own personal Torte crew: Tish Bouvier, Lizzie Bailey, Kat Webb, Flo Cho, Jennifer Lewis, Lily Gill, and Courtny Bradley. You are the best! Thank you for our Zoom chats, your ideas, suggestions, and support. It means the world to me. To author Adrian Andover for this clever title. I love it, but fun fact: We landed on this title long after the book was finished, so I had to race back to the kitchen to test some scone recipes. What would a book titled *Sticks and Scones* be without a single mention of a scone? Jules would never let me live that down.

Also, my deepest gratitude to you. I know there is an abundance of books on the shelves, and I'm guessing your TBR stack is probably piled high. I can't thank you enough for taking the time to read this story and come along with Jules and the team at Torte on yet another murderous baking adventure. I hope inhabiting her world brings you a moment of escape.

to Emigrant Lake

Oregon Shakespeare Festival

The Merry Windsor

Lithia Park

Ashland Police

Torte

A Rose By Any
Other Name

Puck's Pub

The Green Goblin

Ashland

to Crater Lake

Chapter One

They say that you have to let go of the past to step into your future. My future was now. Here, in my hometown of Ashland, Oregon, where organic pear orchards were bursting with fragrant white blossoms, gangly wild turkeys and spotted baby deer stumbled on wobbly new legs in Lithia Park, and the Oregon Shakespeare Festival was back in the swing of entertaining audiences with dozens of performances each week. Our remote location, nestled in the Siskiyou Mountains, blocked any light pollution, which meant that outdoor evening productions at the Elizabethan theater felt like you were being blanketed by thousands of dazzling stars—both human and celestial. One of the things that made living in Ashland unique was bumping into actors while shopping at the co-op or sipping an iced latte at my family's artisan bakeshop, Torte.

Of course, I was biased, but spring in the Rogue Valley had a special touch of magic.

This morning, I was doing my best to make some magic in Torte's kitchen in the form of rising loaves of cinnamon raisin bread, a hearty egg bake, and chocolate hazelnut muffins. There would be a palpable buzz of energy in our open-concept basement kitchen once the rest of the team arrived. For the moment, I was glad for a reprieve because I was doing everything I could to stay upright. Lately, I'd been plagued with dizzy spells. It reminded me of being back on the *Amour of the Seas*, the boutique cruise ship where I'd spent the early part of my culinary career. My years at sea taught me resiliency and how to stay upright in the middle of a storm. The resiliency was a gift I carried with me, but struggling to find my land legs after being permanently cemented to Ashland was an unexpected challenge.

"Are you okay, boss?" Andy, our head barista, asked with a look of concern as I grabbed the counter to steady myself.

I hadn't heard him come in, and I didn't want to worry him or any of my other staff. "Fine," I lied, plastering on a smile and securing a death grip on the countertop. "Too much coffee, that's all."

Andy gasped as he shrugged off his thin jacket. His youthful eyes widened with disbelief. "Honestly, I didn't think I would ever hear Jules Capshaw utter those words. Too much coffee? I would have sworn that you were immune to the effects of caffeine." He joined me at the island, setting down a canister of coffee beans. "I guess it's good to see that you're human."

"It's probably because I haven't eaten breakfast." I motioned to the trays of rising bread and the muffin tins. That was true. I had gotten an early start at Torte. There was something innately calming about the whir of the mixer whipping creamy butter and the aroma of applewood burning in the pizza oven. Mornings before the team arrived were my favorite time in the kitchen. I could linger over a strong cup (or five) of coffee and map out a plan for the day. As Torte continued to expand our offerings, carving out a few moments to set the tone and make sure schedules, orders, and deliveries were in alignment had become critical. In addition to keeping our main pastry cases stocked, we were preparing to reopen Scoops, our summer pop-up ice cream shop, for the season. Uva, our winery, was also in high demand for wine-tasting parties, weddings, and now a new endeavor—live theater.

My best friend, Lance, the artistic director at the Oregon Shakespeare Festival, had his own project blooming—his Fair Verona Players. Never one to pass up an opportunity to entertain, Lance was launching his own spin-off production company. The Fair Verona Players would be staging their first performance in Uva's vineyard in a few short days. Lance had been at OSF—as the locals call it—for nearly a decade. His creative way of combining tradition with innovation in gender-bending Shakespeare productions had made OSF one of the most esteemed repertory theaters in the country. Lately, though, he had confessed that he needed a new challenge—something smaller and more personal that would allow him the freedom to leave his indelible mark on a new generation of actors and patrons. In Lance's words, hosting intimate productions amongst the vines, where patrons and actors could engage and interact in a gorgeous, lush outdoor setting, provided "a space for raw expression."

"There's nothing that can compare with the vulnerability of putting on a stripped-down show," he explained to me when he first pitched the idea of partnering. "This isn't going to be Shakespeare with sequins and glittery lighting, no, no, darling. We're taking plays with a small yet mighty cast and bringing the audience on a journey with us that will leave them forever changed. Creativity does not thrive if we stay stagnant."

Lance had an unmatched gift for embellishing, but I didn't put up a fight. I loved the concept. Watching a show in the vineyard on a warm spring evening while sipping on an earthy glass of our malbec sounded like a dream, and I could appreciate his need to stretch himself. I felt the same way about Torte. It was one of the reasons I had been so intent on expanding our offerings and partnerships at the bakeshop.

The question was had I been too ambitious? Until recently, I thought I was managing our varied projects well, but now I was starting to second-guess myself.

"Jules, are you sure you're good?" Andy asked, waving a hand in front of me to get my attention. His face was tanned from spring skiing on Mount A. There was a touch of auburn stubble on his chin and cheeks. When I had first returned home, Andy was a college student at Southern Oregon University. He had opted to drop out in favor of pursuing his passion—coffee roasting. Mom and I had agreed to support him and do whatever we could to help him grow his roasting operation.

He never called me Jules. Usually Andy was all about the coffee banter, but he stared at me with such an intense gaze that I wondered if I looked worse than I felt.

"No, I promise, I'm fine." I lifted one hand off the counter as proof and pointed to the empty coffee carafe. "I polished off the entire pot before you got here. I just need to eat something." I couldn't tell if I was trying to convince him or me.

"Okay." He hesitated and scrunched his wide forehead

like he was trying to assess whether I was in danger of passing out. "I guess you probably don't want to sample my latest roast?"

"Of course I do." I peeled my other hand free and kept my eyes focused on the built-in brick oven at the far end of the kitchen. As long as I didn't look down or to the side, I should be all right. That could be problematic with the day of baking we had ahead of us, but I didn't want to freak him out. "My egg bake, raisin bread, and chocolate muffins will be done soon. I'll fuel myself and be ready to savor your next masterpiece."

"I'll fire up the espresso machine and be back soon." Andy took off upstairs.

As soon as he was out of sight, I inched along the wall to steady myself. The dizziness came in waves with no predictable pattern. It had been happening on and off for a few weeks. Eating sometimes helped, but if it continued like this, I was going to have to make a doctor's appointment.

My egg bread bowls were ready, so I carefully removed them and rested them on cooling racks. They bubbled with steam and smelled heavenly. The bake was simple. I had halved and hollowed-out crusty leftover buns. Then I cracked eggs in each half and topped them off with a splash of heavy cream, fresh herbs, and salt and pepper. I baked the eggs in the bread, creating a soft creamy center and a perfect vessel for breakfast on the go.

While I waited for the egg bread to cool, I turned my attention to the next item on my to-do list: opening night party pastries. Lance had requested spring pastries and small bites for the first show. We had landed on lemon curd cupcakes, mini coconut cream pies, grapefruit tartlets, and chocolate-dipped almond tuiles for sweet options. Additionally, we would serve crostini with arugula pesto, naan and falafels with roasted red pepper hummus, feta and chicken meatball skewers, and edible Parmesan cups filled with spring vegetables.

I wanted to start on the cupcakes before the kitchen got too busy, so I took a few timid steps toward the pantry and walk-in fridge to gather ingredients. To begin, I creamed butter and sugar together, then I added vanilla, lemon rind, and fresh lemon juice. Once those were incorporated, I sifted in flour, baking soda, and salt, in alternation with buttermilk, until a smooth batter had formed. I filled silicone cupcake trays with an ice cream scoop to ensure that each cupcake would be consistent, and then slid them into the oven to bake.

The egg bowls had cooled enough, so I pulled up a stool and took a seat. The dizziness seemed to be subsiding, and eating could only help. One of our mantras in the bakeshop was "we eat with our eyes first," and my eyes were more than pleased to cut into the flaky layered egg dish. It had a touch of an herbaceous aroma from the fresh sprinkling of parsley and thyme and a perfectly cooked soft-baked egg that oozed as I stabbed it with my fork.

"Good morning, honey." Mom breezed in through the back stairwell. She tugged off a lightweight jacket and hung it on the coatrack before coming into the kitchen. Fine lines etched on either side of her walnut eyes, a sign of her years of wisdom.

"You're here early," I said with a smile, digging my fork into the eggy mixture. "I'm taking a breakfast break; want to join me?"

"These smell as good as they look." She leaned over

the tray to examine the egg bowls. "I already ate, but I'm tempted to be a hobbit and have a second breakfast. Now, if there's coffee, I wouldn't turn down a second cup."

"There was, but I drank it all," I admitted. "That's why I'm eating. I got really dizzy for a couple of minutes. I think I might have to cut back on my caffeine intake."

"This is the third time in a week that you've been dizzy." Mom's eager eyes narrowed. She glanced upstairs, then lowered her voice, her entire face lighting up with excitement. "Could there be another reason you might be dizzy? You know, when I was pregnant with you, that was my first clue."

I shook my head and took another bite of the gooey egg, using the buttery pastry to soak up the runny yolk. "No, it's not that. I did a test." I had actually taken several tests, but I didn't want to share that with her or anyone else yet. When Carlos and I decided to start trying for a baby, I figured I would get pregnant quickly, but thus far that hadn't been the case.

The briefest flash of disappointment crossed her face.

"I'm sorry." She patted my shoulder and tied on a fire-engine red Torte apron with a silhouette of a single-layer torte embroidered in teal blue. When my parents first opened the bakeshop, they decided to pay homage to the Bard by decorating the space in royal colors and adding touches of Shakespeare like the rotating quote on the chalkboard menu upstairs that today read: "Our doubts are traitors. And make us lose the good we oft might win by fearing to attempt."

I nodded but didn't say more. I wasn't prone to worry, and I didn't want to upset Mom, but I couldn't shake the feeling that there might be something wrong.

"I've been in the mood for scones. How does a batch of fresh strawberry scones sound?" she asked, moving to the walk-in fridge for butter.

"I'll never turn down your scones, and I'm happy to chop strawberries if you want to start on the batter."

She proceeded to cut cold butter into cubes. Using cold butter helps create flakiness in scones. The butter melts as the scones bake, leaving little layers of fat in the dough and giving the breakfast treats a tender texture.

We chatted more as she whisked flour, sugar, baking soda, and salt in a large mixing bowl. She used a pastry cutter to add in the cubed butter and worked the dough until it was coarse and crumbly. Next, she incorporated heavy cream, vanilla, and eggs.

Once a thick dough had formed, she folded in the strawberries and turned the mixture out onto a floured surface. She patted the dough into a large circle and cut it into wedges, finishing them with a light brush of melted butter and a sprinkling of sugar.

As she put them in the oven, my stomach growled in anticipation of tasting the light and airy scones.

"I know I don't need to say this, but I'm always here for you, no matter what." Mom closed the oven door. "And for the record it took me a little while to get pregnant with you."

Steph and Sterling arrived together, followed closely by Marty and Bethany, which saved me from having to go any deeper into the subject.

Sterling, our sous chef, had an uncanny ability to read people, especially me. I think it stemmed from our shared grief. We had both lost parents young, leaving an indelible mark on our tender souls. His steel-blue eyes caught mine ever so briefly as he passed me on his way to the sink to wash his hands.

No words were exchanged, just a subtle nod of acknowledgment that told me he must have heard the tail end of my conversation with Mom.

I swallowed back my emotions and gave him a grateful smile.

Bethany removed the custom order forms from the whiteboard as everyone gathered around the island. She tied up her bouncy curls and reviewed the list of specialty cakes for the day. Her pink T-shirt had an illustration of chocolate chip cookie dough and read SERIOUSLY, DOUGH.

"Nice one." Andy came downstairs, balancing a tray of sample coffees, and nodded in approval at Bethany's punny shirt.

Rosa and Sequoia, the final two members of our team, joined us for our morning meeting. Rosa managed the dining room, and Sequoia was a barista, although she had recently started classes at massage school, so I wasn't sure how long we'd be lucky enough to have her on staff.

I liked to gather everyone to run through the rotation and schedules, and sample our daily specials. Steph helped me cut slices of the egg bake, muffins, and raisin bread.

"Okay, everyone, I want your honest input as always," Andy said, passing out the samples. "I paired my latest espresso roast with house-made vanilla syrup, cherry blossom water, brown sugar, and oat milk."

"It smells like I'm walking through Tokyo in the spring," Marty noted, rolling up the sleeves of his button-down shirt. Marty was in his sixties with white hair and a jovial, warm face that reminded me (and all of the kids who traipsed into the bakeshop) of Santa Claus. "This transports me back to a trip my wife and I took many years ago to experience the cherry blossoms." He paused for a moment to breathe in Andy's creation before taking a long, slow sip. A nostalgic smile spread across his face. "Yes, this is why we do what we do. There's nothing that can capture a memory like food."

Andy's cheeks tinged pink with pride. "Thanks, man. I'm glad to hear that."

Steph sipped her coffee in contemplation. She reached for a sketch pad and began drawing the outline of a cherry tree. "This gives me inspiration. What if we do cherry blossom cakes with light cherry buttercream and fresh preserves? We can pipe something like this on top." She held her sketch out for everyone to see.

"I love it." Bethany bobbed her fluffy curls in agreement. "I'm starting on our delivery boxes this week, and I think mini cakes and chocolate cherry brownies would be such a great pairing. Maybe we even do a cherry theme. We could hand paint sugar cookies with cherry blossoms and make cherry bark."

"What about a cherry and arugula pizza with goat cheese?" Sterling asked, looking to Marty for his input.

"Count me in. We could do a cherry bacon jam, too," Marty replied.

Mom raised her coffee in a toast to Andy. "Look at this wonderful collaboration, all from your drink."

Andy shrugged, trying to downplay her praise. "Aww, Mrs. The Professor, stop."

She winked and took another sip of his latte, keeping her proud gaze on him.

The creamy latte with a touch of sweetness from the

cherry blossom water and brown sugar was the perfect antidote for my nausea. It settled my stomach as we went through the plan for the day. Rosa would swap out Torte's window display to mirror our cherry-baking theme and advertise our partnership with the Fair Verona Players. Sequoia and Andy would manage the espresso bar, while Sterling and Marty focused on savory items and lunch specials. Mom, Bethany, Steph, and I would oversee stocking Torte's pastry case with cakes, cookies, croissants, and crumpets.

Everyone dispersed to their workstations. I turned my attention to the lemon curd for my cupcakes. I squeezed fresh lemons from the farmers' market into a saucepan and added butter and cornstarch. I whisked the mixture over low heat until it began to thicken. I made a mental note to swing by the theater later and check in with Lance. I had a feeling that he might want to include some additional items to the menu for opening weekend. The cherry blossom cakes and chocolate cherry brownies seemed like a perfect fit, but I didn't want to alter his menu without touching base. Plus, I never turned down an excuse to walk to "the bricks," as we affectionately called the OSF campus, to see Lance.

The morning breezed by in an aromatic symphony of baking bread, simmering soups, and the waft of coffee coming from overhead. By the time we opened the doors to our first customers, the kitchen was a sea of activity, and the pastry case was a feast for the eyes. It never got old to see Torte humming with happy customers. A group of preschoolers camped out near the chalkboard doodling on the bottom half, which we reserved exclusively for our youngest guests. The corrugated metal wainscotting, red and teal accents, and dainty bouquets of yellow tulips made me forget about my dizziness.

Rosa had changed this week's quote to read: "April . . . hath put a spirit of youth in everything." Shakespeare's words felt fitting for the vibe.

A little before noon, I went upstairs to restock cherry hand pies and discovered Lance in line for coffee. He stood out in his tapered jeans, tailored checkered shirt, and skinny tie.

"Darling, there you are. I was going to come to find you, but it's already been a morning, so coffee is my first priority." Lance greeted me with a kiss on both cheeks before pulling away with his eyebrows arched in concern. "Oh, dear. You're looking a bit peckish today. Are you feeling all right?"

"Fine." I motioned to the counter where Andy had set Lance's flat white. "Too much coffee. Not enough sleep."

"Story of my life." Lance reached for his drink and then pointed to a window booth. "Can you chat for a minute?"

"Yes, in fact, I was going to come see you later."

"How fortuitous." He wiggled his brows and waited for me, making a grand sweeping gesture in front of him. "Beauty before beauty."

I rolled my eyes and headed for a booth. Rosa was stringing cherry blossom branches from A Rose by Any Other Name next door around the window frame. She had already sprinkled petals across the base of the display, making it look like the window was coated in pale pink snow. I couldn't wait to see the finished product. Thanks to Rosa's and Steph's creativity, our window displays had become a talking point for tourists and locals alike.

Lance slid into the booth across from me. His angular cheekbones and dark hair caught the light, casting a halo over him. He wore his hair shorter than normal and had shaved off any trace of facial hair.

"You look like you're backlit for the stage," I said.

He posed with one hand on the side of his cheek. "The light knows where to find me, darling. Always."

I grinned.

"Speaking of the stage. How are things coming along with the menu for opening?" He dipped his pinkie into the foam on his flat white.

"Great. That's one of the reasons I wanted to talk to you, though. We're doing a cherry theme here, as you can see." I motioned to Rosa. "And I wondered if you want us to add a few cherry options to the mix?"

"If it's anything like that, then yes." Lance pointed to one of Steph's tiered cherry blossom cakes on display at the pastry counter."

"Exactly. Although smaller versions for the dessert bar."

"Brilliant. Love it. Love it all." He strummed his fingers together. Then he leaned closer. "Let me tell you what I don't love."

"What?"

"The flack I'm getting for staging *Taming of the Shrew*."

Taming of the Shrew was the inaugural production for the Fair Verona Players. "To be honest, I'm kind of surprised, too. Isn't that play a bit controversial?"

"Are the gender roles a bit, shall we say, problematic?" Lance nodded emphatically. "Yes, obviously, but let me tell you, we've put our own little spin on it. This is not your grandmother's Shakespeare, okay? This is Will Shakes, Ashland style. We've got Katherine as a fierce and independent woman who doesn't take any nonsense from Petruchio and Petruchio as a hapless buffoon who is constantly tripping over his own words. It's a diverse cast, and it's going to be outrageously fun. We need something whimsical and over the top to draw in a new audience. I'm confident that this production and the talent I've pulled together for the Fair Verona Players is going to leave the audience speechless, gasping for breath, and begging for more."

"I love your humility," I teased.

"When you're sitting with greatness." Lance sighed dramatically. "What can you do?"

I shook my head. "You're too much, even for you."

His eyes twinkled, but then he cleared his throat and lowered his voice, his tone turning serious. "Here's the problem. I'm a bit concerned that nefarious things are afoot. I have the sense that someone is trying to sabotage my Fair Verona Players before we break legs. Items have gone missing—costumes, props. Two days ago, we had a little incident where the set collapsed during a fight scene. Thankfully, no one was injured. And then, mysteriously, a prop gun misfired during a scene. I have no idea how the prop gun even made it onto set. Then yesterday, one of our actors took a tumble during a particularly acrobatic dance sequence. We've added a few extra crash mats to the stage, just in case. I'm beginning to wonder if we're cursed. I mean, it's not uncommon for theater gremlins to be up to their antics before opening, but I have a bad feeling about this."

Lance, like most theater directors, was quite superstitious, but I could tell from his fidgety body language and the way that he ran his finger along the rim of his coffee mug that he was worried.

"Who would want to sabotage the show?" I asked.

"That's the question, isn't it?" He blew out a long breath and clutched his coffee. "The problem is that my suspect list is growing, and we open in two days. If these supposed accidents continue to happen on set, I'm concerned that one of my fair actors could end up in serious danger, or worse . . ." He trailed off.

Was Lance merely caught up in theatrics, or was his latest venture teetering on the edge of disaster?

Chapter Two

Opening night for *Taming of the Shrew* came even quicker than I imagined. In addition to Lance's original menu requests, we spent two days incorporating cherry items into the decadent theatrical feast. I was pleased with our efforts. The menu had a little something for everyone, and once we set up the pretty pink tartlets and savory rainbow vegetable and hummus platters in the vineyard, it would hopefully be an enchanting way to welcome theater lovers to Uva.

As Sterling, Steph, Bethany, and I packed boxes of cakes and hand pies to transport to Uva, I went through my final checklist. We would assemble the pizzas, grill the meatballs and falafels, and make the hummus and dips in the kitchen at the winery. Everything else simply needed to be plated or finished with a garnish or buttercream touch-up.

Hosting events outside of the bakeshop was always slightly nerve-racking. The good news was that over the last couple of years, Carlos and I had outfitted Uva's kitchen with everything a chef might need in an emergency. Unlike Torte, the vineyard's kitchen had been converted from a single-family home. José, Uva's previous owner, had done extensive renovations to the property before we purchased it from him. The old, dilapidated barn had been restored to its original glory. Ancient timber beams and a stone fireplace had been salvaged in the process. The barn had served as an event space, including Mom and the Professor's wedding. I couldn't wait to see how Lance would transform it into a theater.

Additionally he and the company would use the house as their greenroom and dressing rooms. José and his family had lived in the house when they managed the vineyard. We opted to convert the kitchen into a working space for events, remodel the tasting room and attached deck, and reserve the bedrooms upstairs for special overnight stays and bridal parties.

Memories of Mom and the Professor's wedding bubbled to the surface as I grabbed a bundle of flat cake boxes. It had been a mesmerizing weekend filled with food, laughter, and plenty of dancing.

I smiled at the thought. Hopefully opening weekend for the Fair Verona Players would be equally special. Now the real work began—transporting the fruits of our labors. The good news was that if we forgot any supplies, Torte was only about a ten-minute drive from the plaza, so worst case scenario, one of us could always run back to the bakeshop if necessary.

"Are you ready for us to start loading the van?" Sterling asked, tying his hoodie around his waist. Both of his arms were full sleeves of colorful tattoos. I knew from our conversations that each piece of ink held special meaning to him, like the hummingbird on his forearm that paid tribute to his late mother.

I crossed off the last item on my list. "Yep. I'll swing upstairs and make sure everything is good and meet you out there." It wasn't as if I really needed to check on the team. They were highly capable and could run the bakeshop without me. There wasn't a day that I didn't feel immensely grateful for our diverse staff. Everyone had their own unique roles and skill sets. I loved that Mom had created an environment where staff members had autonomy and were encouraged to take initiative.

As expected, things were flowing seamlessly in the dining room. Andy circulated with a fresh pot of his spring roast, topping off drinks for customers. Sequoia steamed milk for espressos while Rosa packaged ham and Swiss croissants and double-chocolate muffins. There was a steady line waiting to place orders and outside every patio table was packed with the lunch crowd. Customers sat beneath red sun umbrellas enjoying Marty's flatbread and bowls of Sterling's split pea soup.

"We're leaving for Uva," I said to Rosa and Sequoia as I scooted behind the pastry case to pour myself a cup of coffee to go. "Is there anything you need before we take off?"

Rosa shook her head as she completed the current sale and handed the waiting customer their package in our signature pastry craft bags stamped with the Torte logo. "We should be set. Marty and I will close. Otherwise, enjoy the play. I hope it goes well." She threw her hand over her mouth and glanced toward a group waiting in line near the front door. I recognized a few of them from the theater. "Wait, I'm not supposed to send well wishes, right? It's 'break a leg.'"

I smiled. "I think that only matters if you're in the production, not catering it."

She motioned to the group. "As long as they didn't hear me."

"They're part of the Fair Verona Players, right?" I hadn't been officially introduced to Lance's new troupe yet, although I recognized a few faces from previous OSF plays and from running back and forth between the vineyard and Uva. For the most part, Carlos had overseen efforts to construct a stage and seating in the barn and coordinate rehearsal times. When he decided to stay in Ashland permanently, we both agreed that it was important for each of us to have clearly defined roles. Not that he didn't jump in to help at the bakeshop during busy times and vice versa, but it was critical for each of us to have our own space. I loved collaborating with him, but I'd seen too many family businesses implode over the years because of loosely defined responsibilities.

Rosa raised her eyebrows in a warning. "Yes, and the tension is thicker than Andy's house-made dark chocolate sauce."

"Really." I thought back to my conversation with Lance about the issues on set. "I guess I should probably introduce myself?"

"Good luck." Rosa crossed her fingers. "I'm sure it will go beautifully. I can't wait to see the show myself. I booked tickets for next weekend."

"You used your employee discount, yeah?" That was another perk we offered our team—deeply discounted tickets to any events we hosted, along with meals during their shifts, free coffee anytime they visited the bakeshop, and complimentary ground coffee every month.

Rosa waved the next customer forward. "Of course."

I added a splash of cream to my coffee and secured it with a lid. "Text or call if anything comes up. Otherwise, I'll see you tomorrow." I moved to the door, taking small sips of the almost-floral brew. I could taste fresh peaches, honey, and blackberries in Andy's full-bodied roast. My stomach was still off (probably due to nervous jitters over Lance's big night), so hopefully, coffee would help.

Who was I kidding? Coffee always helped.

A tall, muscular man in his late twenties or early thirties blocked the door and appeared to be holding court amongst his fellow Fair Verona Players. His jet-black hair was swept into a gravity-defying wave that seemed to challenge the laws of physics. The glossy sheen of excessive hair gel that held every strand in place created an immovable, rigid structure. "As I was saying, you need to pull this trainwreck together—now. My costume is a joke, Olive. A joke. I know you've done a lot of *community* theater. This is the big leagues, so either break out your sewing machine and fix it, or I'll make sure that Tom fires you before we even open."

A woman who appeared to be about Mom's age and was holding a pincushion and fabric swatches must have been Olive, the costume designer. Ironically, her outfit lacked any distinct color or flare. She wore a shirt the color of dirt and army green cargo pants. She hunched her shoulders, making her small frame even smaller, like she was trying to take up as little space as possible. Her large, expressive eyes darted around nervously as if she was looking for a way to escape.

The woman standing next to her took charge. She was

much younger, probably in her mid to late twenties, wearing a baggy Fair Verona Players sweatshirt that was at least
three sizes too big for her. It touched her knees, making
it look like she was wearing a sweater dress over her
black leggings. "That's enough, Jimmy. You need to har-
ness this energy and use it in your performance tonight.
Take that rage and put it on the stage. Save all of this for
the show." She made a circular motion and then held her
palm up to signal Jimmy to stop.

I cleared my throat to get their attention, since none of
them had moved from the door as I approached. "Excuse
me. Sorry, I need to get through."

Jimmy's glossy hair caught the light coming in through
the glass windows, making it look wet. He wasn't subtle
in his appraisal of me, running his eyes from my head to
my feet and letting them linger on my chest. "Why the
rush? I can autograph a headshot for you, pretty pastry
lady."

My stomach revolted.

"Gross, Jimmy." The woman who had scolded him
pushed up the sleeve of her sweatshirt to free her hand
and reached out to me. "Don't pay any attention to him.
He feeds off it, and he needs to save it for my stage. I'm
Bertie Parker, by the way. I think you must be Juliet Capshaw, right? I've seen you in passing at the vineyard but
haven't had a chance to meet you."

Her stage?

I wondered what Lance would have to say about that.

"Please call me Jules." I tried to shake her hand but
caught mostly sweatshirt instead.

"Lance has gushed about you," Bertie continued, swimming in the sleeves. "I'm the associate director for the show. You've unfortunately already had the displeasure of discovering one of our lead actors, Jimmy Paxton." She nudged him in the ribs. I couldn't tell if it was a warning signal for him to behave.

"Petruchio," Jimmy corrected, reaching out to try and kiss my hand. "Charmed, I'm sure."

I pulled my hand away.

Bertie sighed with exasperation and turned to the mousy woman. "This is Olive Green, our costume designer."

Olive greeted me with a timid hello in a voice barely above a whisper that seemed to tremble as she spoke. Her khaki clothing made her look like she was trying to fade into the background. I'd met dozens of costume designers over the years, most of whom were much more adventurous in their own fashion. One of Lance's most revered designers, who had recently left for a stint on Broadway, was known for her bold, geometric prints.

"Juliet, uh, sorry, Jules and her team are doing the food for the party," Bertie explained to Jimmy and Olive. "She's married to Carlos and has been kind enough to agree to bake for our little band of misfits for opening tonight."

"Nice; sounds like we'll get to spend plenty of quality time together, then. Lucky you. Lucky me." His tongue darted out to moisten his lips as if he was savoring a delectable treat in his mind. His entire demeanor and blatant disregard for boundaries was unsettling. It was no wonder that Olive shrunk further into herself.

I knew how to handle Jimmy's type—silence. He wanted

a reaction, and I wasn't going to give him one. Maybe Jimmy was the reason for the bad vibes on set. I was surprised that Lance had cast him, but then again, I knew from previous productions that actors' personas on- and offstage could be vastly different.

"Jimmy, move." Bertie forced the door open. "Jules needs to prep for tonight, and we have dress in less than two hours."

Jimmy grumbled but stepped to the side to make room for me to pass.

"We'll see you shortly," Bertie said with a broad, forced grin, physically blocking Jimmy with her petite arm as I stepped past them.

I scooted away as fast as I could, trying to get the awful taste of Jimmy's leering gaze out of my mouth. The only good news was that Jimmy would be onstage, so hopefully we wouldn't have to interact with him much.

The plaza provided a cheerier atmosphere. A group of tourists studied posters and flyers at the informational kiosk about upcoming shows and events. Two guitarists serenaded the lunch crowd, their melody mixing in with the faint gurgling sound from the Lithia bubblers. People dined at outdoor tables at Puck's Pub and across the street at the pizza shop. Spring was definitely upon us. Like the bears that hibernated in caves hidden deep in the Siskiyou Mountains, we were all re-emerging from winter's darkness.

I helped the team load the delivery van, and we took the backroad to Uva, passing wildfire evacuation route signage and warnings to be on the lookout for cougars and deer.

The short drive took us through organic hillsides speckled with family farms and vineyards. Pink, purple, and yellow wildflowers bloomed everywhere—along the roadside and in fields.

"I have to warn you all about Jimmy Paxton," I said as we zipped past beehives and grazing calves. "If he invades your personal space, come find me or Carlos right away."

"He sounds like a real winner." Bethany contorted her face. "I know the type." She let out an involuntary shudder that rippled through her entire body.

"Sadly, we all do," Sterling agreed from the driver's seat.

"Don't worry, Jules," Steph added. She reached out to give Bethany a fist bump, revealing nails painted as black as midnight. "We've got each other's backs. No guy is going to push us around."

I didn't doubt that. And was reminded again how fortunate I was to have such an amazing team.

Once we arrived at the vineyard, I pushed thoughts of Jimmy's lecherous behavior to the back of my mind as we unloaded the van. I stopped for a minute to appreciate the sweeping views.

Nestled on a south-sloping hillside, Carlos's meticulously tended organic grapevines stretched out under the warm afternoon sun, forming a lush backdrop. Chairs and picnic tables were set in rows in a grassy area underneath a large willow tree, inviting guests to take a seat and soak in the idyllic views of Pilot Rock and the summit of Mount A in the distance. The vines and the brilliant hues of the sky perfectly framed its snowcapped peak. I knew that once the sun dipped below the horizon, the mountain would be backlit and appear to glow like it was on fire.

Later, torches would light the path between the outdoor tasting area and the barn. The barn doors were propped open and wrapped in garland with greenery, roses, and peonies. A stage, complete with lighting, rigging, and a trapdoor, had been constructed for the production at the far end of the rustic building. A crew was setting up chairs in neat rows.

I carried a large box of supplies past the long tables situated closer to the tasting room. These would be draped and arranged with platters, cake stands, and bottles of our signature wines. Two of our temporary summer hires were stringing golden lanterns in the trees as I headed in that direction with a tray of grapefruit tarts and lemon curd cupcakes. The lanterns were Lance's request. He'd suggested that golden paper luminaries would help cast a magical aura over the grounds. I had a feeling he was right. Even though they weren't lit yet, watching them swing in the slight breeze added a touch of extra charm.

As if on cue, two vans rumbled up the long gravel drive. Lance and the other members of the Fair Verona Players got out, dragging costumes and extra props with them. Lance held a suit fresh from the dry cleaner on a hanger.

"Do you need an extra hand?" I called out, resting the pastries on the table.

Bertie Parker emerged from the back of the van carrying a huge box while Jimmy started strolling casually toward the stage, his hands empty. "Jimmy, I'm so done with you. Help unload," she commanded. She tried to wave a finger at him, but it disappeared beneath her baggy layers of her oversized sweatshirt and scarves.

Jimmy ignored her and sauntered onward.

"If you don't pitch in and help like the rest of the company, you're done," Bertie shouted.

"Done?" Jimmy whipped around. Her words had caught his attention. "Do you care to elaborate on what you mean by 'done,' Bertie? As associate director, what power do you have?" He paused. "Oh, that's right—none."

Lance and two other men I didn't recognize held Bertie back as Jimmy proceeded past me with his lips curled in a sinister smirk. His sense of entitlement was as invasive as the weeds that Carlos constantly battled between the vines.

"I'm going to kill that guy," Bertie yelled for everyone to hear as the rest of the company unloaded their gear. She turned to Lance and the other men. "You and Tom need to do something about him."

"Focus on the task at hand." Lance tried to appease her, looping his suit over his arm. "We have to run through dress, and then patrons will be arriving. Nothing can be done for tonight, but you have my word that come tomorrow, changes will be made."

"What he's trying to say is that heads are going to roll," one of the men added.

"Tom might be less eloquent in his delivery, but yes, we will reassess tomorrow," Lance repeated.

Bertie stormed away from them, yanking extension cords and boxes with her.

Lance caught my eye and stared up at the cloudless sky in disgust.

I mouthed, "Sorry."

He shook his head and pointed to Jimmy, who was warming up onstage. Then he made a slicing motion across his neck.

My fluttery stomach couldn't take these theatrics.

I knew Lance was a revered director and consummate professional, but at this point, the Fair Verona Players looked like they were doomed before the curtain ever rose.

Chapter Three

We spent the next few hours running back and forth between the house, food tables, and barn. The tension with the Fair Verona Players only escalated as the afternoon wore on. We could hear their arguments about last-minute changes to the blocking over the sound of the blender and mixer.

"What is happening out there?" Carlos asked, wiping his hands on the towel tucked into his apron. His normally easygoing grin faded into a frown as he lowered the volume on the Latin jazz playing on speakers attached to his phone.

"I think it's all stemming from Jimmy Paxton, the actor playing Petruchio," I replied, filling a pastry bag with lemon buttercream. "He has been antagonizing the cast and crew."

"It isn't part of the play?" Carlos swept a lock of dark hair from his eye with a finger. Then he knelt to be even with the counter to appraise the neat rows of crostini. He picked up a piece of the crusty bread, tilting it slightly to examine it and assess how the light played off the carefully arranged sprinkling of fresh herbs. His skilled hands made minor adjustments to the tray—a gentle nudge to realign a garnish and a delicate flick of the fingertips to remove a stray crumb.

As head chef of the *Amour of the Seas*, the boutique cruise ship where we met, Carlos had honed his craft and taught his staff the importance of using a discerning eye to scan every plate before it left the kitchen. This focused attention to detail was vital in ensuring that each guest received a meal that delighted not only their taste buds but also their eyes. It was a skill I had passed on to our younger staff and at Uva. Mentoring a new generation of chefs was more rewarding than I had ever imagined. I knew that Carlos felt the same. He had taken Sterling under his wing in particular, and strutted around like a proud peacock whenever Sterling came up with a new dish that impressed Carlos and the rest of the team. "You must try this. It is the most delectable thing I've ever put in my mouth," he said a few weeks ago, practically pushing samples of Sterling's asparagus tartines.

Carlos's influence was evident in Sterling's ability to blend unique flavor combinations as well as his consummate professionalism. Not to mention his kitchen cleanliness. Not a day went by when Sterling didn't spend careful time going through our closing procedures and checklists. It was critical to maintain an immaculate kitchen for food safety. Additionally, having a well-organized and pristine workspace reduced accidents, ensured employee health, helped our equipment maintain longevity, and promoted customer trust. I appreciated that Sterling took his role of overseeing the kitchen so seriously.

"Isn't *Taming of the Shrew* supposed to be light and

funny?" Sterling asked, watching Carlos complete his inspection.

"Yep. I don't know how they're going to pull it off," I replied with a grimace, as I used a star tip to create a pattern on the top of one of the cupcakes. "I feel terrible for Lance and the rest of the company. Jimmy seems intent on making everyone miserable."

"Maybe he's super method," Steph suggested, grabbing a step stool to reach the top cabinet.

"Maybe, but I don't think anyone else in the company appreciates his method if that's the case."

"Why did Lance hire him?" Sterling asked, continuing to plate the crostini.

A knock sounded on the door.

I turned to see an older gentleman wearing an expensive black suit with a red tie and a matching red rose boutonniere tucked into the front pocket. "Excuse me, sorry to interrupt. I'm Tom Rudolph. Lance mentioned that I might be able to find a private reserve bottle of wine somewhere around here?"

"Of course, come in," I said, welcoming Tom into the busy kitchen. Tom and I hadn't been formally introduced, but I knew his name well. When Lance first floated the idea of the Fair Verona Players, he knew he would need investors. Tom had stepped forward from the beginning and become the company's biggest benefactor. "I'm Jules Capshaw. I've heard so much about you." I brushed powdered sugar from my hand before extending it in a greeting.

"Likewise." Tom's grasp was firm, but clammy. "Lance speaks quite highly of you. In fact, your pastries are legendary. Since I'm newer to the Rogue Valley, I must admit that I haven't had the chance to stop by the bakeshop yet, so I'm looking forward to getting a taste tonight."

"Feel free to sample anything." I motioned to the counter, which was packed with sweet and savory options. Then I introduced Tom to the rest of the team.

"I don't want to keep you. It's clear that you're in the middle of preparations, but I will admit that I am a bit of a wine snob, and rumor has it that you have a few special bottles of reserve in the cellar. Could that be true? And might I bother you for a glass of something off the menu? Perhaps a higher price point? My palate is used to fine wine. I blame it on family genetics. My mother owns shares in a variety of vineyards in Napa, although we're both quite impressed with the surprisingly good quality being produced here in the Rogue Valley." Tom's voice took on a coy tone. His eyes flickered around the kitchen like he was subtly gauging the reactions of my staff.

His insincere attempt at humility didn't fool anyone, especially Carlos. While Carlos had high standards for his food, he had little tolerance for the idea that the quality of a glass of wine or a three-course meal should be judged by price. Trying to impress food critics was never his style. He believed firmly that an old family recipe for a simple soup or an unassuming homemade loaf of bread was the reason people should come to the table.

"Food is memory and love and connection. It isn't Michelin stars," he would say again and again to our staff on the ship. It was one of the things that drew me to him from the start. We agreed on the transformative power of a good, handcrafted meal served with love. There was no denying the emotional quality of food. As chefs we were innately connected to the process of preparing a dish or pastry with gentle care. Everything that left Torte's kitchen was a reflection of each one of us. The personal touch, intimacy, and authenticity imbued in our food was what resonated with customers and kept them coming back year after year for burnt almond birthday cake or Mom's Saturday morning cinnamon rolls.

Carlos used that same approach in wine making, tapping into the nostalgia of his formative years in Spain to infuse a hint of saffron and paprika into his blends.

I could tell from the way Carlos's nostrils flared ever so slightly that Tom had touched a nerve. "Let me take you down there," I said to Tom, reaching for the key to the cellar door that we kept on a hook next to the aprons.

"Many thanks." Tom gave everyone a half bow and followed me to the basement.

When we purchased Uva with Lance, we inherited a small collection of private reserve wines from the previous owners. Their library wasn't extensive. It was primarily bottles they had acquired from conventions and partnerships. We rarely opened anything in the cellar. In fact, I couldn't remember the last time I'd been downstairs.

"This way," I said to Tom, leading him through the tasting room. It took up most of the main floor with a long burgundy bar with stools and ample space for guests to spend an afternoon tasting. The wall behind the bar showcased our blends, sparkling stemware, and a collection of photos from the original farm and homestead. Cozy chairs and couches were interspersed for lingering over a bottle and charcuterie board.

We had extended our seating options with the large attached deck that allowed for additional intimate tastings in the spring and summer. I loved the view from the deck that looked out over the hillside onto acres and acres of grapevines.

There wasn't much in the basement. I flipped on the lights. "Be careful on these stairs," I cautioned Tom. "They're original from when the house was built in the early 1900s."

"Noted."

We primarily used the basement for storage and a cool space to keep any overstock of our seasonal wines. The cellar was tucked in the back corner of the basement. I unlocked the door and turned on the lights. The space had been thoughtfully designed with sturdy wooden shelves that cradled a nice array of select wines. It was Lance's idea to have a secret "speakeasy" in the basement. We never opened the room to the public, but Lance had used it on occasion for private tastings.

The walls were constructed of weathered brick, making the small room with its exposed wood ceiling feel like a cocoon. A rectangular antique table with plenty of scuffs and dings sat in the center of the room, surrounded by four intentionally mismatched chairs and a handwoven rug. Two vintage barrels had been repurposed to serve as decoration and potentially extra space for tasting guests, although that made it quite cozy.

An assortment of wine bottles was artfully displayed on the far wall, each with a label telling the story of a far-off vineyard from growing regions around the world.

"Oh, this is quite nice." He drew in a long breath through his nose. "I do enjoy the scent of oak and earth. It gets the olfactory senses firing, doesn't it?"

"I get the earth smell for sure," I replied, turning on the iron sconces, which cast a golden glow over the room.

"Shall I sit?" Tom pointed to the table.

"Feel free." I ran my hand along the shelves. "Is there a particular style or region you're interested in?" The compact space was efficiently organized. Something I couldn't take credit for but appreciated. Each section of shelving was meticulously labeled by region, vintage, and varietal.

"I'm surprised you keep the key hanging out in the open. This is a fairly impressive selection." Tom studied the dusty bottles. "I would lock it up tight if I were you."

"It's just our team. No one else has access to the kitchen."

"You can never be too careful," Tom scolded. "Take, for instance, the company. I don't trust anyone, aside from Lance, that is. As an investor, I have to keep my eye on my money at all times."

I couldn't tell if he was speaking figuratively or if he literally kept watch on his cash.

"Can I see that Torgiano Rosso from Umbria to start and then we can go from there?" Tom nodded to the section of Italian wines.

For someone who didn't want to inconvenience me, he had certainly made himself comfortable quickly.

"Why don't you trust the company?" I asked as I removed the bottle from the shelf.

"The better question would be, what would make me trust anyone in the company?" Tom folded his arms across his chest and waited for me to open the bottle.

I poured a small taste into a glass and handed it to him.

He made a big production of examining the wine before holding the glass to his nose, closing his eyes in exaggerated concentration, and then proceeding to take a
series of deep, ostentatious sniffs.

It was almost comical. "Jimmy seems to be getting
under everyone's skin," I said, trying not to laugh.

Tom opened his eyes and swirled his glass with great
gusto, watching the wine's legs dance down the sides.
"Jimmy should watch his back."

"Why?" I brushed dust from my fingers.

He had yet to taste the wine. His eyebrows rose and fell
in a choreographed display of discernment as he sniffed
again. It was a good thing that Carlos hadn't been the one
to bring Tom to the cellar. Carlos wouldn't have been able
to disguise his disgust at Tom's spectacle. "There are a
number of people out to get him at the moment."

"Out to get him," I repeated.

Tom finally placed the glass to his mouth and took a
pretentious sip, puckering his lips and swooshing the liquid
like it was mouthwash. "A nuanced bouquet. I'm getting
underripe peapods and petroleum along with meaty, bony,
brothy, earthy notes."

Was he making up words?

"Would you like a glass? Or I can send you with the
bottle if you prefer," I said, hoping that he'd take the hint
that I didn't have time for an extended tasting session at
the moment.

"The bottle will be fine." Tom stood. "I've taken too
much of your time already."

I pressed the cork into the bottle before handing over
the vintage wine and waiting for Tom to exit the small
space and then locking the door.

He cleared his throat and stared at the door handle. "I must say that I feel compelled to suggest that you really might want to consider tighter security measures. As a man of business, I would hate to see you taken advantage of by employees with questionable morals."

"I'm not sure what you mean." I didn't need a lecture, especially from him.

"The cellar. It's not a wise move to store the key in plain sight. I couldn't help but notice you have it hanging on a hook out in the open in your kitchen. One scheming employee could wipe out your collection." He waited for me to go up the stairs first. "Your cellar is more extensive than I would have expected, and I would hate for you to lose valuable vintages thanks to a staff member who realizes what a treasure trove is hiding in the basement."

"I'll take that into consideration," I said, to end the conversation.

Tom and I clearly had different philosophies about business ownership. I trusted my team. They were like family. They had autonomy in their roles while still collaborating. I wasn't worried about any of them stealing wine from the cellar. I knew them well enough to know that if anyone was interested in a bottle, they would simply ask. And, quite frankly, I didn't care about rare vintage wines.

Listening to Tom's untrusting perspective made me appreciate how grateful I was for Torte and everyone connected to it.

Chapter Four

Tom's impromptu private tasting had put me behind schedule. I went outside to find Lance and confirm the timing for the first round of appetizers and drinks. The gates would open an hour prior to curtain to allow time for everyone to grab a glass of wine, have a bite to eat, and mingle. There would be no service during the performance, but we would refill the tables once the show started so that theatergoers could help themselves to more small bites and wine refreshers during intermission.

I weaved along the stone pathway between the house and the barn. Solar lights would illuminate the walkway later. Bees hummed on wild bunches of lavender and rosemary. A garden snake darted between my feet before disappearing into the grassy outdoor tasting area.

Inside the barn, most of the cast had dispersed for hair and makeup. Jimmy remained onstage with two members of the crew.

"Ed, you're going to get me killed," Jimmy said to a guy wearing classic stagehand attire—black slacks, black work boots, and a black T-shirt that read CREW.

"Dude, you missed your mark and tripped." The guy,

who I assumed must be Ed, ripped off a strip of duct tape that he used to secure a cord on the stage.

"I'm Jimmy Paxton. I don't miss my marks, Ed," Jimmy shot back in a piercing tone.

Ed sniggered. "Sure. Keep telling yourself that."

A young woman, also wearing a CREW T-shirt, handed Ed a pair of scissors. "Actually, Ed, he didn't. I was watching the timing, and it was perfect, Jimmy. Flawless." She shot Jimmy a shy smile. "You're brilliant. You never miss a beat, Jimmy."

"Of course, you would say that." Ed rolled his eyes and stuffed the scissors in his toolbelt. "We need more electrical tape. It's in the van, can you go get it?"

The woman gave Jimmy a wistful look. She flipped her long ponytail and started to move toward the side of the stage.

"Hey, stay where you are. I'm not going to let him treat you like that." Jimmy strolled toward her in one fluid motion, like a prey animal about to pounce. "Ed, is that any way to speak to the women on the crew? I thought we were more evolved than having the ladies grab us coffee."

Ed yanked another piece of tape with force, his eyes locked onto Jimmy. "Sophie is the assistant set designer. If I need tape, she gets the tape. It has nothing to do with her gender. It's her job."

"Sorry, Soph, some people are just stuck in the Dark Ages." Jimmy put his arm around her, pulling her tight to his chest.

Her cheeks flushed with color as she smiled up at him with a doe-like gaze.

"Sophie, the tape." Ed pointed to the van. "Now. We're running behind."

Jimmy squeezed her shoulder. "Don't worry. We'll catch up and get cozy after the show, babes."

Sophie bobbed her head. "That would be great. I'll wait for you. I'll make you a plate of snacks. I'm sure you'll be famished by then. You put everything you are onto the stage. It must be so draining."

I cringed.

Ed looped the roll of industrial tape over his wrist and then ran his hands through his hair in exasperation. I didn't blame him.

What did Sophie see in Jimmy?

I mean, I knew he was the star of *The Taming of the Shrew*, but aside from that, his personality was anything but charming, and he was the last person on the planet (short of maybe Richard Lord, Ashland's self-appointed king and my personal nemesis) who should be giving a lecture on misogyny.

Sophie hurried off to find the tape.

"If anything goes wrong on the set tonight," Jimmy said, sticking a finger in Ed's face, "it's on you. Everyone will know you did it."

"Did what?" Ed knelt and started hammering a nail into the stage.

I glanced around for Lance. Where was he?

"Tried to kill me," Jimmy shouted, looking directly at me.

I gasped, even though it was obvious that was exactly the reaction Jimmy was looking for.

"You are entirely too much, man. Entirely." Ed pounded the floorboard.

Jimmy puffed out his chest and towered over him, egging him on. "Hey, you want to go? You want to fight?"

Ed tucked the hammer into his tool belt and stood. "Don't tempt me. That's a fight you wouldn't win."

I was about to say something in hopes that I might defuse the situation, but Lance appeared on the side of the stage. He immediately commanded a graceful control, strolling up the stairs as if he had all the time in the world. He cleared his throat as he clapped his hand on Jimmy's shoulder. "Excuse me, gentlemen. I hope I'm not interrupting, but you're late for makeup, Jimmy. They need you— now. Olive made adjustments to your costume, and she said it would take at least twenty to thirty minutes to get you fitted."

Jimmy made one last thrust at Ed. Then he gently smoothed his expertly coifed hair and strolled off the stage toward the house.

For the run of the show, the actors would change and get in hair and makeup in the house, where the upstairs rooms had been transformed into dressing rooms. They would stay there until everyone was seated. Then they would return during intermission. Lance didn't want them to break character or be seen coming and going from the house by the audience members. Fortunately, Lance's vision for the show didn't involve any elaborate costume changes like some of his previous productions at OSF. The dressers for those performances had their own intricate choreography behind the curtain that rivaled anything patrons saw on the stage.

"We have to maintain authenticity even if we don't have the same level of sets, underground tunnels, and back exits here," he had said during one of our early brainstorming meetings.

Using the house was no problem. We wouldn't open the tasting room, since the food and drinks were being served outside, so as long as the show ran on schedule, the audience should be none the wiser.

Ed flipped the roll of tape like a circus performer warming up for their opening act. "Lance, you've got to do something about that kid. He's going to tank the show intentionally. I wouldn't put past him to pull a stunt tonight that gets him or another member of the cast in trouble."

"What kind of trouble?" Lance asked, reaching down to hand Ed a nail that fell out of his pocket.

I couldn't hear what Ed was saying, but from the way he pointed to Jimmy's mark and then to the steep drop-off at the edge of the stage, I caught his gist.

Lance seemed like he managed to calm Ed down, and by the time Sophie returned with an armful of electric tape, the mood was lighter.

I waited for him to finish giving Ed and Sophie final instructions before wandering over to him. "How's everything going?"

He threw his hand to his forehead. "Burning up. Or perhaps I should say that I'm ready to burn it all to the ground."

"Please don't do that. Carlos has poured his blood, sweat, and tears into the vineyard. He would be devastated. So would you." I pointed above us to the strands of golden twinkle lights wrapped around each roof beam and then to the potted boxwood trees covered with more lights flanking either side of the stage. "Your vision has come true. Everything looks amazing. The food and wine are good to go. It's going to be a spectacular night."

"Thanks for the pep talk. You're right, but now I have to keep my cast from ripping each other to shreds." He jumped down from the stage. "Shall we walk back to the house?"

I looped my arm through his. "Yeah. I happened to see the exchange between Jimmy and Ed."

Lance fanned his face. "I thought we could get away with keeping him in the show tonight, but now I'm not sure."

"Is there anything else you can do?"

"No, it's too late. His understudy is stuck in Mexico. His flight got canceled. You know how small the Medford airport is. He won't be back until sometime tomorrow at best. We're such a small operation we don't have swings or standbys. Unless it's me, and trust me, I've been giving the thought some serious consideration." He tapped his chest and pressed his lips together in a frown.

"Wait. What? *You* might step in or Jimmy?" I couldn't contain my surprise.

"It's not my first choice, but as you know, the show must go on. If duty calls . . ." He trailed off.

We stopped at the food tables. It looked like a scene from *Alice in Wonderland*. Pretty pink platters of sweets and bunches of wildflowers mixed in with tea lights and greenery. The bucolic countryside stretched as far as my eye could see.

"I overheard Ed say something about Jimmy potentially sabotaging the show," I said, catching a flash of a baby bunny's little white cottontail near the giant oak tree. "I don't get it. Why would he do that? Doesn't he want this role?"

"Who knows? He's unhinged." Lance swiped a cherry macaron with almond buttercream and cherry preserves from the dessert table. "I'd like to rip his head off, if you want to know the truth, but for now I just need to get through opening night. Come tomorrow, I'll have a new plan. He's skating on thin, thin ice." He tore off a piece of the French cookie with his teeth. "Or, should I say on thin icing?"

I chuckled. "Hey, at least you still have your sense of humor."

"That's all I have at the moment," he muttered through a mouthful of the macaron.

"Do you think Jimmy's behind the mishaps during rehearsals? You mentioned the play being cursed. Is it him? Could he be stealing costumes and messing with the set and props?" I asked as we walked toward the house. I had to be intentional about each step, careful not to squish the western fence lizards sunning themselves on the path.

"I would put money on it. But, as you mentioned, I don't understand his motivation unless he's gone full method with his embodiment of Petruchio."

"Could that be it?" I knew that Lance had worked with a handful of actors over the years who took their craft so seriously that they became the characters they were playing on the stage during the show's run.

"He's not the type. And if he is method, he has work to do. As you'll soon see, my take on Petruchio is an update from the Bard's sexist beast. Jimmy is an utter buffoon in our production, but my notes have never included being nasty to everyone he encounters." Lance paused as he polished off the last bite of the macaron. "No, there's more to the story that I can't seem to grasp."

"How is he onstage?"

"A dream. A delight. Funny. Impeccable timing." Lance threw his hands up in desperation. "He's a conundrum, that one." He stopped in front of the porch. "I'm going to check upstairs to see how hair and makeup are faring with him. Is there anything else you need from me before the curtain rises, metaphorically?"

"Actually, yes. I want to make sure we're set for timing." I pulled out my notes and reviewed them quickly. I didn't want our supporting role to throw off his staging. There were many similarities with putting on a production like *Taming of the Shrew* and catering a feast. Instead of costume changes and perfectly timed marks and special effects, in the kitchen we had the ovens down to a science, ensuring that wood-fire pizzas and ham and cheese hand pies were served piping hot. Just as a choreographer planned dance routines, my team meticulously organized every minute of tonight's service, preparing, baking, and plating dishes simultaneously with fluidity.

"It looks good. Just reiterate to your staff that patrons are not to be anywhere in the vicinity of the house and tasting room during the performance. As long as we keep this pathway clear and keep people in their seats, we should be fine."

"Not a problem."

He kissed my cheeks. "I'm off, then, darling. Ta-ta."

"Break legs," I called after him. I wished there was something more I could do. I knew how hard Lance had worked to get the Fair Verona Players off the ground. It was stressful enough to launch a new theater experience without your lead trying to tank the show.

The one thing that I could control was the food. Even if things went wrong on the stage, the appetizers and desserts would be perfect tonight. I could guarantee at least that much.

Chapter Five

I spent the next hour garnishing, plating, and styling our theatrical spread. Our beautifully orchestrated menu was completed and staged beneath the glow of the lanterns and the electric flames of the flickering tea lights. I stood back to observe, pleased with how well my team had executed Lance's vision.

Patrons began arriving, and soon the vineyard was filled with the sounds of happy laughter and clinking wineglasses. I mingled with familiar faces as I poured our earthy merlot and watched the sun get swallowed up by an invasion of twinkling stars. Carlos and Sterling illuminated the lanterns and twinkle lights inside the barn, which cast a lustrous glow over the neat rows of chairs.

Lance took the stage when the sun had fully set with a glass of wine in one hand. He had changed into a well-fitting navy suit with a canary yellow tie and matching shoes. "Welcome, welcome to the inaugural production of your Fair Verona Players."

The audience applauded enthusiastically as the last few stragglers topped off their wine and took their seats.

"You are in for a wild ride with a Kate and Petruchio

like you've never seen." Lance addressed his adoring audience and raised his glass. "Hold on to your wineglasses and buckle up for an evening of hilarity as our Fair Verona Players take you to Padua in the Italian countryside near Verona, where we open with a nobleman playing a trick on a beggar and setting the stage for the play that we know and love as none other than *Taming of the Shrew*."

Lance's introduction sent the audience to their feet with cheers and whoops.

The energy was electric as the stage lights went out and were immediately replaced by pulsing purple and orange flashes. Madonna's "Lucky Star" blasted through the speakers, and the ensemble, in a mashup of Tudor and '80s garb paraded down the aisle.

It was impossible not to get swept up into the celebratory atmosphere. Even Jimmy was on his best behavior. The show exceeded my expectations and that of the entire audience. During intermission, everyone was talking about what a visionary Lance was—that he had managed to blend a tribute to Madonna songs with a gender-bending cast and yet still keep Shakespeare's material recognizable was a monumental feat.

The audience, myself included, gave the cast a five-minute standing ovation when the actors took their final bow. Lance hadn't oversold his remake on the problematic Shakespearean comedy. The show was an '80s dance party—intertwining pop beats from Wham! and Billy Joel with Elizabethan sonnets and soliloquies. This might go down in history as the best show Lance had ever directed, which was saying a lot, because he had won nearly every regional and nation theater award and accolade.

No one wanted to leave. We kept pouring wine and

bringing out the last of the desserts as everyone gushed about the show.

Arlo, Lance's boyfriend and the current fiscal director at OSF, beamed with pride, and Mom and the Professor couldn't stop talking about Lance's revolutionary approach to Shakespeare.

"He is single-handedly going to bring along a new generation of theater lovers, and I could not be prouder to say I was here to witness it," the Professor said with admiration. "That production belongs on the big screen. I wouldn't be surprised if Madonna herself makes an appearance."

"I love that you know Madonna." I'd never heard him talk about an affinity for '80s pop before.

The Professor wrinkled his forehead and ran a finger along his beard. "Now, Juliet, how can you say that, with lyrics like, 'Poor is the man whose pleasures depend on the permission of another.' The bard couldn't have said it better." His eyes twinkled with mischief.

"Now I'm really impressed."

Mom grinned as she leaned into his shoulder, wrapping her cashmere shawl over her left arm. "I'll have you know that I have discovered Doug dancing to the beat of 'Holiday' in the kitchen on more than one occasion."

"How did I never know about your Madonna obsession?" I asked with real shock.

"It's a bop, as the kids say." He winked and adjusted his tie. As usual he had dressed for the occasion in a gray suit and loafers. His tie featured a treasury of Shakespearean insults. I had to squint to read some of them, like "Thou odoriferous stench" and "Pestilent complete knave."

"Did I just hear the Professor say 'a bop'?" Andy passed

by with an empty tray. He stopped long enough to offer the Professor a fist bump of approval and to check in with me. "Hey, sorry to bug you, boss, but have you seen the key to the wine cellar?"

"Not recently."

"That guy Tom is asking for another bottle of private reserve, but the key isn't on the hook," Andy said, glancing around like he expected to see him.

"I'll come in with you and take a look." I thought back to earlier when I had let Tom into the cellar. I knew I returned the key to the hook because of what a big deal he had made about safety measures. Part of me wondered if he had taken it himself to prove a point. He was the type. He probably thought it was a good way to teach me an "important business lesson." I needed to introduce him to Richard Lord. They would get along swimmingly. Richard and I hadn't gotten off to good start when I first returned home to Ashland. He owned the aging Merry Windsor Hotel, which sat across the plaza from Torte. Since my first day back in Ashland, he had attempted to try and insert himself into my professional and personal life. I knew the reason—Mom. Richard had been close to taking possession of Torte. Mom's generosity had left her in a precarious financial position, and Richard had swooped in with a pitiful offer to buy the bakeshop out from under her. Unbeknownst to her, the deal would have left her with nothing.

Thankfully, Mom caught on, and I had saved money during my years on the *Amour of the Seas* that I invested. We were able to save Torte, which made me enemy number one in Richard's eyes. There was no need for animosity or competition. Richard's offerings of microwaved oatmeal and slice-and-bake cookies at the Merry Windsor were vastly different from Torte, but that didn't stop him from constantly accusing me of trying to copy him.

In addition to attempting a hostile takeover of the family bakeshop, he made it his mission to make me and everyone else in his sphere miserable.

I wound my way along the dimly lit path, guided by the stars, moonlight, and the solar lights. Chatter of frogs and crickets echoed in the valley, bouncing off the mountains to the west. I was thrilled and relieved that the show had gone off without a hitch, mainly for Lance's sake. He had put so much of his own time and money into the Fair Verona Players.

I still couldn't quite wrap my mind around how different Jimmy had been onstage. Lance was right. Once the curtain went up, Jimmy was an entirely different person. I had to credit his acting ability—or maybe his shift in personality had more to do with Lance's careful direction.

Movement flashed out of the corner of my eye. I turned to see someone, or something, disappear amongst the grapevines. I hoped it wasn't a black bear. This was the time of year when they woke from their winter slumbers and began meandering down into town and the surrounding farmland in search of spring berries.

It wouldn't have been one of my staff, and no one else was supposed to be up this way.

I shrugged it off, but stayed on high alert as I continued toward the deck. I let myself in the side door. The tasting room was empty, as was the kitchen, although I could tell that the tear-down-and-clean-up processes were already in full swing by the stacks of empty dishes on the counter and in the sink. Sterling's clipboard with the closing checklist noted that everyone would be responsible for bringing loads from the vineyard.

I smiled at his efficiency. Multiple items had already
been completed and checked off the list.

I could hear footsteps above. Someone was moving
about in the dressing rooms. I was surprised that any of
the actors had opted to linger inside, given that everyone
outside was eager to congratulate them on a stellar opening show.

There was no sign of Tom.

The last thing I wanted to do was spend twenty minutes hearing him pontificate on his wine knowledge. I'd
rather give him the key and let him go find his own bottle.

I scribbled a quick "You are awesome" on the clipboard
and went to grab the key.

Andy was right—it wasn't on the hook where I'd left it
a few hours ago.

Classic.

It had to be Tom.

But then again, why not just help himself versus making a big show about our lack of safety procedures?

I sighed and hurried through the tasting room.

The lights were off in the stairwell. I turned them on
and made sure not to take the stairs too fast, even though
the only thing I wanted to do was get Tom a bottle of what
he had deemed to be superior wine and get back to the
party.

A tingling feeling spread up my spine as I descended
the rickety stairs, letting out a sigh when my feet landed
on solid ground. The basement was plunged in darkness.
The only light was from the staircase. I could see that the
cellar door was partially open.

Tom must have let himself in.

I inhaled through my nose and squared my shoulders, preparing myself to kindly yet firmly kick him out.

I knew that he was financially tied to the Fair Verona Players, and I didn't want to ruin a business relationship for Lance, but Tom had overstepped.

I pushed the door open, expecting to see Tom seated at the table with his nose buried in a glass of vintage wine.

Instead, Jimmy was sprawled on the floor with a corkscrew stabbed in the side of his neck and a pool of blood surrounding his head.

Chapter Six

I clutched the door frame, a tidal wave of dizziness assaulting my body.

You're imagining this, Jules, I tried to tell myself. That had to be a pool of burgundy wine, not burgundy blood, surrounding Jimmy's head. Right?

This couldn't be happening.

I dug my nails into the wood, forcing myself to breathe.

That was Jimmy. And he was dead.

Definitely dead.

I inched closer, knelt next to his lifeless body, and checked for a pulse. There wasn't one, which wasn't a surprise given that his eyes rolled up toward the ceiling in a vacant gaze.

I inhaled slowly and deeply, trying to force myself out of the rhythm of shallow breathing.

I wasn't an expert, but from the gash in his neck, it looked as if the corkscrew had delivered the fatal blow.

I had to get the Professor—fast.

Bright yellow spots clouded my vision when I stood up. I blinked hard and squeezed my eyes shut tight.

My knees threatened to buckle as I ran up the stairs, keeping a firm grasp on the railing.

The tasting room was empty, but I could hear music in the kitchen—thank goodness. That meant that someone was here.

Sterling heaved a huge tub of ice onto the counter next to the sink as I stumbled into the room. "We have a problem. Where's the Professor?"

"Jules, what's wrong?" Sterling dumped the bucket of ice in the sink and ran to me. "Are you okay?"

It was like my tongue refused to work. My mouth felt gummy and pasty, like I'd been chewing on a sheet of fondant. "It's Jimmy." I pointed behind me to the stairwell. "He's dead."

"What?" Sterling gripped my shoulders and steered me over to a bar stool. "You need to sit down, Jules. I'm going to go find the Professor, or Thomas, or whoever I can. Don't move. I'll be right back." With that, he sprinted out of the kitchen and vanished.

I nodded. He didn't need to worry. My legs were failing me. They quivered and shook like the floor was erupting beneath me.

I had to use the counter as a crutch to steady myself as I sat down.

Who could have killed Jimmy? And why?

I placed a hand over my mouth, hoping to keep my nausea at bay.

What was he doing in the cellar?

Had the killer planned their attack? Or had it been a crime of convenience? Maybe they found Jimmy in the basement and decided to strike.

"Julieta, what is it?" Carlos's voice interrupted my spiraling thoughts.

I turned to see him standing in the doorway, holding a box of empty wine bottles. "It's Jimmy, the actor," I said, although my warbly voice sounded like it was coming from someone else. "He's been stabbed—in the neck. I think he's dead. Actually, I'm sure of it."

Carlos set down the wine box. His dark eyes filled with concern as he came closer, studied my face, and massaged my fingers. His tone was calm and even. "Keep breathing, mi querida. It will be okay."

His touch helped center me.

"That's good. Nice and slow." The tender, steady quality of his voice made me want to collapse in his arms and disappear.

I wiggled my toes, trying to make a connection with the floor in hopes of grounding me in the reality.

"You found him?" Carlos asked, releasing his grasp.

I nodded.

"Should I get Doug?" He reached for a glass and filled it with water.

"No, Sterling is already on his way to find him."

"Drink this." He placed the water in front of me. "Are you sure that Jimmy is dead?"

I nodded again. "There was so much blood, and he wasn't moving."

"Sí, it's okay." He squeezed my hand and pointed to the water. "You need to drink this slowly and try to relax. I will go downstairs and check on Jimmy while we wait for Doug to arrive."

I must have looked even worse than I felt. Between

Sterling and now Carlos telling me that I needed to sit, I wondered if I was in danger of toppling over.

Sterling and the Professor rushed past a few minutes later, but I remained cemented in the chair. I didn't need to see Jimmy's body again, and I wasn't sure I could manage the stairs without my knees giving out this time.

I sipped the water as Mom, Andy, Steph, and Marty all filed into the kitchen, carrying platters and cake stands.

"Juliet, we heard that one of the actors is injured," Mom said, approaching me with a look of concern. She took off her shawl and wrapped it around my shoulders.

"It's Jimmy." I told her and the rest of the team what happened. I had barely finished when the sound of wailing sirens reinforced how dire the situation had become.

Mom sat next to me as paramedics and police officers ran past the kitchen on their way to the scene of the crime.

Could I have been wrong?

Was there a chance that Jimmy was still alive?

Maybe his injury wasn't as bad as I thought.

But then images of the corkscrew and the pool of blood flooded my head.

I blinked hard to try and force them away.

"Honey, how are you doing?" Mom asked, putting one hand on my knee, which I couldn't stop bouncing.

"Okay, I guess." The truth was that the entire kitchen appeared blurry. My eyes couldn't focus, everything was tilted and fuzzy. I could hear the clatter of plates and silverware, and the hum of the dishwasher, and see flashes of movement as the team deftly continued cleanup procedures, but it was like I was underwater, watching through foggy swim goggles.

"Juliet?" Mom cleared her throat and raised one eyebrow.

"Yeah, sorry. I feel terrible. I should have stayed down there with him. I just took off. What if I'm wrong? Maybe he was okay, and I left him there. Maybe I should have tried CPR or rescue breathing. What if I didn't do enough?" I massaged my arms, thankful that she had lent me her shawl without asking if I needed it. The room suddenly felt like I was sitting in the walk-in freezer.

"You did enough. You came to get help," she said with a firm, sad smile. "The only thing you could do in the situation."

"But I should have applied pressure or removed the corkscrew."

She squeezed my knee harder. "No, that's the job of the professionals. You did exactly what needed to be done. This is what Doug and the first responders are trained to do. You could have made it much worse if you removed the object or even applied pressure to the wound."

I appreciated that she was trying to make me feel better, but I couldn't stop seeing Jimmy's lifeless body in my mind.

After what seemed like hours but was probably more like minutes, the Professor came into the kitchen. His suit jacket was draped over his left arm. I could tell immediately by his solemn stare that the news wasn't good. "I'm afraid I must report that Jimmy is deceased."

A hush fell over the kitchen.

Even though the logical part of my brain already knew it was true, hearing the Professor speak the words out loud made it suddenly real.

I placed my head in my hands and exhaled.

The Professor loosened his tie. "I want to assure you that there was nothing that could have been done. The stab wound punctured his carotid artery. It was not a survivable injury."

It was like the Professor was reading my mind.

"Do you have any idea when it happened?" Mom asked, rubbing my back the way she had when I was young and woke up with nightmares.

I was wondering the same thing, not only for my own peace of mind but also because I was curious to know the window of time he'd been killed in. That might determine a suspect list.

"It's too soon to have a definite answer, of course," the Professor replied. "The coroner will have to determine the time of death, but I would surmise that Jimmy has been dead for at least an hour, if not longer."

"Really?" I sat up straighter. That had to mean that he had gone immediately to the cellar after his performance. Could he and the killer have planned to meet up? Did that imply that his death was premeditated?

Lance rushed into the kitchen with Arlo on his heels. His face was flushed and his eyes darted in every direction, like he was expecting to see Jimmy standing near the sink. "Are the rumors true? Please tell me that this is a terrible prank."

The Professor folded his hands together and shook his head slowly.

"Jimmy Paxton, my shining star, Petruchio, is dead?" Lance laced his fingers together and exhaled with a long whistle.

"I'm afraid so," the Professor replied.

Lance met my eyes as his mouth dropped in disbelief. Then his gaze drifted to the pantry. "Where? In here? I don't understand. I saw him mere minutes after curtain. How? Who?"

"These are things that will have to be determined. We are in the very early stages of the investigation." The Professor held up a finger to the paramedics signaling him near the door. "If you'll excuse me for a moment. I'll want to hear your thoughts and recollections on Jimmy's movements, but it appears I'm needed first."

"I can't believe it." Lance paced from the counter to the sink. "Well, to be fair, that's not entirely true. Jimmy had a habit of making fast enemies rather than friends, but I can't wrap my head around the how. The show just premiered. The killer must have been waiting for him here." He paused and glanced around the room as if expecting to see someone dressed in black waiting to jump out from behind the island. "Where was he killed?"

"Downstairs," I replied.

"Don't tell me that you found him?" Lance gasped and fanned his face.

Arlo stood near the apron rack, fiddling with one of the apron strings. "Oh, no, Jules. How terrible."

I nodded, not trusting myself to speak.

"Was it gruesome?" Lance asked.

I nodded again. "He was stabbed in the neck with a corkscrew."

Mom cleared her throat in warning.

"Sorry. Sorry." Lance shot me an apologetic grimace. "I don't need the gory details."

"Jimmy was there for the final bow, right?" My memory

was hazy. I had been so caught up with the rest of the audience in the standing ovation that I hadn't paid attention to where or how the cast had made their exit.

"Yes. He would never pass up an opportunity to bask in the adoration of his cheering fans." Lance peeled off a cupcake wrapper and broke the cake in half. "I saw him right after. He passed by my seat. I was in the front row, and I gave him my seal of approval. You can't fault what that man left on the stage. He owned that role. In fact, I was thinking to myself that I couldn't possibly entertain the thought of firing him after what he did tonight."

"What about the rest of the cast and crew?" Arlo interjected.

"Fair point, fair point." Lance swiped a taste of buttercream. "He was a menace offstage, but I found no fault in that performance. I was mentally reviewing what I was going to say at the cast party."

"You were going to keep him in the show in spite of his behavior?" I asked.

"Have you ever seen a better interpretation of Petruchio? He wore those tight short shorts and knee-high rainbow socks like a true '80s icon. His energy was addictive. You could say it was inspired. I knew he had it in him, but that was next level," Lance countered. "I fully intended to keep him in the role and brainstorm ways to temper his antics, but it appears that someone beat me to the second part, and I think I know who."

"You think you know who killed him?" Arlo sounded incredulous. "Maybe you should have led with that."

Lance gave him a coy shrug. "What, and miss an opportunity for a big reveal?"

"Who do you think killed him?" I blurted out. My patience was running thin.

"I dearly hope that I'm wrong, but I watched Sophie follow him along the path until they vanished in the darkness. They were heading straight here, and you'll never guess what she had in her hand."

"A corkscrew," Arlo offered.

Lance licked the tip of his finger with a flourish. "Exactly. She had a bottle of wine in one arm and a corkscrew in the other. I hate to say it, but my lovestruck assistant set designer just might be our killer."

Chapter Seven

It took a while for the Professor to finish securing the crime scene, so my team proceeded to bring in platters, wineglasses, and empty bottles. Sterling and Andy took over dish duty while Steph and Bethany packed up the remaining leftovers and Marty sorted wine bottles for recycling.

I felt terrible sitting and watching them work while I sipped water, but no one would let me help.

"I'm not an invalid," I said to Carlos, who passed by me with tablecloths and napkins draped over his arm. "I can do something."

"No, you sit and just rest." He kissed the top of my head. "We have this under control. There's nothing for you to do, anyway." He motioned with his free hand toward Andy and Sterling. They didn't have to say a word as they rinsed, washed, and dried in a perfectly synched rhythm. "You'll just be in the way, mi querida."

That was probably true, but sitting and doing nothing other than replay my every movement before finding Jimmy's body wasn't helping. I untied my ponytail and massaged my temples. Who could have killed Jimmy? And why?

There was a possibility that one of the cast or crew was fed up with his inflated ego and stabbed him in a moment of passion. But that seemed unlikely. Jimmy's self-absorption might have been annoying, but leading someone to kill him? That was another story.

Detective Kerry entered the bustling kitchen shortly after midnight. She wore Thomas's baggy Ashland Police Department sweatshirt over her black cocktail dress. Thomas was my dear childhood friend and Kerry's partner in work and life. As the Professor scaled back on his detective duties, Kerry and Thomas had taken the lead. The transition had been practically seamless, since they had shadowed him for years and took a similar approach to community-centered police work.

Her body gave a little shudder as she approached me. "The basement is chilly."

"I know. We only use it for storage for that reason," I replied, glancing at the clock above the sink. "You all have been down there for a while, too."

She nodded and rubbed her hands over her arms. "Can I have a word? Maybe we can talk in private in the tasting room?"

"Of course." I followed her to the adjoining space.

Kerry took a seat on one of the chairs next to the fireplace and waited for me to pull up a chair next to her. "Doug told us you found the body. How long ago was that?" She didn't bother with small talk, which I appreciated.

I would have been exhausted even without Jimmy's murder. Working baker's hours meant that typically I was up before dawn. I didn't want to do the math to figure out how long I'd been awake. Just thinking about it made me yawn. "Yes, I found him," I said to Kerry, covering my mouth with my hand.

She readjusted her long red ponytail and made a note on a yellow legal pad. "Do you know approximately what time that was?"

"I'm not sure exactly. The show had just finished. All the actors had left the stage. We hung around for a while, chatting about the production. Mom and the Professor were there. Andy came outside to tell me that the key to the cellar was missing, so I went inside to find it, and that's when I found him. I'm guessing it was around ten forty-five or maybe eleven."

Kerry jotted down notes as I spoke. "Tell me more about the missing key."

"It's weird," I admitted, pointing to the door that led downstairs. "We rarely go down to the cellar. In fact, I can't remember the last time I was in the basement, but before the show tonight, Tom Rudolph asked for a bottle of reserve."

Kerry looked up from her notes, her inquisitive green eyes meeting mine. "Who's Tom?"

"He's an investor. I think he's an official partner in the company. Lance will be able to tell you more, but he's a bit of a wine snob, and apparently our Uva wines weren't up to his standards."

She tapped her pencil on the top of the pad. "Did he say that?"

"He didn't have to. You should have seen him tasting the bottle I opened earlier. It was a production on its own. He was so pretentious and went on and on about the legs of the wine and his tasting notes. I guess not realizing— or maybe caring—that he was basically calling Uva's wine inferior the entire time." I shook my head at the memory.

Kerry laughed and rolled her eyes. "I know the type."

"Anyway, he made a big deal about the cellar key and how we were making a huge mistake by leaving it in the kitchen."

"Interesting." Kerry tapped her pencil on her notebook. "How did he know where the key was located?"

"He saw me take it off the hook. It's not a secret. We leave the key hanging next to the aprons. It's hardly like we have huge issues with people trying to break into the cellar. The only people who are ever in the kitchen are my staff. Tom scolded me like I was a child for leaving the key out in plain sight. He gave me a lecture about how I should tighten my control. Let's just say I'm not a fan of that, or him."

"Uh, no. That's not cool at all." Kerry scrunched her eyes together and scowled. She shifted in her chair and held her pencil ready to write again. "Did Tom seem like he was assessing the space? Did you get the sense he could have been scoping out the basement?"

I hadn't considered that. "You mean like he might have been formulating a plan to lure Jimmy down to the cellar and kill him."

"Your words, not mine." She tilted her head and raised one eyebrow.

"Maybe." I hesitated. "I don't know. He was really into the wine, so I guess that was my focus. I didn't really have time for a lengthy tasting, so I wasn't paying attention."

"What did you do after the tasting?" Kerry scribbled something on the page. "And where was Tom?

"We both came upstairs. I put the key back on the hook

and finished setting up." I glanced at the cellar door. "Tom was with me. It's not like he camped out downstairs."

Kerry closed her eyes briefly and placed the back of her palm over her mouth. "Sorry. I'm slightly off center tonight."

I could only imagine. I felt the same, and I'd only been in the cave-like room with Jimmy's body for a few minutes. Kerry had been downstairs examining the scene for nearly an hour. It gave me even more empathy for her line of work. I spent my days (whether frenzied or not) baking rhubarb crisps and citrus scones. Kerry faced death as part of her occupation, by choice. I served a little taste of joy into the world with raspberry cupcakes, and she ensured that justice would be served when it came to Jimmy's murder.

I was struck by the juxtaposition, and I appreciated that she was opening up. When she'd first arrived in Ashland, she had kept her emotions close to her chest. A few years ago, she never would have admitted that she was feeling off.

"Can I get you something?" I asked, leaning closer.

"No. I'll be fine." She swallowed hard and continued with her questions. "You're sure you returned the key?"

"Positive." I nodded emphatically. "Tom made another comment about being cavalier with our wine collection. At the time I thought he was under the impression that our reserve wines were valuable, but now I'm not sure. He's the reason that Andy came out to get me."

"Why?"

"According to Andy, Tom asked to be let into the cellar to get another bottle after the show. That's when Andy realized the key was missing."

"Did you see Tom when you went down to the cellar for the second time?"

"No. Come to think of it, I haven't seen Tom since the start of the play. Lance had him and a few other donors stand up and be recognized before the show started, but I never saw him again after that."

Kerry's well-defined eyebrows rose ever so slightly. "He wasn't waiting for the special wine downstairs when you returned, and you haven't seen him since?"

"Nope. Unless I missed him in the frenzy of activity, but I don't think I did. I came into the kitchen and checked for the key. It wasn't there, so I assumed that since Tom knew where we kept it, he had decided to let himself into the cellar. Then I went downstairs, found Jimmy, and came right back up here to the kitchen. I haven't left, and I haven't seen any sign of Tom." As I relayed the information to her, I wasn't so sure about Lance's theory that Sophie killed Jimmy. Tom also had a motive, and he had the opportunity. If he wanted another bottle of reserve, why had he disappeared?

Kerry finished asking me a few more questions. She closed her notebook and stood. "You're free to go once you're done with your closing procedures. Doug thinks it might be a long night, but there's no reason that you or your staff need to stay."

That was a relief, but I felt bad for her. "What about you and Thomas?"

She rubbed her sleeve. "He's probably freezing down there, but he insisted that I take his sweatshirt. I can't seem to regulate my temperature right now. One minute I'm freezing, and the next I'm burning up. I'm worried I might be coming down with something, but I need to push through."

"Do you?" I asked with sincerity, as I moved the chair back in its spot next to the hearth. "I've been feeling the same way lately, and maybe it's a sign from the universe that we're doing too much."

She sucked in a breath and squared her shoulders. "Maybe, but a man has been murdered. It's not like I can take a nap while there's a killer running loose. The first hours after a crime are critical, so it's going to have to be a lot more coffee for me."

"That I can do for you. Coffee is my middle name." I put an arm around her shoulder. "Thanks for all that you do for our community. I don't know how you do it. Ashland is lucky to have you, and so am I."

She squeezed my arm and brushed away a tear. "Don't make me cry, now. I have work to do."

"Fine." I gave her a half hug before pulling away. "But it's all true. You know that I care about you and I'm here if you need anything."

"Same." She didn't elaborate. She didn't need to. I knew that our friendship was equally important to her. Once things were calmer, I would find a date for a girls' night where we could sip some wine, hang out, and catch up.

Carlos was completing the last of the checklist when Kerry and I returned to the kitchen. "Julieta, you look so tired. It is time to take you home, isn't it?" He looked at Kerry for confirmation.

She nodded. "You've all been cleared to leave."

"Wait." I held up my index finger. "Not until we make a fresh pot. If you and the Professor and Thomas are going

to pull an all-nighter, the least we can do is keep you caffeinated."

"Sí, and feed you." Carlos opened the fridge. "Please
help yourself to anything."

We waited until the coffee brewed, and Carlos explained what each of the Tupperware tubs neatly stacked
in the fridge contained. Kerry promised to make sure the
Professor, Thomas, and anyone else working the case
knew they could make themselves at home in the kitchen.

I spent the short car ride home staring out the black
window into the star-drenched darkness. I appreciated that
Carlos didn't try to prod or force a conversation. We were
content to sit in the comfortable silence.

Once we were home, I slid under the covers, collapsed
into his arms, and drifted off into a less-than-restful sleep.
Images of the stage crumbling, wine bottles breaking,
and rogue corkscrews flying over the audience danced
through my fitful dreams. The problem was that Jimmy
was really dead. This wasn't a nightmare I could wake up
from.

Chapter Eight

After a night of tossing and turning, I woke long before the sun would rise. I didn't bother trying to get back to sleep. I knew it was futile, so I pulled on a pair of jeans and my favorite hoodie, and tiptoed downstairs.

I didn't want to wake Carlos or Ramiro, so I left them a note and headed outside to walk to Torte. I revered my morning walks. The air smelled damp from dew and sprinklers that had given backyard gardens an overnight soaking. I passed by the sprawling lawns of Southern Oregon University, where families of deer were huddled beneath redwood trees. The faintest hint of pinkish light tinged the sky. Stars flickered overhead, ready to make their retreat. Everything held the aroma of spring, fresh grasses, blooming bunches of flowers, and the crisp morning air. I drank it in and reminded myself that this was a new day.

I continued to Siskiyou Boulevard, passing the Carnegie Library and fire station, letting thoughts of Jimmy's murder consume me. Maybe instead of trying to squash the images, it was better to embrace them.

I barely registered the historic houses with their grand

porches and flowering baskets as I made it to the plaza, where the architecture shifted to Tudor-style buildings with welcoming façades and rows of antique streetlamps illuminated my path. Walking through downtown always felt like I was living in the pages of a storybook with the forested mountains tucking in the charming storefronts. London Station was decked out for the shifting season with buckets of sidewalk chalk, watering cans, terra-cotta pots, and seed packets. The record store displayed a collection of retro vinyl, and the vintage resale shop featured flowered sundresses for spring.

At Torte, I paused to admire Rosa's window display with its dainty cherry blossoms and pretty pink cake stands filled with blushing macarons and miniature tarts. Next door, A Rose by Any Other Name was still dark, as were the rafting shop and Puck's Pub. It would be another couple of hours before the plaza was humming with life. That was fine with me. I liked it this way. The bakeshop was my sanctuary—my happy place. Hopefully this morning it would provide respite. I needed to bake. Mom had always said that the easiest way to work out any problem was by kneading sticky bread dough, and that was exactly what I intended to do. There was nothing that compared with the calm of the kitchen, where I had to be fully present with my hands coated in flour, the aroma of caramelized sugar and cinnamon filling every room with a sweet, nurturing tranquility.

That's just what the doctor ordered, Jules.

I unlocked the basement door, turned on the lights, and warmed up the ovens. The team had left the kitchen spotless last night. Custom cake orders and the wholesale delivery list were posted on the whiteboard. A new bundle of applewood was stacked next to the wood-burning pizza oven, and the countertops glistened. Everything was in its place and ready for the day.

The flutters in my stomach had returned, but that didn't stop me from brewing a pot of coffee before gathering ingredients for two of my morning bakes. The first would be a sweet brioche filled with the first strawberries of the season. I also wanted to bake chocolate tahini cookies for our daily special.

For the brioche, I warmed milk, added a touch of sugar and yeast, and then set it aside to activate while I poured myself a cup of strong brew. Our signature Torte spring roast was a full-bodied coffee with notes of peaches and pomegranate and a spicy brown sugary finish. Andy had crafted the blend based on customer feedback. He spent two weeks perfecting the brew, taking copious notes, and making minor tweaks and adjustments to the roasting process. Admittedly, I was a fan of all his creations, but his spring brew was quickly becoming my new favorite.

After enjoying a few undisturbed moments with my coffee, I melted butter and whisked it together with the frothy yeast. I used a scale to weigh the dry ingredients. That would ensure accurate measurements for my strawberry brioche. Once a sticky dough had begun to form, I sprinkled the countertop with flour, rolled up my sleeves, and began kneading.

The tension I had been holding in my neck since discovering Jimmy's body fell away as every muscle in my arms fired. The dough was warm and stretchy. I put my weight into it as I formed a ball, massaged it, and repeated the process again and again. I thought about how many

problems I had worked out in the dough over the years—
my angst about leaving Carlos on the *Amour of the Seas*
and striking out on my own in Ashland, battles with Richard Lord over whether or not the town could support two
ice cream stands, worries about the bakeshop's future.

Mom's advice was correct. Visions of Jimmy faded, too.

Customers often commented on how lucky we were to
work in an artisan bakeshop and get to sample the fruits
of our labor every day. That was true, but for me, the
gift was this. I couldn't imagine another career path that
would allow me to spend time in a moving meditation
every morning, just me and the bread dough.

It was cheaper and much more delicious than therapy.

Not that I was opposed to therapy—I'd benefited from
it myself many times over the years—but I sometimes
wondered if we should start our own version of baking
therapy. Allow guests into the kitchen once a week for
quiet contemplation and sensory healing.

I smiled at the thought as I smeared, rolled, and twisted
strawberry preserves into my dough. I finished each loaf
off with pearl sugar and set them in greased baking tins
for another rise.

Next I gathered tahini, cocoa powder, maple syrup,
flaxseeds, almond flour, sea salt, baking soda, vanilla,
dark chocolate chips, and sesame seeds for my cookies.
I wanted a gluten-free vegan option for the pastry case. I
began by whisking tahini, cocoa powder, and the syrup.
Then I sifted in the dry ingredients. Once a batter had
formed, I stirred in the chocolate chips by hand. I rolled
the batter into two-inch balls and coated them with sesame seeds before using a spatula to flatten each cookie.
The cookies would bake for ten minutes and then need to

cool before serving because after cooling they would develop a soft brownie-like texture.

I swiped a taste of the batter. The nutty flavor from the tahini and sesame seeds paired with rich chocolate created a lovely balance.

Andy showed up just as I was putting the first trays into the ovens. "Morning, boss. That was wicked last night." His eyes were red and puffy, like he hadn't gotten much sleep either. He ran his fingers through his hair and stretched his arms overhead, trying to wake up.

"I know. I think I slept a total of five minutes. By the way, I'm sorry I missed you. Kerry was taking my statement. Were you there long?" I checked the brioche, which had risen nicely and was ready to bake.

"No, Thomas interviewed me and Sterling and then said we could take off. Carlos told us to go, I hope that was okay."

"Oh yeah, of course. I'm glad you left. It was already going to be a late night without having to stick around for a . . ." I trailed off.

"I know what you mean." Andy caught my eye, then his gaze drifted to the coffeepot. "Are you drinking boring, regular coffee this morning, boss?"

"It's your spring blend, so I wouldn't exactly call that boring, but I guess if that fits your definition, then I'm guilty as charged." I tried to wink, but my face contorted in a weird half grin. "I couldn't wait for you, though. I needed caffeine ASAP."

"I hear you on that." Andy unzipped his SOU football sweatshirt. "I've got a couple of ideas for a special that I'll bring down for you to try in a few minutes."

"Hey, before you get started, I never had a chance to

ask you about Tom last night, what with all of the police activity."

"He's a demanding dude," Andy said. "I felt bad pulling you away from the party, but he insisted that he needed another bottle and would only take one from the private reserve."

"Did you see him after he asked to get in the cellar?"

Andy considered my question. "No. Thomas asked me that last night, too. I wish I had been more observant, but it was controlled chaos at that point. You know how it is at the end of an event. We were bringing stuff in from outside. Everyone was running around, starting closing procedures, and Tom came into the kitchen basically demanding to be let into the cellar."

"That's when you realized the key was missing?" A blast of heat hit my face as I slid the loaves of brioche into the convection oven.

"Kind of." Andy tilted his head back and forth, like he was trying to decide if that was true. "Tom was the person who mentioned that the key was gone. I didn't give it much thought at the time because, like I said, we were busy and tired, and everyone wanted to clean up and get home, but I have a distinct memory of Tom standing next to the aprons and pointing at the empty hook."

"Hmmm."

"Right?" Andy swiped a taste of the cookie batter. "That's crazy good, boss."

"Thanks." My timer for the cookies dinged. I turned on the oven light to check them. "And what did you do after that?"

"I told him I would check with you. I knew you had taken him to the cellar earlier for a private tasting, so I figured that you probably stuck the key in your pocket. I left him in the kitchen, went outside to get you, and then I never saw him again."

I grabbed a silicone potholder and removed the first tray, resting it on the counter to cool. "He wasn't in the kitchen after you came to find me?"

Andy shook his head. "Nope. I didn't see him for the rest of the night. I don't know where he ended up, but it is weird that he wanted in the cellar so badly and then he vanished, right?"

"My thoughts exactly."

Andy went upstairs to fire up the espresso machine. I finished reviewing my to-do list until it was time to check the brioche loaves. They were a pale golden color, not quite done, so I returned them to bake a bit longer while I removed the cookies from the tray and put in the next batch.

I wasn't sure what the rest of the day had in store for me, but I knew one thing—I was going to try and find Tom. Perhaps he'd had one too many glasses of wine and simply wanted to keep his buzz going. Or perhaps there had been another reason he was lurking in Uva's kitchen.

Chapter Nine

As promised, Andy returned shortly with an iced cold brew with rice milk, vanilla, almond, cinnamon, and brown sugar. "Here you go, boss. This should go nicely with the tahini chocolate cookies, but I should probably try one to make sure, yeah?"

"Yeah. Me too." I took the drink and handed him a cookie. "This is exactly what I needed this morning, you are such a gem," I said, raising the glass in a toast and taking a sip of the creamy cold drink. It settled my stomach and went down so easy that I could have had a dozen.

The mood in the bakeshop was muted even after the entire team had arrived. Jimmy's murder had cast a pall over all of us and our guests, who had heard rumors of his death. Constant, hushed conversations replaced the normal happy banter of a typical Saturday. It was almost like you could feel the shock and grief reverberating throughout the kitchen and dining room. My team, myself included, moved slower. Customers lingered over egg and ham frittatas and Dutch babies with spiced apples, somberly rehashing last night's events.

Shortly after opening, I took a tray of strawberry swirl

brioche and cardamom buns upstairs and was surprised to find Lance chatting with Andy at the espresso bar. He was dressed in running clothes, but I had never seen Lance so much as jog. Maybe Arlo was encouraging him to train with the SOU softball team.

"You're making this a habit," I noted, pointing to the clock. "You better be careful. If we keep spotting you before noon, you're going to get a reputation for being a morning person."

Lance knocked back a shot of espresso like it was whiskey. "Darling, do not even start with me. Erase those terrible words from your beautiful lips. If I'm ever deemed a morning person, kill me." He set his espresso glass on the wood bar. "Hit with me another, Andrew. I need all the caffeine to get through me this ungodly hour."

"What are you doing here this early?" I asked.

"Duty calls." He motioned with his head toward the police station across the street. "The Professor asked if we could have a convo about Jimmy."

"I wonder if that means he learned something new. Or maybe he already received the coroner's report?"

Lance slugged another shot of espresso. "Your guess is as good as mine, although I don't think it's breaking news, because he set up this meeting last night. I assume that he's in desperate need of my help and insight, which is quite fortunate since Arlo was going to force me to do his morning workout routine with the team."

"Somehow I don't think anyone can force you to do anything you're not into, but I was curious about the attire." I motioned to his running shorts and warm-up jacket.

"Me sweating? Can you imagine?" Lance shook his head as his smile faded. "Honestly, I am sweating over

Jimmy's death. It's unfathomable. I barely slept last night, replaying the evening over and over and wondering if I failed to notice a glaring detail and if I'd shared everything of importance with the Professor."

I was glad he had steered the conversation back to Jimmy's murder. "Didn't the Professor take your statement at Uva last night?"

"He did." Lance set his glass on the bar and gave Andy a half bow, momentarily shifting tone again. "You've outdone yourself once again, our local boy wonder barista. I believe that two drinks shall suffice, but I'll be back if not."

Andy saluted him. "We're here to keep you caffeinated."

"Care to join me until the cavalry arrives?" Lance pointed to an empty booth and then proceed to make his way in that direction like a debutant at a ball. He gracefully glided between tables with a perfect regal posture, his chin lifted just high enough to portray confidence. Every step was deliberate and measured. He extended his hand when greeting other early risers with practiced charm.

It was as if the dining room was his own personal stage.

"Do tell, what have you heard? I'm on pins and needles waiting for more news." Lance rested his chin on his hands and leaned in, dropping the act once we were seated and no one was paying attention.

"Not much," I answered truthfully. "You mentioned Sophie last night, but I am curious about Tom." I went on to explain about the missing cellar key and Tom's vanishing act.

"Plot twist." Lance's eyes sparkled with anticipation

while the rest of his body remained composed. "Tom, what a sneaky tomcat."

"How well do you know him?"

"Not well. He approached me about the possibility of being a part of this new endeavor through none other than the dearly departed."

"Through Jimmy?" I clarified.

"Yes. Keep up. We've got a lot of ground to cover here." He snapped his fingers and scowled in mock disapproval that I had asked for clarification. "They did a production together in Washington a few years ago. Tom moved to the Rogue Valley recently and had been looking for artistic investment opportunities. He and Jimmy reconnected, and Jimmy introduced him to me. Or that's the story they fed me."

"The fact that they knew each other before seems suspicious."

Lance strummed his fingers on his chin. "I absolutely agree. Something smells fishy, and it's certainly not the bakeshop."

I made a face. "I hope not. We don't have salmon cakes on the menu today."

Lance wiggled his brows. "What we do have on the menu is a meeting with Ashland's finest detective. I'll be sure to butter him up and see if there are any other nuggets I can extract from him. After my tête-à-tête, I think it will be time for you and me to pay a visit to Mr. Rudolph. What do you say?"

"Do you know where to find him?"

"Please." Lance looked at me with utter exasperation. "It's *me* you're talking to."

"How could I possibly forget?" I bumped the top of my forehead with my palm.

"Don't worry, darling. It happens to the best of us." He patted my hand. "Now, scurry off to the kitchen like a good little mouse, and then we shall go hunting for tom-cats."

"But cats chase mice, not the other way around."

"Details. Details." He waved me away. "I'm meeting the cast at Uva around noon for an emergency sesh. If I have time, I'll come to find you after I've had my chat with the Professor. Otherwise let's regroup later this afternoon. Ta-ta!"

I left him and returned downstairs. So, Jimmy had encouraged Tom to invest in the Fair Verona Players. That was an unexpected piece of news. Money was a powerful motive when it came to murder, though I wasn't exactly sure how it would factor in here.

"Any word on tonight's show?" Marty asked, stacking bagged loaves of sourdough and cracked wheat for morning deliveries. His normally jovial expression had a touch of melancholy. "Everyone is upset about the murder. It's hard to imagine how the show goes on, but then again, I guess that's the adage."

"I agree. It's so surreal." My stomach lurched at the memory of the pool of blood around Jimmy's head. I inhaled slowly and forced myself to focus on Marty. "I was just chatting with Lance upstairs. I should have asked him, but it completely slipped my mind."

"That's okay. I'm sure you have plenty to think about." Marty smiled kindly, his rosy cheeks dimpling. "One of our wholesale clients asked if there would be food and drinks at tonight's performance. I told them I would check with you. I'm assuming you'll be pouring wine, but we're not doing a spread like last night for every show, are we?"

"No." I glanced at the whiteboard. "I put in an order for extra bread, as we'll prepare some boxed snacks and desserts for purchase if the show goes on tonight, but nothing like last night."

"That's what I thought. Thanks for the confirmation. I'll let them know." Marty continued packaging the bread.

I went through the menu for Uva. In theory, *The Taming of the Shrew* was due to run for the next three weekends with shows on Friday and Saturday evenings and a Sunday matinee. Our summer vineyard staff and volunteers would pour wine and sell premade Torte treat boxes, like a sweet dessert option with chocolate tahini cookies, lemon tarts, assorted macarons, and savory small-bite boxes. But there shouldn't be a need for any additional staffing. We would prepare everything at the bakeshop and deliver it to Uva daily, just like any other wholesale client.

For the snack boxes, we would offer guests three savory options and a dessert box. The first would include a miniature sourdough baguette with a cup of our house-made chicken salad, spiced nuts, and a cherry almond sugar cookie. The second choice was a classic peanut butter and jelly sandwich on our wheat-berry bread, layered with thinly sliced apples and granola. That would come with salted kettle chips and a dark chocolate brownie. The final savory box featured a hummus wrap with pickled veggies and a lemon cupcake. Finally, the dessert boxes would have a rotation of whatever we were baking at Torte.

I got started on the chicken salad while I waited for Lance. I used shredded rotisserie chicken as a base. I finely chopped celery, white onion, green onion, and fresh herbs. I added those to the chicken and creamed in Dijon mustard and mayonnaise. Then I seasoned the mixture with salt and pepper and fresh lemon juice before adding halved red grapes and sliced almonds. The salad would develop in the fridge as the flavors married together.

The peanut butter and jelly and the hummus wraps would be assembled on-site at Uva, but I tasked Sterling with doubling his hummus recipe so that we'd have plenty for the bakeshop and the play.

With that task complete, I turned my attention to our specialty orders. Graduation and wedding cake requests had already started to roll in. I had a feeling that the summer season was going to be particularly busy. Mom and I had talked about hiring a couple more support staff as June approached. Ramiro would be winding down the school year in a few weeks. It had gone by in such a flash, I couldn't believe it was almost time for him to return home to Spain. And I wasn't sure either Carlos or I were going to be able to cope with a teen-free house. I had gotten used to stocking the fridge, baking extra batches of cookies for his friends, sitting down to our weekend family board game sessions, and hearing all the details about his school day.

Having Ramiro live with us for the last year had been the best decision ever, and I could already feel my heart beginning to break at the thought of not getting to see him every day.

Bethany delicately added buttercream roses to the top of a two-layer birthday cake. "Jules, do you have a second?"

"For you, always." I smiled and focused my attention on

her work. It was a good distraction. Pre-grieving Ramiro finishing his stint in American high school wasn't going to serve me well, especially after the emotional roller coaster I'd been on for the last twenty-four hours. "Those are so real that I almost can't believe it's frosting."

Bethany's dimples creased as she smiled with pride. "Really? Thanks. That's high praise coming from you."

"Are you kidding? I can barely keep up with you and Steph these days." I bent over to examine her work more carefully. Her piping skills were flawless. It had taken me years to perfect my technique, but Bethany was a natural. Her precision and attention to detail showed in her fondant designs and painstakingly delicate piping of rosettes.

"We joke all the time about how we won the pastry lottery getting to have you as a mentor, Jules, so nice try." Bethany smiled as she switched a nozzle on a piping bag filled with sky blue buttercream.

"Well, aside from our mutual lovefest, what else can I do for you?" I noticed that she had a spot on her workspace for all her tools—spatulas, carving tools, piping tips. Her organization was as impressive as her artistry.

"I wanted to talk about a revamp for the Unbeatable Brownie this summer." She gnawed on the side of her lip.

"Ooohhh, tell me more."

Bethany had started her baking career in her tiny home kitchen by preparing and delivering boxes of her delectable brownies. Mom and I had met her at the annual Chocolate Festival many years ago and had fallen head over heels in love with her brownies, her talent, and her infectious positive energy. We had offered her a role at Torte with a small percentage of ownership. It was a decision I never regretted.

We had continued her tradition of offering boxes of dark chocolate and sea salt brownies, cheesecake brownies, and every other flavor combination under the sun. The boxes were popular amongst our regular clientele and tourists. They always sold out, so I was very curious to hear what she had in mind for a revamp.

"The dessert boxes you're doing for the theater got me thinking that we could offer Torte subscriptions where customers either pick up or get a box of brownies and weekly specials that are exclusive to the boxes every week." She sucked in a breath. "What do you think?"

"I love it. That's such a great idea."

"Okay, cool." Her freckled cheeks flushed a light shade of red. "Steph and I have some sketches to show you. We'll put together a couple of sample boxes today and see what you think. If you like them, I can post on our social media and see what kind of response we get."

"I can't wait," I said sincerely. I loved that my staff was empowered to come up with ideas, and I also loved that Bethany (and the rest of the team) was constantly thinking out of the box when it came to the bakeshop and trends. In this case, I guess technically speaking, she was thinking in the box.

Sterling and I then talked through lunch specials and everything else needed for Uva. "How are you holding up, Jules?" His steel eyes felt like they were piercing through my soul.

"I'm okay. I've been better, honestly, but you know, it's good to be here, doing something." I leafed through the wedding cake orders for next week. "And there's certainly plenty to do."

He tilted his head to one side and nodded, but I could

tell from the way he tightened his lips that he didn't agree. "You don't always have to be okay. You're human. You've just been through a major ordeal, and you spend an inordinate amount of time worrying and caring about all of us. What would it feel like to give that back to yourself?"

I gulped. How did he always know the right thing to say?

Sterling had become like a brother, and his words cut through me, piercing my already tender heart.

"Fair point," I managed to say, willing myself not to cry. "Thanks for checking in. I promise I'm working on taking care of myself."

He gave me a one-sided smile. "I'm going to hold you to that, Jules."

"Deal." I could tell he was letting me off the hook for the moment. It seemed to be a recurring theme. The universe was sending me loud and clear messages about my need to focus on self-care.

Sterling returned to the stove. Marty left for bread deliveries, and Bethany and Steph were in the decorating zone, so I wandered back upstairs to see if by chance Lance and the Professor were still meeting. It was a longshot. Neither of them was still at Torte.

Rosa passed by me with a plate of egg and avocado toast. "Jules, Lance asked me to tell you that he was urgently needed at Uva and could you please meet him there as soon as you have a minute."

"He's at Uva already?" It was shortly after eleven. Lance had mentioned meeting the cast at noon, but there was no reason I needed to be there for that.

She repositioned the tray and made room for a couple of teenagers waiting for their hot chocolate orders to squeeze by us. "That's what he said. He didn't have time to find you but stopped me to make sure that I relayed the message. I was about to come downstairs after I dropped off this order."

"Thanks for letting me know."

She lifted the tray and headed toward a table of eager diners.

I stared out the front windows to the plaza. What was Lance doing at Uva? The vineyard wouldn't open for tasting for another hour. A group huddled in front of the Lithia bubblers with their phones in hand, ready to record friends taking a sip of the healing waters. It was a daily tradition to watch unsuspecting tourists drink from the sulfuric fountains.

Saturday morning held a leisurely vibe. No one appeared to be in a hurry as they stopped to admire pastel spring floral arrangements at A Rose by Any Other Name next door. There was already a small line at the rafting window where adventure seekers could sign up for a day of whitewater on the Rogue. A family with young children on tiny bikes rode past on their way to Lithia Park.

What had changed with Lance? Why the sudden need to go to Uva? Could it have to do with his conversation with the Professor?

There was one simple way to find out—I would check in with the team to make sure I wasn't needed and then take the first load of baking and snack box supplies to the vineyard. If Lance was in that much of a hurry, there had to be a good reason, and I had a feeling it was connected to Jimmy's murder.

Chapter Ten

I loaded the delivery van with tubs of chicken salad, hummus, brownies, and all the other supplies needed to assemble the snack and dessert boxes and made the short drive to Uva. Carlos was tending to a new crop of grapes when I pulled into the driveway. The sight of him in his fitted jeans and casual chambray work shirt brought a different kind of fluttering to my stomach. His skin was naturally tanned from so much time spent under the southern Oregon sun, and his dark hair was covered with an Uva baseball cap. Every time I saw him, whether he was wearing weathered jeans or a suit and tie, I fell a little more in love with him.

He snipped the vine and then looked up and spotted me. I parked on the side of the driveway and got out of the van.

"You are here early. The tasting room doesn't open for another hour," he said, tucking his pruning shears into his back pocket and greeting me with a long kiss. "We missed you this morning."

"Sorry, I couldn't sleep."

"I figured. This is nothing new, mi querida." Carlos pulled away and studied my face. "How are you now?"

"Fine. Better. I don't know. Maybe that's just a story I'm trying to tell myself to be functional." I looked around the house and grassy outdoor tasting area for any sign of the Professor's investigation. There wasn't any crime scene tape or a police officer posted in front of the tasting room. I wondered if that meant they were done with their inquiries here.

"Sí, it is understandable." Carlos massaged my thumb with his fingers. "Is there anything I can do?"

"I have supplies for tonight. You could help me unload. The real reason I'm here is to meet Lance. Have you seen him?"

"Lance?" Carlos wrinkled his nose in confusion.

"Yeah, isn't he here?"

"No." Carlos looked from the vineyard to the house. "Unless he's inside. Maybe I didn't see him. I was down in the bottom half of the acreage earlier. Why would he be here now? I thought they were meeting at noon."

"I don't know. He and the Professor were supposed to connect at Torte. We were going to talk after, but he left and asked Rosa to tell me to meet him here."

"He must be inside, or in the barn. I was down in the vineyard pruning." He pointed to the van. "Are you ready to unload first?"

"I don't want to keep you from pruning."

He rolled up his sleeve and glanced at his watch. "This is a good time for a break. The tasting room volunteers will be here soon."

In the summer we used a combination of volunteers and part-time employees to staff the tasting room. Volunteers poured wine for a few hours in exchange for a few bottles for themselves. Our volunteers tended to be teachers, stay-at-home parents, and retirees who were looking to have a little social interaction without the responsibilities of a full-time job. It was a win for everyone. We were able to offer extended tasting hours, and our volunteer crew received a mini course in viticulture and complimentary wine to bring home to share with friends and family.

As head chef on the *Amour of the Seas*, Carlos was known for his wine dinners. He had never formally trained as a sommelier, but his palate was pristine, and he had a deep appreciation for small farms and serving seasonal food that was grown naturally and prepared by hand. These skills had translated seamlessly into wine making. He took classes, connected with other vintners, and spent nearly every waking hour amongst the vines, singing to the grapes like they were his babies. Lance often joked that I had to keep an eye on him; otherwise, he was going to fall in love with another woman—his beloved grapevines.

"Do you want a ride?" I asked Carlos.

"No, I'll walk and meet you there."

I smiled as I watched him work his way past Adirondack chairs and picnic tables on the path that led up to the house. When Carlos told me that he was ready to give up his vagabond lifestyle on the *Amour of the Seas* and move to Ashland to be with me, I never would have believed that he would end up so happy. I had worried that Ashland would feel small and stifling after over a decade of sailing from one adventurous port of call to another. I was worried that I would hold him back, that he was giving up what he loved for a chance at rekindling our love.

It just goes to show that sometimes the problems we create in our imagination turn out to be works of fiction. Carlos was clearly at home with the vines. He spent hours tinkering with his grapes. I could see how the connection to the land had changed him. His wanderlust had been transformed by the grounding force of the lush Rogue Valley. Our daily rhythm was different than it had been on the ship, and yet in some ways very similar.

He talked about the grapes like they were members of our extended family, singing to them softly as he snipped away dead sections of the vine, and dialing in the exact amount of water they needed to survive, yet not without effort. "It's the struggle that breeds the best vintages," he had once said.

His words had lingered. It was a perfect metaphor for life, especially our life. It was because of our struggles that we had reached this contented point. I found myself grateful for the challenge of our years apart. If you had asked me when I first left the ship, I never would have imagined that my endless tears and months spent questioning our relationship and my future would have led to where we were now. Those experiences had allowed us to grow together.

I let out a soft sigh as I steered the van into a parking space in front of the house and noticed Lance's EV parked near the gate. Lance had a collection of vehicles ranging from this latest electric obsession to a retro Range Rover. He quietly operated his own personal car lending library for temporary actors who needed transportation during their stay in Ashland. Lance would "check out" vehicles to them at no charge and tuck gift certificates to local restaurants into the glove box.

While he had grown up with enormous wealth and family fortune, he had made it his mission to anonymously donate large portions of his trust to causes near and dear to his heart, as well as invest in small businesses throughout the Rogue Valley. Very few people knew about Lance's philanthropic tendencies, which was exactly the way he wanted it.

"Thank goodness you're here." Lance rushed to greet me before I had a chance to get out of the van. He was still in his running gear. "We have a problem. A serious problem."

"What?" My heart thudded in my chest as I stuffed the keys in my pocket and closed the van door.

"It's Sophie." He pointed to the tasting room.

"I don't understand." Pointing to the empty room did nothing to clarify his meaning.

Lance waved his hands in circles like he was trying to will me to catch up with whatever he was trying to say.

Carlos strolled up to us, rubbing a stalk of rosemary between his fingers.

"Oh, good. You're here, too, perfect," Lance said in a rushed tone, clapping Carlos on the back. "We need all the help we can get right now."

"What's going on?" I repeated, looking around in every direction. Nothing seemed out of place, but Lance's bulging eyes and fidgeting had the tiny blond hairs on my forearms standing at attention.

Had there been another murder?

Was Sophie okay?

Did I need to call the Professor?

"I got a frantic, nearly incoherent phone call from Sophie while I was meeting with Doug," Lance explained, gesturing wildly with his hands. "She was inconsolable, muttering about being responsible for Jimmy's death."

"Wait, she admitted to killing him?" I looked at Carlos in disbelief. Had I heard Lance wrong?

"She wasn't making sense. She was rambling on about how she couldn't live with herself. She would never be able to forgive herself, and she couldn't go on."

"That sounds like a confession," I said, noting internally that it also sounded like Sophie was in a bad place in terms of her mental health. "Why are you here, though?"

Lance pointed to the house. "To find Sophie. She's—holding vigil. I can't get her to budge."

"What did Doug say about this?" Carlos asked. He sounded as confused as I felt.

"We agreed that it would be best for me to approach Sophie alone. I'm sure he has his reasons, but he doesn't seem to think that she's a 'flight risk'—his words, not mine. He's on his way and has been in contact with a licensed therapist, but in the meantime, she's glued herself to the cellar door."

"Glued herself?" I tried to piece together everything Lance was saying. Could this be an open-and-shut case? But if Sophie had confessed to Jimmy's murder, wouldn't the police want to arrest her immediately? Something didn't make sense. Actually, pretty much nothing made sense.

"Not *literally*, darling, but like I said, she's not budging. Maybe you'll have better luck. Woman to woman, so to speak."

"She's downstairs?"

Lance pointed the way.

"I'll unload the van," Carlos wisely suggested. "When Doug and the police arrive, I'll let them know you're in the cellar."

I followed Lance downstairs. Sure enough, Sophie was slumped against the cellar door. Her clothes and hair were disheveled, making me wonder if she'd slept here last night. She had her knees tucked entirely into her oversized crew sweatshirt.

She wiped her nose on her sleeve and squinted at me as we approached.

"Sophie, you remember my friend Jules?" Lance asked, practically purring like a cat with his soothing tone.

She bobbed her head, brushing away tears from her splotched cheeks, not meeting my eyes.

"I thought it might be easier for you to talk with her. Jules has had her fair share of heartbreak." Lance was laying it on thicker than our buttercream.

"Can I get you anything?" I knelt next to her, ignoring a wave of dizziness that came with bending over. "A glass of water? Tea? A sandwich?"

"No. Thank you, though." She sniffed, sucking air in tiny bursts through her nose. "I don't know that I'll ever be able to eat or drink again. He's dead. He's really dead."

"You're in shock. It's normal to feel like that," I said, in what I hoped was a calm and even tone.

"I can't believe it's true." She rocked against the wall, causing the shelves to rumble slightly. "I keep thinking it's a bad dream and I'm going to wake up any minute, you know?"

"It sounds like you two were close," I prodded.

Lance hung back near the stairs, close enough to hear our conversation but far enough away to not feel like he was looming over us.

"I loved him." Sophie buried her head in hands and broke down.

"It's okay to cry." I put my hand on her shoulder. "It's your body's way of releasing and healing."

"But it's my fault. If it weren't for me, he'd still be here," she gasped between sobs. "I did it. I'm responsible. The police can arrest me now and put me out of my misery. I don't deserve to be alive while he's dead. I can't believe what I've done. I can't go on another minute like this. It's me. I'm the reason that Jimmy Paxton, the man I loved, the man I was going to marry, is dead."

I couldn't believe it, Lance was right.

Sophie wasn't even attempting to conceal her guilt. She had killed Jimmy and was understandably overcome with regret. Dozens of questions competed for space in my brain, but one rose above the rest: If she had loved him and intended on marrying him, why would she have killed him?

Chapter Eleven

"Would it help to talk about it?" I asked Sophie, who continued to try to calm herself by clutching her knees to her chest and rocking back and forth.

Lance nodded in approval and twisted his index finger to signal that I should keep her talking.

Sophie sniffled, her shoulders heaving in rhythm with her sobs. "It's so awful. He can't be dead. He can't be." She shook her head so hard it made mine hurt. "Nothing will help. Not talking about it. Not anything. The only thing that would help would be the ability to travel back in time. If I could do that, Jimmy would still be here."

I had the sense that we were going to be there a while, so I sat down next to her. "Can you walk me through what happened last night?"

She tucked her hand into her sleeve and then used it to dab her tears. "It started right before the show. He was freaking out about issues on the stage, and Ed wouldn't listen. Jimmy wasn't the problem. I mean, I know, I get that he had an ego, but that's just because of his brilliant acting. He was a genius. You must have seen that last night.

The audience loved him. Without Jimmy, the play would have been flat."

I didn't necessarily agree. Lance's ensemble cast deserved equal credit, but arguing that point with Sophie in the state she was in wasn't going to get us anywhere, so I nodded at her to continue.

"Weird things have been happening in rehearsals." She yanked a loose string from her sleeve. "Accidents, mishaps, even a prop gun misfired. There aren't any guns in the production, so we still don't know how it ended up on the stage."

That matched everything Lance had relayed.

"Jimmy was convinced that someone was trying to kill him."

"Really?" I couldn't contain my surprise. Jimmy had suspected that someone wanted to hurt him. That could explain the accidents on set, or it could also mean he was delusional and assumed that anything or everything happening onstage was directly connected to him.

She smeared her mascara, trying to dry her tears. "Yes. All of the incidents onstage were connected to him. He told me that he was sure they weren't accidents." She used air quotes to emphasize "accidents."

"Why would someone want to kill him?" I asked.

She shrugged. "I don't know. That's what we were trying to figure out. He asked me to be his eyes and ears, and honestly, I was freaked out. At first, I thought maybe he was being kind of dramatic about it. You know actors and their superstitions."

Lance coughed and cleared his throat.

Sophie looked at him like she was realizing he was in the cellar for the first time.

"Apologies. The dust is triggering my allergies." He fanned his face, brushing away any imaginary pollutants.

"Anyway, once I started paying more attention, I realized that Jimmy was right. Every accident on set involved him. First there was the trapdoor that didn't latch. Jimmy fell through it during rehearsals. Fortunately the crew had already placed mats beneath it for the next scene, but if they hadn't been ahead of schedule, Jimmy would have been seriously injured or worse." She paused. "The rigging fell and nearly crushed him. Someone changed the sets around and made him slam into one of the dance platforms. The accidents kept escalating, but I never saw who was doing it."

"You were helping him figure out who was trying to kill him, but you killed him?" I couldn't contain my confusion any longer.

Sophie recoiled and threw her hands up. "No, what? I didn't kill him."

"But you said you were responsible and the police should arrest you."

"For telling him to meet me here, not *killing* him," she wailed. "I would never kill him. I loved him. I should have urged him to go to the police. Or I should have called the police myself. He wasn't paranoid. He was in danger, and I could have done something about it."

That made much more sense.

Lance caught my eye and motioned for me to keep asking her questions. He looked like he was waiting to audition for a part in his running gear.

"You told him to meet you in the cellar?" I asked Sophie.

Her breath wavered unsteadily, her inhales hitching

and faltering like an old car stubbornly refusing to start. "Yeah, which is why this is all my fault. I told him that I would keep a close eye on the cast and crew during last night's performance. He felt like things were escalating too. He was worried that whoever was trying to kill him was going to do it during the performance. Ed had me spooked. I'm sure that he moved Jimmy's mark. I think his goal was to try and get Jimmy to fall off the stage. We just needed proof. I tried to film him when he was putting tape down, but he caught me, and I had to make up a lie on the spot about getting footage from the audience's perspective."

"Do you think Ed was behind the other accidents, too?" I asked.

She tilted her head up and down in a silent yes. "It had to be him. As the lead set designer, he had access to everything—the set, props, costumes, lighting, sound."

Lance gave a slight jerk of his head, affirming Sophie's statement.

Her tears had subsided. "Ed has been trying to kill Jimmy for weeks, and he finally succeeded last night. If only I hadn't told Jimmy to meet me here. Ed must have gotten to him first . . ." She couldn't finish.

"Do you have any sense why Ed would have wanted to kill Jimmy?" I shifted on the cold floor. It was stuffy in the small room. I was starting to feel a touch claustrophobic.

"Why wouldn't he? Jimmy had everything Ed wanted— fame, adoration, fans, talent, that hair, and gorgeous eyes. Jimmy's career was about to break wide open. He had an audition for a pilot in LA that was going to make him a household name."

Lance arched his eyebrows in astonishment.

"Does Ed covet the spotlight?" I asked. Most of the crew members I had met over the years relished their roles behind the scenes, but maybe that was different for Ed. One of the things that I loved most about the theater was that there was a place for everyone, whether you wanted to be belting out tunes center stage or mending a broken skirt seam backstage with a flashlight between your teeth.

"I don't think he wanted the spotlight; he just hated that Jimmy had the spotlight. I know that he was intentionally sabotaging Jimmy and putting him in danger. I don't know what happened between them last night that made him finally snap, but I know that he killed Jimmy."

"How do you think he found out that you two were meeting here after the show?"

"I wish I knew." She massaged her temples. "He must have seen me, or maybe he overheard us. I told Jimmy that I was going to document the performance on my phone. That way we could review it afterward and see what Ed was up to. Jimmy was extra cautious with his blocking. I don't know if you picked up on that last night, but he was careful to watch each step and stay far away from the edge of the stage. He was even worried that the lighting or rigging was going to fall on him, so he made sure to stay underneath it for as little time as possible."

I hadn't picked up on any of that. Jimmy's performance had been flawless, so to consider that he had simultaneously been concerned about his well-being made it all the more impressive.

"We agreed to meet in the cellar as soon as he had done his required postshow appearance. The cast is supposed to mingle with patrons for a few minutes after closing and then we were going to meet here. He wasn't going to bother getting out of costume or makeup, because we didn't want to run the risk of Ed getting wind of what we were up to."

"But he never made it back outside again, because he was killed," I said aloud.

"I know, and by the time I came down here, the police had already arrived and were trying to revive him." She stared at the ground like she was imagining Jimmy's lifeless body.

For the first time since she'd revealed her theory of Ed being the killer, I questioned her story. Where had she been between the time the play ended and when I'd discovered Jimmy's body?

As if reading my mind, she kept talking. "I got stuck outside with Bertie. If only I would have made an excuse to get away from her faster, Jimmy might still be alive."

"When was this?"

"During the standing ovation. I was heading for the cellar when Bertie stopped me. She had extensive notes about changes she wanted to implement. I tried to get away from her as fast as possible, but she's my boss, so I couldn't exactly just leave. It felt like we were talking forever, but at the time, I wasn't super worried, because I knew that Jimmy was probably going to be signing a lot of headshots and playbills. As soon as I finished documenting everything Bertie wanted changed, I came straight here, but like I said, Jimmy was already—already dead."

I patted her arm as tears spilled down her cheeks again.

"I couldn't have been talking to Bertie for more than ten minutes," she said through sobs. "Ed must have used the opportunity to strike. I heard that he stabbed Jimmy with a corkscrew, that's so brutal. It must have been a painful way to die." Her flat gaze remained focused on the spot where I'd discovered Jimmy.

"The police assured me last night that Jimmy likely died quickly." I wasn't sure that information would be helpful, but it felt important to share. Sophie was obviously distraught over his death. That much I believed.

"I hope that's true." Her wide dark eyes met mine. "I also hope they make Ed pay for what he's done."

"We can't say for sure that Ed killed Jimmy." I tried to reason with her. "At this point, everyone is a suspect, including both of us." I figured including myself might help her open up even more.

"But I never made it to the cellar last night. How could I have killed him?" she wailed. "Bertie will back me up. She can tell them that we were together when Jimmy was killed. I know that Ed can't say that. He doesn't have an alibi."

"How do you know?" I studied the wine racks, briefly considering the possibility that Jimmy's killer could have hidden out in the cellar lying in wait. But it was impossible. There was nowhere to hide. The shelves were only as deep as the wine bottles. No one could have squeezed behind them. The only other things in the room were the table and chairs. Maybe the killer hid underneath the table, but that didn't make sense either. They would have been hiding in plain sight.

"Because I saw him on my way to the cellar." Her tone shifted as she sat up straighter.

"You saw him where?"

"He was leaving the winery and headed back to the stage." She pointed upstairs. "He must have already killed

Jimmy at that point and was trying to get outside again before anyone realized what happened."

"You saw Ed leaving the tasting room?"

She nodded. "Yes, and he was acting super shady. He was carrying big boxes. He was looking all around him, trying to make sure that no one noticed him. I don't think anyone did, except for me. What I didn't realize at the time was that Jimmy was already dead."

"Do you know when this was?"

"I checked my watch when Bertie finally made it through her endless list of everything she wanted changed. It was ten forty-five when I left her by the food tables."

"Did you tell the police this last night?"

"I can't remember. Last night was a total blur." She squeezed her eyes tight as if trying to block out the memory.

Again her response struck me as odd. If she really believed that Ed had killed Jimmy and she had seen him fleeing the scene of the crime, wouldn't that be the first thing she told the police?

There was something she wasn't telling me, but the sound of footsteps brought a halt to a conversation.

The Professor, Thomas, and Kerry appeared in the doorway. Lance moved out of the way.

"I was told that we might find you here. I'm so pleased that you've been in such good hands with Juliet and Lance." The Professor removed a Moleskine notebook from his tweed jacket and stepped closer.

Thomas turned off the walkie-talkie attached to his belt, and Kerry whispered something to Lance.

I took that as my cue to let them take over. "Come by the bakeshop anytime, if you ever need to talk," I said to

Sophie, pushing myself to my feet and catching the Professor's eye.

He gave me a subtle nod of appreciation.

Lance and I went upstairs to give them privacy. I wasn't sure how much of Sophie's story I believed, but one thing I knew for sure was that this wasn't an open-and-shut case. Instead of shrinking, my suspect list was growing rapidly.

Chapter Twelve

Lance reached for a container of heavy cream and poured a generous splash into his cup of French press. "Carlos, you are a godsend, my friend. Thank you for this."

Carlos smiled in acknowledgment. "I thought Doug, Kerry, and Thomas might be in need of some sustenance while they investigate." He arranged a tray of fresh fruit, berries, slices of sourdough, and honey butter, along with French press, cream, and sparkling water. "It sounds like they'll be in and out for most of the day."

"That reminds me, I forgot to ask you earlier," I said to Lance. "What do you want to do about tonight's performance?"

"The show must go on, darling. There's no question. I've already called Jimmy's understudy. He landed late last night and is ready to step in. The cast is meeting me here in an hour for a quick dress rehearsal. People have paid for a show, and a show is what they will get."

I expected that would be his response.

"Of course, we'll hold a moment of silence and reflection for Jimmy and cooperate with the police." Lance stirred his coffee and pondered for a minute. "It's a shame that Jimmy's understudy was stuck in Mexico yesterday. Otherwise, it would have been quite Shakespearean to have the starlet waiting in the wings to bump off the lead."

"What did you think of Sophie's explanation?" I asked Lance, plucking a red grape from the bunch and popping it in my mouth. "You mentioned being concerned about the weird accidents on set. Do you think that there's a chance she's right? Could one of the members of the Fair Verona Players—cast or crew—been trying to kill Jimmy and finally succeeded last night?"

"Failed attempts?" Carlos looked at me and then Lance for clarification.

"Sophie is convinced that someone was trying to kill Jimmy," I said, grabbing more grapes. The sweet, sugary, juicy bites were like a little hit of energy. "She thinks that the accidents during rehearsals weren't accidents at all."

"Is this true?" Carlos whisked whipping cream with vanilla bean paste and fine sugar.

"I'm afraid so." Lance plunged a stir stick into his coffee and swirled in the cream until it turned a light shade of toffee. "Although she's not correct about not taking the incidents seriously. We filed reports for each accident, and I have been watching the stage like the red-tailed hawks that frequent the vineyard. It's most distressing to have anything go awry and a surefire way to kill any creative energy. The irony is that Sophie never came to me. If she was so concerned about Jimmy's safety and well-being, wouldn't it make logical sense that she inform me?"

"Maybe she was worried that you would think she was overreacting," I suggested.

"Perhaps. Or could it be that she's so lovesick that

it made her sick?" Lance raised an eyebrow. "Sophie's reaction to Jimmy's death has me questioning its authenticity. I wonder if she's picked up a trick or two watching actors run lines. That felt too on the nose for me. It felt like a performance, and not a particularly great one, I might add."

"I had that sense, too. Part of me believes her, but I don't think we got the entire story." I reached for another grape. "How well do you know Ed? If Sophie was telling the truth about seeing him leaving the tasting room last night, do you think there's a possibility he could have done it?"

"Anything is possible at this stage, isn't it?" Lance blew on his coffee before taking a timid sip. "It's no secret that Ed was not a fan of Jimmy's. You witnessed that firsthand yesterday, but Ed is a professional. I can't fathom why he would put his career in jeopardy, especially because he and I had a chat about making changes. He was aware of my intention to replace Jimmy. Why kill him?"

"Maybe he didn't plan to," Carlos suggested. The muscles in his arms flexed as he whipped the cream. Carlos was old-school when it came to method. If given the chance, he would always opt to use his hands over modern equipment. When he was running a kitchen with a huge rotating staff on the *Amour of the Seas* and serving multiple courses to hundreds of guests, that wasn't possible. Since being in Ashland, he embraced cooking slowly, juicing lemons and kneading pizza dough with his hands. It was the same approach he used in the vineyard.

He caught me staring at him and shot me a flirty grin as he dipped his pinkie into the fluffy whipped cream and licked it off his finger. "Could they have gotten in a fight that went too far?"

Lance and I nodded in unison.

Carlos added the whipped cream to his breakfast spread and turned on a calming classical playlist.

"I considered that," Lance replied first. "A corkscrew as a murder weapon does have a certain *Hamlet*-esque ring to it."

I shuddered.

"Sorry." Lance grimaced.

"It's okay." I buttered a slice of sourdough. "What we need to learn from the Professor is the actual time of death. Then maybe we can try to place where everyone was when Jimmy was killed and start ruling out suspects instead of constantly adding more."

"Excellent point," Lance agreed. "I'm also quite curious about the supposed footage that Sophie recorded last night. It's probably a long shot, but there's an outside chance that she could have caught something while filming."

"Filming?" Carlos looked at me for clarification.

I filled him on what Sophie had shared.

"That reminds me of something," Carlos said with a slight gasp. Unlike Lance, he had no propensity toward exaggeration. "I saw him, too."

"You saw Ed?" Lance asked. He slathered honey butter on two slices of bread, filled them with berries, and smashed them together to make a sandwich.

"Sí. Sí." Carlos nodded like he was replaying the scene in his mind. "I had come around on the deck with empty trays. I didn't want to disturb the cast, because I knew you were using the main tasting room entrance for them to go upstairs to change." He motioned in that direction. "I almost missed him, but I caught a flash of someone running toward the vineyard. It took me a minute to process what

I was seeing. At first, I thought maybe it was an eager fan trying to sneak onto the deck to get an autograph, but then I realized it was Ed. I recognized his crew shirt and his headlamp.

"When was this?" Lance set his coffee on the island and paced from the door to the stove. "Because Ed shouldn't have been anywhere near here. He was supposed to be in the wings for the entire show, and then postshow, he should have been going through his closing checklist."

Carlos shrugged. "I don't remember exactly. I came up to the house to check on the kitchen and get trays to make carting everything back inside easier. It couldn't have been long after the play was done. Maybe ten or fifteen minutes. Julieta and I were chatting with Helen and Doug and enjoying the lively atmosphere." He paused and turned to me. "You got wrapped up in a conversation with your mom. It was not long after that. People had begun to disperse, but most of the cast hadn't come back outside yet."

"This changes everything," Lance said, rubbing his hands together like he was trying to warm them up. "What was Ed doing on the deck and running through the vines? That sounds very nefarious."

"Was he running toward the vines?" I asked.

Carlos handed Lance a napkin. "Sí, I came along the path and took the side stairs to the deck so I could enter the tasting room through the sliding doors. I noticed movement and looked up to see him running away."

"So it definitely wasn't a fan hoping for an autograph." I took a bite of my bread. The tangy sourdough balanced beautifully with the creamy honey.

"No, no." Carlos shook his head. "I don't think I was

explaining myself well. That was just the first thing that came to my mind, but I'm sure it was Ed. He was tall, bulky, wearing a crew shirt and a headlamp. He was also carrying boxes."

"That's Ed," Lance confirmed, dabbing his chin with the napkin as he went in for another bite of his berry creation.

"This is my point," I said through a mouthful of bread and butter. "Five minutes ago, we were sure that Sophie was the killer, now Ed."

"You're right. We need a more exact window for the time of death from the police," Lance said.

At that moment, Thomas came into the kitchen. He was dressed for duty in his blue uniform, shorts, and hiking boots. No matter the weather, Thomas wore shorts. Even in the dead of winter when the plaza was coated in layers of snow and ice, Thomas could be spotted walking his beat in his signature shorts with running tights.

I caught a glimpse of Kerry and the Professor escorting Sophie out of the tasting room. They flanked her on either side, but I couldn't tell if her hands were cuffed.

"What's going on?" I asked, peering around Thomas to try and get a better look. "Are you arresting Sophie?"

Thomas ran his hands through his hair, which he had grown out. It fell in loose waves over his eye. "Geez, Jules, can't a guy beg you for a cup of coffee before you launch into it?"

"Sorry." I gave him a sheepish smile and poured him a cup of French press.

"Manners, darling, manners." Lance waved a scolding finger at me.

"Lance, you have no room to speak." Thomas raised his mug in a toast. "This is your influence."

"Moi?" Lance patted his chest. "Never."

Thomas generously buttered a slice of bread. "Thanks for the snacks, Carlos. At least there's one adult in the room."

"Hey." Lance's mouth hung open. "We're only trying to help you solve your case. You should be thanking us."

"The Professor actually tasked me with giving you an update." Thomas took a huge bite of the sourdough and glanced at the tasting room to make sure everyone was gone. "We are not making any formal arrests at this point, but the Professor and Kerry are taking Sophie to the station for further evaluation."

"Evaluation?" I blurted out.

He lowered his voice. "They want to do a well-check before they release her. The Professor has some concerns about her stability in the short term. She's taken the death hard, and he doesn't want to send her off on her own without resources and support."

That didn't sound like they thought she was a suspect, more like they were worried about her mental health. The Professor's perspective on detective work had always focused on the community. He saw himself as a connector and made it his mission to ensure that he disseminated information about resources to anyone and everyone who needed it. Sometimes that meant giving tourists directions and restaurant recommendations, and sometimes it meant delivering food and supplies to the unhoused, doing well-checks on seniors living alone, and hosting bike safety workshops at the elementary school.

"Is there a time of death?" Lance asked.

"Not yet." Thomas savored the buttery bread. "This is delicious, by the way. Is that honey in the butter?"

"Honey grown here at the vineyard," Carlos replied with a hint of pride. He had partnered with the neighboring farm to raise honeybees. His hive had expanded, which was great for pollinating the grapes, and one large benefit was that we were able to reap the rewards of the harvest with jars of organic honey, free of additives and infused with the floral scents of our growing region. He had become an advocate for pollinator populations, which were essential for the health of the vines. Often in the evenings when he and Ramiro and I shared quinoa bowls with sweet potatoes, chickpeas, and grilled veggies drizzled with Uva honey, he would talk about how the bees were helping him become more attuned to the rhythms and cycles of nature.

"It's really good," Thomas said through a mouthful.

"You should tell him about Ed," Lance said to Carlos.

Carlos proceeded to relay what he had seen last night, then Lance interjected and gave Thomas a word-for-word recap of my conversation with Sophie.

Thomas listened but didn't take notes on his iPad. Instead, he enjoyed the bread and coffee. I wasn't sure if his lack of notetaking was because we were sharing information he already knew or if it was because the police had a suspect in mind and were getting ready to make an arrest.

Once Lance had finished, Thomas brushed his hands on his navy shorts. "Thanks for the intel and for the snack and coffee."

"Is that it?" Lance scoffed. "You're going to leave us with nothing?"

"Not nothing. A little patience, please." He clicked on his iPad and motioned for us to come closer. "Come take a look at this."

We gathered around the counter. Thomas played a shaky video that had clearly been shot on a phone.

"Is this Sophie's footage?" I asked.

"Yep. Just wait for a minute, pay attention to the left side of the stage." Thomas tapped the iPad with his finger.

We watched with rapt attention. Clearly, Sophie was not a professional videographer, but she had zoomed her phone onto the side of the stage where Bertie and Olive were huddled together with handheld flashlights. Bertie was holding what I presumed to be the script, scanning it as Jimmy and the other actors belted out their lines for the audience. Olive stood ready with a small sewing kit. It looked like she was poised to spring into action if the cast happened to have any costume fails.

The footage was grainy from being zoomed in and from shooting in the dark, but both women were easily identifiable.

"This part," Thomas said, tapping the screen again to point out where we should be looking.

In the video Jimmy took his final bow as the audience erupted with applause.

I hadn't noticed it last night, but Jimmy jumped off the stage and quickly vanished in the darkness.

My eyes drifted back to Olive and Bertie as Thomas touched the top of the screen again. "Right, here, see?"

Sure enough, Olive nudged Bertie, and both women exited the stage and followed Jimmy.

Lance threw his hand over his mouth and gasped. "Well, well, this changes everything, doesn't it?"

Thomas's lips pursed into a thin line. "I'm not sure I'd go that far, but I will say that this footage only expands our suspect list. The Professor asked me to share it with you, and now I'm due to have a conversation with Olive and Bertie. In the interim, we'd appreciate you keeping a close eye out. Report anything and everything that comes up."

Lance saluted. "Consider it done."

Thomas turned off his iPad and took an apple on his way out the door.

New questions pounded my head. Who was telling the truth and who was lying? Sophie claimed that Bertie cornered her after the show. Was she attempting to establish an alibi? And if Bertie and Sophie weren't together, what were Bertie and Olive doing when Jimmy had been killed, and why were they following him?

Chapter Thirteen

"What now?" Lance asked, pouring himself another cup of coffee.

"I guess it's back to work." I motioned to the kitchen, which needed organization before we opened the tasting room.

"Well, that's no fun," Lance scoffed. "Where's your sense of adventure?"

"My sense of adventure involves being ready to serve tonight," I bantered back.

Disappointment washed across Lance's angular jawline. "Carlos, whatever will we do with our pastry muse?"

Carlos held up both hands. "No, no, do not put me in the middle of this debate. I have to prepare the tasting room to open soon, but before that I must return to the vines. There's always more pruning to do." With that, he mouthed "Good luck" to me and removed himself from the conversation.

"I'm serious," Lance said, shifting out of theatrical mode. "We can't simply sit around and do nothing."

"Don't you have rehearsals this afternoon?"

He glanced at his watch. "Fair point. I'm planning to

gather the cast and crew early to discuss how we move forward without Jimmy and make sure his understudy is up to speed. But you've given me a new mission. I'm assuming you suggest we use rehearsals as a chance to spy on our ever-growing list of suspects?"

"I'm not sure I'd put it exactly like that, but yeah. We're both here. I have to prep food and desserts. You meet with the cast; I'll keep an eye out and my ears open while Thomas and Kerry continue their investigation. We can reconvene later."

"Excellent." Lance gulped the rest of his coffee and set his empty cup in the sink. "Let's meet up outside a little before three."

"That works for me." I gathered the dishes and took them to the sink.

He kissed my cheeks. "Good luck, and do be careful." Then, in a rare show of tenderness, he held my gaze. "I don't know what I would do without you, Juliet Montague Capshaw. You know that, yes?"

"Yes." I leaned into him. "The feeling is entirely mutual."

"Well, lucky us." He waved his hand with a little flourish and danced out of the kitchen. "Until later."

I watched him stroll casually into the tasting room. I wasn't averse to snooping with Lance, but I really did have plenty of work to do.

The jingle of bells in the tasting room signaled that our first customers had arrived. I took that as my cue to assemble the theater boxes. I started by placing the stack of flat boxes on the island and folding each side until I had a pile that reached almost as high as the stainless-steel pot rack hanging from the ceiling. I started on the dessert boxes first, carefully placing cupcakes, brownies, and tarts on paper doilies and then securing the lids.

The bread and fruit had helped. My stomach felt relatively calm as I worked.

I stacked the dessert boxes on the far counter and turned my attention to the savory boxes. I scooped chicken salad into reusable containers and added miniature baguettes, spiced nuts, and cherry almond cookies. Each box would serve at least two people. They would need to be refrigerated until the performance. We didn't have a walk-in or large pantry spaces at Uva, but fortunately, we had an oversized fridge that easily had enough room for the boxes.

The list of suspects swirled through my mind as I rolled hummus wraps. Sophie had admitted to arranging a meeting with Jimmy in the cellar. Ed was seen fleeing the scene. Tom had requested access to the cellar, and now there was video evidence of Bertie and Olive following Jimmy after the show. Not to mention Sophie's claim that one of the Fair Verona Players had been trying to kill Jimmy, and Tom's prior connection to the star. There was no one above suspicion at this point.

Any one of them could have killed him. They were all in the vicinity of the tasting room after the show. It would have been easy enough to slip downstairs, stab Jimmy, and sneak out again without being seen. The only people around would have been my staff, who were focused on the event.

It seemed impossible that Jimmy's colleagues could have killed him, but at the same time, it wasn't as if he had done much to earn their respect or affection. I'd witnessed him being awful to Olive and Ed. I was curious about his history with Tom, and how he'd come to encourage Tom to invest in the Fair Verona Players. I needed to learn more about Tom's financial connection to the company and if he stood to gain anything with Jimmy's death.

Bertie seemed like she had been trying to be the peacekeeper between Jimmy and the other members of the small company, but could that be an act? She was trying to climb the theater ranks. If she saw Jimmy's unprofessional behavior as a threat to her future career, could she have resorted to drastic measures?

And then there was Sophie. She confused me more than anyone else. Her outward adoration of Jimmy was apparent, but as Lance suggested, it was possible that she may have harbored other feelings for the star. I was sure that there were holes in her story, I just didn't know what they were and why she was lying.

I sighed as I rearranged boxes in the fridge in a delicate balancing act. Working with limited space was a skill I had learned early on in culinary school. It was the premise for the philosophy of "mise en place," or "everything in its place," and something I had taught my staff. Every knife had its own spot on the magnetic strip hanging beneath the cupboards, every ingredient and spice was labeled and organized alphabetically, and every member of our team had a station. I appreciated the challenge of finding a place for everything and everyone in the kitchen.

My thoughts drifted to the murder as I rotated a stack in the back to make more room.

Did the weapon matter?

I shuddered at the vision of the twisty metal impaled in Jimmy's neck.

Why a corkscrew?

Was it simply a matter of convenience?

Had the killer made a deadly decision in the heat of an argument? Or maybe there had been a physical fight, and they had grabbed the corkscrew to defend themself. I knew I left the corkscrew on the table after opening a bottle for Tom, so it was certainly plausible that the killer had skewered Jimmy in a rash act of passion.

Could Jimmy's death have been a spur-of-the-moment crime? It seemed to make the most sense, or it alluded to his killer being a terrible planner. I couldn't imagine a premediated murder with a corkscrew, but then again, I couldn't fathom the concept of putting an end to someone's life.

Regardless of whether he was brash or entitled, Jimmy didn't deserve to die. The thought made me that much more resolved to do anything I could to bring his killer to justice.

A timid knock interrupted my thoughts. I turned to see Olive standing in the doorway. Her sewing kit was tethered to her hand the way a child might hold a security blanket. Again, she was dressed in a drab, monotone outfit of matching shades of dirt brown.

"Sorry to disturb you," she said in such a low voice, I had to crane my neck to hear her. "I was told I might be able to get some water."

"Of course, come in." I closed the fridge. "Do you want a glass for yourself, or should I bring out pitchers for the cast and crew?"

Her skittish gaze darted around the empty kitchen. Was she looking for something or someone? Finally, after what felt like a minute, her eyes landed on the row of black Uva aprons hanging on the wall next to the stove.

Was she looking for the cellar key?

I waited for her to answer, but she continued stare at the neatly pressed aprons.

"Is this where he was killed? Here in the kitchen?" She squinted and wrinkled her nose as she tore her gaze away from the aprons. "I don't see any crime scene tape or an outline of the body, but this is the spot, isn't it? This is where he died."

Her question took me off guard. "Jimmy?" I asked, reaching for a glass of water.

She moved toward the wall and appraised the stitching on the aprons. Our Uva logo was embroidered in cream on the top right corner. "Nice work. This was done by hand."

I wasn't sure how to respond. "Thank you" didn't seem appropriate, given that I ordered the aprons from a supplier, and her behavior was odd. She went from bombarding me with questions about the murder to complimenting the stitching on our aprons.

"Rumors are spreading out there," Olive continued, rubbing the hem of an apron between her index finger and thumb. "I heard that he was killed in here, in the kitchen. Was it with a cleaver or a knife? Was it bloody?"

I gulped down the bile rising in the back of my throat at the image of Jimmy's punctured throat.

"Not here, exactly." I made an executive decision and began filling water pitchers, mainly to give my brain something other than the crime scene to focus on. Was it my imagination, or did Olive almost sound excited about the possibility that Jimmy had been murdered in my kitchen? And why had she homed in on the apron rack? In fairness, the aprons were the only clothing items in the kitchen, and she was a professional seamstress, but everything about her seemed off.

"Was it down in the cellar? That's the other rumor I've heard going around. Or was it upstairs? Are there bloodstains?" She took an apron off the hook to appraise it more closely. "I like the contrast of the topstitching on these."

"Yes, he was killed downstairs." I didn't want to elaborate, since I wasn't sure how much information the Professor had shared publicly yet.

"I suppose the police have that area blocked off. It must be hard to function as a business. Do you give a dead-guy discount? I can't imagine many people wanting to sip their wine in a place where a dead body was discovered hours ago, but then again, you might get a crowd of gawkers. Murder is hot these days. Maybe you can find a way to capitalize on that. A murderous merlot and a tour of the crime scene." Olive looked pleased with her suggestion, like she was offering me an inventive marketing idea, rather than suggesting I profit from her colleague's death. "You found him, that's what I heard. Was it bad? Is it true that his eyes were rolled back in his head? Did you get a good look at the wound?"

I couldn't tell if Olive had a dark sense of humor or if she was obsessed with the macabre.

She returned the apron to its hook and peered into the tasting room. "Maybe you'll sell more wine today if you give everyone the inside scoop on the murder. Like I said, people love a good crime. Have you seen how many true crime TV shows and podcasts there are these days? You could start one of your own."

That was the last thing I would ever consider. Obviously

Olive was one of the "people" she was talking about. I wanted to erase Jimmy's murder from my mind, and she wanted to turn it into a full-scale production, complete with blood spatter and a bird's-eye view of the body.

I filled one pitcher and began filling the next, trying to shift the conversation away from the gory details of Jimmy's death. "Did you know Jimmy well?"

"I wish I could say I didn't know him, but this was my fifth show working with him." She stopped herself, shook her head, and held up one finger. "Strike that. What I should say is working in spite of him."

"He seemed like he had a bit of an ego."

"A bit?" She threw her head back and let out a cackle. "That is an understatement. His ego was absurd."

"Although his performance onstage certainly resonated with the audience." I had to admit, Jimmy had won me over last night. Or rather, I had forgotten about Jimmy the person and become captivated by his interpretation of Petruchio. That was where Sophie and I agreed. There was no denying his ability to completely embody a character.

"If you like that sort of thing, I suppose, but no amount of supposed 'talent' excuses his atrocious behavior. I'm not the least bit shocked that someone killed him. He had no friends among the company."

I turned off the tap and went to the freezer for ice. "Do you think someone in the company killed him?"

"I can name about twenty people who wanted him dead, so the answer to that is—yes." She tapped the tip of each of her fingers like she was mentally reviewing everyone she considered a possible criminal.

"Do you really think someone killed him because of his

ego?" I agreed with Olive about Jimmy's personality, but I was still struggling to see how that translated to a motive for murder.

"It was much more than that." She peeked into the tasting room again to make sure no one was coming our way. Then she put a hand to the side of her lips. "I probably shouldn't be saying this, but did you know he was involved in a number of enterprises that were not legal?"

Enterprises?

That was an interesting choice of words.

"Like what?" I scooped ice into the pitchers.

"The rumor mill has been working overtime on that. You know how it is with theater people." She paused for a minute and checked behind her. "I've heard too many stories to count about Jimmy's financial situation, blackmail, bankruptcy, and even issues with some of the women on the cast and crew."

My thoughts immediately went to Sophie.

"He was not a nice guy."

"But these are rumors, right?" I tried a more rational approach.

"Most rumors are born from truth," Olive said with a hard gaze. "Surely you know that, living in a small town like Ashland."

I wasn't sure I agreed with her statement, but I wanted her to keep talking. "Jimmy was in financial trouble, does that mean he was being blackmailed or blackmailing someone else?"

Olive shrugged. "I don't know, but I do know that he was in serious trouble, and as we know from Shakespeare, love and money are the ultimate entanglement."

Now she was starting to sound like the Professor.

"Jimmy's brash attitude was probably the final straw." She twisted her pincushion and took out a needle. "I'm convinced that the real reason he was killed had more to do with his bank account than his personality. No one would kill a guy just for having a big head. Who cares about that? You know what people care about?"

I started to reply, but she didn't wait for me to respond.

"Money." She jabbed the needle into the pincushion so hard I thought it might come out the other side. "Mark my words, that's why he's dead. Cold, hard cash—it gets you every time."

"What kind of financial trouble was Jimmy in?"

"How would I know?" she scoffed, sounding offended. "I'm the costume designer. I mend hems, but I have two working ears that no one seems to notice. I hear things. I hear a lot of things."

"Like what?"

"Like him talking to the bank and trying to move around funds and . . ." Olive clammed up. "I should probably get back to rehearsals. Chances are good that one of the actors has split a seam by now."

"Should I bring some food, too?" I asked, motioning to the platter of bread and fruit. "Do you think everyone is ready for an afternoon snack?"

"Whatever you think. Ask Bertie. She should be taking over, since Sophie didn't show up for work today."

I was about to ask her opinion of Sophie, but she beat me to it.

"That young, flighty woman claims to have a huge crush on Jimmy. She followed him around like a puppy, neglecting her responsibilities. But I don't buy it. If you ask me, I would put my money on her."

I pretended not to follow. "Put your money on Sophie for what?"

"For killing him," she said with a hint of irritation. "Sophie trotted after Jimmy like a sycophant. She wanted everyone to think that she was starstruck and lovesick."

"Wait, are you saying that you don't think Sophie had a crush on Jimmy?"

"That's exactly what I'm saying. Sophie played her dewy-eyed role beautifully. Everyone in the company believes that she was desperately in love with Jimmy. I'm sure her next performance will be that of grieving lover, but she doesn't fool me."

"Why?"

"Because her insincere flattery was a smoke screen. She wanted something from Jimmy. I don't know what, but what I do know is that young woman was as much in love with Jimmy as I was."

I tried to control my reaction by focusing on refilling the snack tray Carlos had put together earlier.

"My guess is that she learned she wasn't going to get whatever it is that she wanted from him and decided that she would have to kill him instead." She pretended to stab herself in the neck with the needle. "You know what they say about a woman scorned."

How did she know that Jimmy had been stabbed in the neck? Was it simply a coincidence that Olive had pretended to stab herself? Was that information out to the public? I couldn't imagine the Professor releasing any details about the crime scene to the Fair Verona Players. She hadn't known that he was killed in the cellar, so how would she know that he'd been impaled by a corkscrew?

Unless she was the one who had stabbed him.

Chapter Fourteen

"You think Sophie killed Jimmy," I repeated Olive's words back to her.

"I just said that," Olive retorted with irritation as she stuffed the needle into the pincushion a final time.

"What makes you think that Sophie had an ulterior motive? I obviously don't know her well, but from the outside, it seemed fairly obvious that she was obsessed with him."

"Costume designers hold everyone's secrets." Olive patted her sewing kit. "It's ironic because people don't pay any attention to those of us who work behind the scenes, but they should."

Was it my imagination, or did her tone sound threatening?

"Sophie wasn't in love with Jimmy. She despised him. I'll give her credit for putting on a good front, but I'll be stunned if the police don't arrest her. I'm not counting on her returning to set anytime soon." She observed the water pitchers. "Are these ready? I'll take them, since apparently I'm going to be responsible for more than costume fittings and touch-ups for the remainder of the run."

"I'll help you walk them down," I offered, handing her the pitchers and glasses while I balanced Carlos's fruit and bread tray and a basket of cookies and nuts.

Olive was tight-lipped as we strolled along the pressed gravel path toward the barn. Fragrant bunches of purple lavender bloomed on both sides of the path. Bees and hummingbirds flitted between the aromatic herb and the rosebushes. The afternoon sun warmed the grass and make everything smell like summer.

It was hard to believe that Jimmy was dead and that a terrible crime had occurred here last night. However, once we rounded the pathway to the main outdoor wine-tasting area and the barn came into view, I was immediately reminded that this wasn't an average idyllic Saturday afternoon with the vines.

Thomas and Kerry were seated in the front row, watching rehearsals. Uniformed officers flanked the stage.

Olive's body went rigid. "Why are the police here?"

"They said they'd be here most of the day continuing their investigation," I replied. Her reaction was odd. I was sure that Lance had informed the cast and crew about what to expect as the interrogations continued.

"They're wasting their time if you ask me," Olive said, avoiding the main aisle that would take her past Thomas and Kerry. "We all know that Sophie did it. They should arrest her and let us all move on with our lives."

I had the sense that nothing I said would change her mind, so I set up the water station and arranged cookies, bread, fresh fruit, and other snacks for the performers and crew. Olive hung behind me like a shadow. She didn't offer to help, but mirrored my movements. I almost got the sense that she was using my body as a shield.

Why was she so skittish about Thomas and Kerry seeing her?

Did she have something to hide?

I put a basket of cookies next to Carlos's fruit and bread platter.

Thomas turned around, caught my eye, and motioned for me to come join them.

Olive let out a low whimper and ducked.

"What's wrong?"

"Nothing. I dropped my pincushion." She pretended to reach down to the ground to pick up the pincushion, safely secured to her wrist. Then checked to make sure that no one was looking and darted to the right side of the stage. "I need to get backstage to do some touch-up before tonight's performance."

I watched her retreat and then vanish behind the curtain. Our conversation left me with way more questions than answers. How was Olive perceived by the rest of the company? Did they ignore her? Could she know more about Jimmy than she was letting on? Particularly his finances?

Or had she committed the murder herself and was acting skittish because she worried about getting caught?

I sighed and went to join Thomas and Kerry in the front of the makeshift auditorium.

"Hey, Jules, how's it going?" Thomas asked, scooting his chair to make room for me.

"Fine, I guess." I sat next to Kerry. "I had an interesting conversation with Olive just now, but I have no idea what to make of it."

"She's next on my list." Thomas tapped his iPad and pointed to the stage. "We're waiting for them to break, and then Kerry and I have some follow-up questions for a few members of the cast."

"What did Olive say?" Kerry asked, staring toward the right side of the stage.

When I turned my head in that direction, I was shocked to see Olive looking straight at us. If her goal was not to be seen by Thomas and Kerry, she was failing. She hung on the side of the stage with half her face shielded by the curtain. Her eyes were lasered on the front row. I couldn't tell if she was curious about Jimmy's murder and hungry for details or if she was apprehensive that Thomas and Kerry were here to interrogate her.

I tried to ignore Olive's intense observation as I filled them in on her theory that Sophie had faked her interest in Jimmy.

"But she didn't say why she thinks Sophie would have pretended to be in love with him?" Kerry frowned and glanced at Thomas.

Thomas noted something on his iPad.

"No. She said she thought that Sophie had other reasons for wanting Jimmy dead but didn't elaborate." I peered in Olive's direction. She had vanished.

"Interesting." Kerry cleared her throat and looked again at Thomas, who gave her a slight nod as if to signal that it was fine for her to share more. "This stays between us, okay?"

"Okay." I nodded seriously. "Of course."

"Our conversation with Sophie revealed something very similar. In fact, you could say basically the same sentiment, only flipped." Kerry uncrossed her legs and shifted in her chair. She was dressed in a casual skirt and a lightweight button-up shirt, while Thomas preferred his standard uniform with shorts and hiking boots. I'd rarely seen him out of uniform. "Sophie told us that she believes Olive had a very clear motive for wanting Jimmy dead."

"Really?" That was a shift from what Sophie had said to me.

Kerry leaned against the back of the chair. "According to Sophie, Olive and Jimmy had a very vocal fight last night, just before curtain. Have you heard anything about this?"

I shook my head. "They were arguing earlier in the afternoon, but I was in the kitchen prepping right before the show, so I didn't see a fight, and I haven't heard any chatter from my staff either, but that doesn't mean it didn't happen. We were preoccupied with setting up for the event."

Thomas made another note. "That's one of the questions we're going to be asking once they take a break. We'll see if anyone else can corroborate Sophie's statement."

I thought about my conversation with Olive. "I wouldn't be surprised. Olive was very irritated with Jimmy, and he was rude and dismissive to her, although that doesn't seem unusual. I think he was that way with everyone, but she made it sound like the entire cast ignores her and basically acts like she doesn't exist."

"Huh." Kerry nodded but didn't sound like she believed that.

"Did Sophie elaborate on Olive's motive?"

"We aren't at liberty to share that information." Kerry pressed her lips together and caught Thomas's eye as if to remind him that was the case.

"Yeah, fair enough." I watched as Jimmy's understudy ran through new blocking on the stage with Ed.

"Anything else you can add?" Thomas asked.

"I did hear something about Ed." I kept my voice down. I didn't want to interrupt the actors as they prepared for tonight's show, or have them overhear my thoughts about the suspects. An understudy's role was to train for situations like this, but I couldn't imagine how much pressure it must be to have only a few hours to get ready for curtain, especially stepping in under circumstances like this.

"Go ahead," Kerry encouraged.

"Sophie believes that he was intentionally trying to sabotage Jimmy. She claims that he was behind the accidents and mishaps on set, but she thinks they weren't accidents—that he was trying to kill Jimmy and failed. At least, unless that changed last night," I said. "Maybe you heard that already from her, but I can confirm that Ed was seen leaving the cellar last night, according to Sophie and Carlos."

"Do you know what time?" Thomas held his fingers ready to type.

"I don't know for sure. Sophie told me that she saw him running away from the cellar out into the vineyard, and Carlos confirmed that he spotted Ed around then too."

They shared another look.

Then Kerry clutched the side of her chair. Her face went as white as the thin clouds embracing Grizzly Peak.

"Are you okay?" I asked.

She inhaled deeply and pressed her hand to forehead. "Just another touch of dizziness. Like I told you, I've been feeling off."

"I wonder if we have a touch of the same stomach bug?"

"Maybe." She didn't loosen her grip on the chair.

Lance strolled to center stage and clapped twice to get

everyone's attention. "That's a wrap, folks. Let's take a brief hydration break, and I'll see you onstage in fifteen minutes."

The cast scattered.

Thomas reached out a hand to help Kerry to her feet. "That's our cue. Thanks for the intel, Jules. We'll keep you posted."

I watched Thomas support Kerry's waist as they approached the crew. Then they split apart. Thomas took Ed to the food table, while Kerry pulled Olive aside.

Olive claimed that Sophie had the most likely motive for killing Jimmy, and Sophie claimed the opposite. Her story had changed dramatically, which made me wonder if she was scrambling to shift suspicion to anyone other than herself.

I wished I had asked them about Sophie. Had the Professor made an arrest, or was he really worried about her well-being? I sighed as I stood, blood rushing to my head and causing tiny little dots to cloud my vision.

Not again.

I sat back down and tried not to pass out.

"Juliet Montague Capshaw, what's going on?" Lance appeared at my side like a magician. "You don't look well, darling."

I gulped and blew out a breath. "I'm a little dizzy."

"It's the sun. To think Arlo wanted me to run this morning. In this heat?" He pointed to the sky and fanned his face.

It was a perfect afternoon, with temps in the mid-seventies, powder blue skies, a thin layer of clouds, and a light spring breeze.

"You're probably dehydrated, too. Let's get you inside."

"No, I'm fine," I protested, but my legs buckled when I stood.

"Nope. You're not fine." Lance pressed the top of my shoulder. "Stay here. I'll be back with water and reinforcements."

"Okay." This time I didn't put up a fight. The dizziness was much worse. Black spots continued to dance across my line of sight, making me feel like I was staring down a dark tunnel. My peripheral vision started to fade. Sounds nearby became distant and muffled. Conversations and noises were indistinct, like the birds outside were mingling and mashing together with jumbled words coming from the stage.

A profound weakness washed over me, as my extremities began to tingle.

The next thing I knew, my vision went completely dark.

Chapter Fifteen

"Juliet, Juliet, wake up."

I felt someone shaking my shoulder.

"She's coming to."

I tried to force my eyes open, but it felt like my eyelids were glued shut.

"Juliet, are you with us?"

I blinked hard and squinted. My arms felt heavy.

"She's okay. She's okay." Lance's fuzzy figure stood over me. I could make out a crowd of worried onlookers nearby. "Back up, people. Give us a little space, and someone go get her husband, Carlos, inside."

I tried to move my head forward, but it felt like it was floating above my body. "What happened?"

"You fainted. Don't move too fast. Just take a minute to get your bearings, and keep breathing slowly." Lance immediately controlled the situation. His flippant attitude vanished in crisis. "You look like you're getting a bit more color in your cheeks."

I pressed a hand to my cheek, more than anything in hopes of feeling real. This was like a bad dream. I wanted to pinch myself.

"Carlos is coming," Lance said in a calm and even tone. "Oh, and here's Thomas with water."

Thomas ran over with a half-full glass of water. His cheeks were flushed with worry, and his eyes narrowed in concern. "Have you eaten anything today, Jules?" He handed me the glass and put two fingers on my wrist to check my pulse.

I nodded. "Yeah, earlier. I had some bread and butter and grapes."

"Kerry's getting you a cookie. You might have had a blood sugar drop or heatstroke, although it's not that hot." He put his hand to my forehead. "Are you cold, chills, shaking?"

"No." I held a steady hand out to prove my point.

"You mentioned dizziness to Kerry. Should we call an ambulance?" Thomas knelt on both knees and held up his index finger. "Follow my finger with your eyes." He proceeded to assess my entire body.

"Please, no. I'm fine. I swear." I rotated my shoulders and held my head high.

"Julieta, what is it?" Carlos was breathless. His face was etched with worry as he sank to his knees and reached for my hand.

"I'm better, I swear." I made an X over my heart. "Just a little dizzy spell."

"I think you should take her home," Thomas suggested, getting up and placing a hand on Carlos's shoulder. "She should get out of the sun. I would recommend a dark room, a wet washcloth on the forehead, and some electrolytes."

"Sí, I will take her home now." Carlos moved to help me up.

"There's no need for that," I protested. "I can take a sun break in the tasting room. There's so much to do—the boxes for tonight, the tasting room."

"No. This is not up for debate." Carlos shook his head. "Sit for a minute. I will go direct the volunteers, and then we'll go home."

I could tell that I wasn't going to win the argument, and quite honestly, everything felt off-center, like I had been on the ship for months and was trying to find my footing on solid ground. The vineyard appeared to have wavy lines running through it in a mesmerizing pattern like the grapes were dancing and swaying. The leaves and tendrils on the vines curled and rippled as if caught in an invisible current of water.

"Carlos is right." Lance sat next to me and patted my knee. "You're overdoing it, Jules, and you're going to burn yourself out. I need your clever brain to help figure out whodunit. Remember we're on the case, and we need those gray cells firing on all cylinders. Go home, take a long nap, and come tomorrow, you'll be back on your feet and ready to scour Ashland's mean streets for criminal activity."

"Mean streets, excuse me?" Thomas stared at Lance like he was speaking a foreign language. Then he tapped the shiny badge on his chest. "I take great pride in keeping Ashland's streets safe and friendly."

"Metaphorically speaking, of course." Lance gave him an apologetic nod. "I'm trying to give her a pep talk and motivation to get herself well."

"Leave the mean streets to the professionals," Thomas said with a twinkle in his eyes. Then he paused. "But, before you go, I do have one question for you."

"Yeah, anything." The lines in my vision gave an undulating quality to everything I could see. It almost looked like the vineyard was morphing into a breathing canvas.

"You mentioned you spent time with Olive earlier, correct?" Thomas asked.

"That's right." I didn't trust myself to nod. If I kept my line of sight focused on Mount A in the distance, things seemed less blurry.

"And during that time, did you notice any strange behavior?" Thomas scrolled through his iPad.

"Like what?"

He found the page he was looking for, reviewed his notes, and then studied me. "You began feeling unwell shortly afterward, correct?"

"Yeah, I guess, but I've been having little dizzy episodes for a while now," I admitted. "You heard me talking to Kerry. I've been wondering if we both have the same touch of the flu."

"But you haven't passed out until now, and would you consider this worse?"

"That's true."

Thomas hesitated.

Lance jumped in. "What he's hinting at is, did you notice Olive trying to lace your food or drink with something?"

I blinked again. "What?"

Thomas tilted his head to one side. "I'm not hinting at anything. I'm asking if you saw any odd behavior."

"No." I shook my head.

Bad idea.

The movement sent another wave of dizziness through

my body. I willed everything to stop spinning and dug my heels into the ground.

I felt like I might pass out again at any minute.

Could Olive have slipped me something? Panic bubbled in my stomach and spread to my limbs. My fingers felt numb and tingly. I scrunched my hands into fists and let them go to try to bring the feeling back. But no. We had spoken in the kitchen, but I didn't eat or drink anything. She couldn't have drugged me.

Kerry showed up with a cookie, which I nibbled on, mainly to appease everyone. Carlos returned shortly with the keys to the van and instructions for Lance.

"Sterling is on his way. He'll take over food service for this evening. The volunteers will stay until a few more of our staff finish up at Torte."

"Don't worry about it," Lance assured him. "I have my OLCC card. I will happily pour if need be. Take care of our Juliet." He planted a soft kiss on the top of my head. "Rest up, darling. You're going to be just fine in no time, but for tonight you will let your devilishly handsome husband wait on you hand and foot—understood?"

I fought back tears.

Why was I suddenly emotional?

It was just a touch of dizziness, but I appreciated how kind and concerned Carlos, Lance, Thomas, and Kerry were. While it was embarrassing to pass out, the experience reconfirmed how lucky I was to have such wonderful family and friends. I was humbled that everyone was looking out for me.

Carlos followed Thomas's instructions to the letter. He took me straight home, had me change into comfy pj's, and tucked me in bed with a cool washcloth and a glass of Gatorade.

"I'll be downstairs if you need anything. Call for me, and I'll come to you." He pressed his lips to mine. "Get some sleep, mi querida."

I didn't think I would be able to sleep in the middle of the afternoon, but my dark bedroom and the cold washcloth did the trick. It didn't take long to drift off into a deep, dreamless sleep.

When I woke, the light outside the window was dusky.

I looked at the clock and realized I'd been out for nearly five hours.

I sat up and stretched, noticing the aroma of sautéed onions and garlic coming from the kitchen. I got up slowly, expecting to be overcome with dizziness, but I felt fine.

The nap had done me good.

I went downstairs to find Carlos and Ramiro dancing to the Gipsy Kings and stirring something on the stove that smelled so delicious I wanted to devour it immediately. "What smells so good?"

Carlos turned with a wooden spoon in one hand. "You look like yourself again. You have color in your cheeks, and your eyes are bright. Are you feeling better?"

"Much." I sat at the kitchen table. Fading evening light filtered through the large bay window above the sink, illuminating pots of fresh herbs—mint, parsley, cilantro, basil, and lemongrass—that I had seeded over the winter. "I can't believe I slept for that long."

Ramiro wiped his hands on a dish towel and wrapped me in a giant hug. "I'm so sorry you're not feeling well. We have been cooking all afternoon. This sauce is the best medicine. It's our family secret."

I hugged him back. "It smells incredible."

Carlos stirred his sauce. "Sleep and our secret sauce is what the doctor ordered."

"What's the secret?" I tried to get a peek of the bubbly mixture on the stove, but Carlos shooed me away.

"It's a ragu with veggies and herbed chicken sausage. We'll serve it with cavatappi pasta, some Romano cheese, a salad, and bread. We can curl up and watch a movie. Ramiro is going to get you set up in the living room. We can eat out there together, sí?"

"That sounds lovely." I smiled at both of them, grateful to have such wonderful men in my life.

"Why don't you go get comfortable on the couch? I'll bring you a sparkling water," Ramiro said, already opening a can of fizzy strawberry lime water.

"I'm not an invalid," I teased.

"Sí, but I have been tasked with taking care of you. You must not let me fail at this important responsibility." He caught Carlos's eye.

Carlos ruffled the top of his son's head. "You are already a pro."

"There's a book on the table for you, and I'll light the fire," Ramiro said with a hint of pride. "Would you prefer a tea?"

"A sparkling water sounds great." I pressed my hand to my chest. "You both are too sweet."

Ramiro followed me to the living room with the water. He got me set up on the couch and started a fire. "It's still cool at night so we thought this might help. Do you need anything else?"

"No. I'm all set." I lifted the flavored water to my lips, getting an immediate hit of strawberry. "Thank you."

"It is my pleasure. You've done so much for me this year." Ramiro's voice cracked slightly. "You've made this my home, and I don't like seeing you unwell."

Tears spilled. There was no hope of containing them.

Ramiro's face blanched. "Oh no. I didn't mean to make you cry."

"These are happy/sad tears," I managed to say through my sniffles. "I'm going to miss you so much when you leave in a few weeks. This has been the best year of my life. I don't know what we're going to do without you."

He scrunched his lips together, unable to hold in his emotions either. His face still held a hint of the young boy he had been, but it was morphing into adulthood with the same angular jawline as his father's. "It will be hard to leave."

Carlos swept in, carrying a plate of pasta, salad, and homemade bread. "Why the sad faces?" He set the plate on the coffee table in front of me.

"We're talking about what a wonderful year it's been with Ramiro here," I said, wiping away tears.

Carlos pulled me to my feet and drew Ramiro closer. "Family hug."

We held each other tight as the fire began to crack and pop and tears continued to flow. I was enveloped by the aroma of the woodsmoke and their strong, steady embrace. We had carved our own little family this past year, and whether Ramiro was in Ashland or Spain, that bond would remain.

After we were all a blubbery mess, Carlos finally broke apart. "Okay, now it is time for some pasta and a movie and cuddling on the couch, my loves."

"You're going to make all of my single friends jealous," I teased. "Men who openly cry and cook, that's the dream."

"This is why you married a Spaniard." His eyes twinkled with flirtation.

I followed his advice and tucked myself onto the couch, feeling grateful for Carlos, Ramiro, and the fact that the room wasn't spinning.

It was probably time for me to go back to the doctor. I wanted to get to the root cause of my dizziness. It wasn't very functional to have a head chef in danger of passing out in the kitchen. But I couldn't stop thinking about Thomas's question regarding Olive. Could she have snuck something into my water glass when I wasn't looking?

Odds were good that since I'd already been suffering from dizzy spells, this wasn't anything new, but then again, Jimmy had been killed last night, and Olive was on the suspect list. I couldn't be too careful.

Chapter Sixteen

The next day I felt much more like myself. I woke to the smell of sausage and grilled onions. After a long shower with a refreshing eucalyptus and peppermint shower soother, I pulled on a pair of capris, a thin rainbow-striped sweatshirt, and my tennis shoes and headed downstairs to find Carlos and Ramiro busy in the kitchen again.

"Buenas!" Carlos greeted me with a coffee and a kiss. "How did you sleep, mi querida?"

"Really well." I breathed in the scent of the eggs sizzling in olive oil on the stove. "And suddenly, I'm starving."

Ramiro sprinkled fresh parsley on the dish. "We're making you my favorite—huevos rotos."

"I should pass out more often," I teased, sliding into the breakfast nook. Huevos rotos, or "broken eggs," was a classic Spanish dish made by sautéing Yukon gold potatoes with garlic and herbs until they were soft and tender inside and crispy on the outside. The potatoes were topped with sausage and pan-fried eggs, and seasoned with salt, smoked paprika, and fresh herbs.

My mouth began watering the minute Ramiro served me a plate with a side of buttered toast. "This looks amazing." I dug my fork into the soft yolk, letting it ooze over the potatoes.

Ramiro poured himself a glass of fresh squeezed orange juice and a coffee and sat next to me. "How is it?"

"Um, it's pretty much the best thing I've ever tasted."

He ran his fingers through his thick dark hair and scrunched his face. "You're saying that to be nice."

"Nope. Well, wait, let me check something." I devoured another bite, sopping up the runny yolk with the potatoes and stabbing a piece of sausage. The potatoes were like a cross between French fries and oven baked wedges. My mouth tingled from the smoky paprika and spicy sausage finished with the silky, buttery egg. "Yep, I'm sticking with my statement. This is the best breakfast ever."

"You're going to give him a big head," Carlos said, wiping the edge of his plate with a napkin. Even at home, he couldn't take the professional chef out of himself, making sure the presentation was flawless.

"It's a sign that maybe I will have to be a chef." Ramiro scarfed down his eggs and went in for seconds before I had finished mine.

"Are you seriously considering culinary school?" I asked, adding a small scoop of whipping cream to my coffee.

Ramiro shrugged and tried to sound nonchalant. "Maybe. It's a possibility, but I still have a year to figure it out."

Carlos met my eye as he joined us at the table. "You must follow your own path. If it leads you to the kitchen, I will be very happy, but I do not want to you to do this for me."

"You don't have to worry about that." Ramiro scoffed

and rolled his eyes as he went in for another bite of huevos rotos. "You've told me this a million times."

"We want you to do something you love, not something
you feel burdened by," Carlos added, looking at me for
confirmation.

I bobbed my head in agreement. Living with us this
year meant that Ramiro had spent lots of time at Torte,
Uva, and Scoops. The topic of him pursuing a culinary
career had come up fairly consistently. I didn't get the impression that Ramiro felt pressure to follow in his father's
footsteps, but Carlos was adamant that Ramiro explore
every possibility before deciding on a career path. I appreciated his concern and that he was being intentional about
giving Ramiro space to make his own choice. I had also
witnessed Ramiro come alive in the kitchen. Food was in
his blood, and I had no doubt that if he decided to attend
culinary school, it would be because of that passion, not
pressure from his dad.

"I know this, Papa." Ramiro ended the discussion by
telling us about the theme for prom. "It's enchanted forest. I don't know what that means, and do I get my date
flowers?"

Enchanted forest sounded quintessentially Ashland.
Our little corner of the Rogue Valley was a mecca for
artists, entertainers, outdoor lovers, and modern hippies.
"Yes, to flowers," I said to Ramiro. "I can pop into A
Rose by Any Other Name and ask Janet what's popular
these days."

"Thanks. That would be great. We don't have prom in
Spain." Ramiro used his toast to scoop up the remains of
his breakfast.

"It's mainly an excuse to dress up and dance all night."

I thought back to my proms with Thomas. At the time, I never would have imagined that we would both end up back in Ashland with different people, and yet still remain friends. I appreciated having a friend in my life who knew me when I barely knew myself. It was a gift to have the shared experience of our youth and now meet each other as adults.

We finished breakfast. Ramiro headed out to meet friends for spike ball in the park. Carlos insisted that he drive me to Torte and made me promise that I would call him immediately if the dizziness returned.

At the bakeshop I made sure to switch to decaf. Hopefully, whatever had been ailing me was in the past, and I could concentrate on baking and digging deeper into Jimmy's murder.

An opportunity arose shortly after we opened, when I bumped into Sophie—literally. She was huddled at the far end of the pastry counter with the hood of a Fair Verona Players sweatshirt draped over her head and her face buried in her phone like she was trying to stay incognito.

"Sorry," I said, repositioning a tray of raspberry cream croissants. "I didn't see you there."

She looked up and realized it was me. "Oh, hi, Jules. No, it's my fault. I'm trying to avoid being seen."

"By anyone in particular?" I checked around us. There was a short line for coffee and pastries, and a handful of tables were occupied. Sundays tended to be slower. Things would pick up for brunch, but the first few hours of opening usually brought in a steady trickle of customers needing a coffee or cardamom bun fix after a morning run or mountain biking session through Lithia Park.

"The entire troupe." She gnawed on her thumbnail.

"Let me put these pastries away." I pointed to one of the window booths. "Why don't you grab a seat? Did you already put in an order, or can I bring you something?"

"That's so nice of you, but you don't need to go to any trouble."

"It's no trouble. It's my job."

She gave a half nod. "Okay, if you're sure. I was just going to get a coffee and an egg sandwich."

"Great. I'm on it." I ducked behind the counter, placed the fresh tray of filled croissants in the case, and warmed up an egg sandwich. This was the opportunity I had been hoping for. I wanted to get a better sense of whether her grief was legit.

Sophie tugged off her hood as I slid into the booth and handed her the egg sandwich with melted Monterey Jack cheese, sliced avocado, and thick heirloom tomatoes. "This smells so good." She cradled the coffee with her hands. "I need something—anything—to make me feel real. Everything feels so wrong right now."

"I understand." I hoped my tone sounded soft. "For what it's worth, our philosophy here at Torte is that coffee and pastries might not be able to solve your problems, but sometimes having coffee with a friend is as good as therapy."

"That's good because I could use some therapy. I'm not sure this is even reality." She pressed her finger into the breakfast sandwich, leaving an indent in the top of the biscuit. "Like, is this real? It smells real. It probably tastes real, but my mind can't comprehend much right now."

"Do you want to talk about it? I'm not a therapist, but I'm happy to lend a listening ear." I wondered if the Professor had put her in contact with a trained psychologist.

She tugged on the strings of her sweatshirt. "It's impossible to believe that he's really dead, you know? I keep thinking I'm going to see him walking through the plaza or get a text from him, and then every time that happens, I have to remind myself."

"That's very normal. You're in shock and likely will be for a long time. My dad died when I was young, and still to this day, I'll have moments where I see a flash of someone from behind or smell someone wearing his cologne and have to stop myself from running up to hug them."

"Really?" Sophie's voice wavered. "I don't know if that makes me feel better or worse."

She was so young. I wanted to wrap her in a hug, but I had to remind myself that it could be an act. She could be a killer.

"There's no escaping grief. It evolves and shifts with time, but loss stays with us," I said, feeling a familiar tightness in my throat. "I think in some ways it's beautiful. It's a reminder that we loved and were loved. I never thought I would say this, but there are days now where I welcome grief. I know it sounds strange, but it helps me feel connected to my dad. I've learned to make space for my sadness and find ways to celebrate him, like baking his favorite cake on his birthday. Things might feel out of balance now. That's normal. Give yourself time."

She bit into the egg sandwich. Melty cheese dribbled down her fingers. "That's a good way of looking at it. Although I'm not sure I was loved. I loved Jimmy, but I don't think he was in love with me."

Her demeanor and words made me question Olive's perspective. Unless Sophie was a stellar actress, her grief felt raw and authentic. If I didn't know anything about Jimmy's murder, I would have pegged her for a young woman with a broken heart.

"Did he know how you felt?" I asked, handing her a napkin. "Were things serious?"

"Yes, of course. Not that things were serious, but that he knew how I felt." She wiped her fingers and then fiddled with the string on her sweatshirt. "I mean, it's no secret that everyone had a little crush on Jimmy. His charm was captivating; it would be pretty impossible not to fall under his spell."

I wasn't sure that was how I would categorize his personality, but then again, Jimmy Paxton was not my type. It was clear everyone in the troupe had struggled with Jimmy's abrasive personality. One of the reasons I'd fallen hard for Carlos early on was his tender heart and lack of toxic masculinity. Carlos wasn't afraid to be vulnerable or express his love for me, Ramiro, and everyone in his sphere. I couldn't imagine falling for someone as brash and self-absorbed as Jimmy, but then again, I wasn't in my early twenties.

"People think that he had an ego, but that comes with being on the stage. He was really kind and totally different when we hung out alone."

This was an interesting revelation. She and Jimmy had spent time alone.

"Did you hang out often?" I asked.

"Not as much as I would have liked, but his schedule was always busy with rehearsals, side gigs, and auditions." She nibbled on her sandwich.

"I didn't realize he was auditioning." My eyes drifted outside to the plaza where a volunteer crew watered the hanging baskets overflowing with colorful geraniums.

"Yeah, he had a big break. He was heading to LA soon to shoot a pilot."

She had mentioned this at Uva, but I had forgotten to ask Lance whether he or the rest of the staff knew about Jimmy's potential departure. I made a mental note to ask Lance about it when I saw him next, but I wanted Sophie to keep talking.

"He was so excited. I was there when he got the call from his agent. He was like a little kid at Christmas, bouncing off the walls. This was the real deal. If the pilot went well, the show had a good shot of being picked up for network TV."

"That would have meant he would have to leave Ashland, though, right?" A new thought entered my mind—could Jimmy's departure from *Taming of the Shrew* give anyone a motive for killing him? It seemed like a stretch, but it was something to consider. Could the killer have benefited in some way from Jimmy remaining in the production and in Ashland?

Someone like Sophie, who was desperately in love with him?

"Yeah. He was planning to tell leadership after opening."

"Do you know when he was going to leave?"

She shook her head and ripped off a piece of the breakfast sandwich. "I don't know, probably in a couple of weeks. He mentioned that he'd be able to do next weekend's performances too, but he wasn't sure after that. Depending on the timing, he was looking into the possibility of flying up to do the show on the weekends. It's not a long run, so it seemed like there might have been a way to make it work if Bertie, Tom, and Lance were on board."

"But you don't think he had spoken with them before he was killed?"

"No." She circled her shoulders like she was trying to loosen the tension in her neck. "I know he hadn't, because he wanted to work the angle of doing both the pilot and keeping the lead in the show. He's a working actor, like most of the troupe; he needed the money."

"Do you have the sense that anyone would have been resistant to the idea? Jimmy was so good in the role. I can't imagine that Lance and the rest of the executive team wouldn't have done everything in their power to try and find a way to make it work."

"You would think, but there were a few members of the company who were out to get him. I told you about Ed. I'm still convinced that Ed was behind the accidents, but he's not the only one."

"Anyone else in particular?"

She rested her elbows on the table. "I told the police about this, but I don't trust Olive."

"Olive?" It was interesting that the two women were putting the blame on each other. "Why?"

She leaned closer and darted her eyes toward the Lithia bubblers in the center of the plaza. "Olive and Jimmy had a huge falling out. He caught her doing something she wasn't supposed be doing."

That was about as vague as possible. I waited, hoping Sophie might expand and say more.

"The police know, so I think it's okay for me to share this." She paused and looked around the dining room.

Was she worried that someone was listening to our conversation?

"Jimmy caught Olive reselling costume pieces."

That wasn't what I expected her to say. "Like underground costume trafficking?" I chuckled, imagining Olive sneaking down a long dark alleyway with a pile of fluffy rainbow tulle skirts in her arms.

"Basically, yes." She gestured with her palms open, like she was trying to convince me. "None of the costumes or props are to leave the set or dressing rooms. That's standard across all productions. Sure, there are always actors who will pocket a memento, and occasionally they'll speak with wardrobe and the costume designer to arrange to keep a piece, but that's a rarity. Most of the costumes get repurposed. It's an expensive part of the budget, and everyone in the company knows that. It was made clear to all of us from day one of table reads that anything used on set stays on set."

I was aware of this practice. Often audience members assumed that when sets were taken down, they were destroyed, but the reality was that many elements in sets and costumes were reused in future productions. Generic set pieces like tables, chairs, fake swords, and candelabras could be in a variety of different shows. Similarly, costumes were often altered and repurposed. Every item from a performance, whether it was a prop plastic apple or organza gown, was itemized and tracked. Reselling pieces was a violation of Olive's contract.

"She's been making a ton of money on the side, illegally selling pieces that OSF lent to the Fair Verona Players. Jimmy caught her in the act, confronted her, and warned that he was going to alert the executive team."

"Did he tell the team?" I asked.

"No. They got into a wicked argument about an hour before the show. That's how I found out. I overheard them backstage. He never had a chance to go to the police or tell anyone else because he was killed. At first I thought maybe Ed did it, but the more I think about it, I'm sure that Olive killed him to keep him silent about her secret side gig." Her voice grew shriller. "It makes perfect sense. She realized that Jimmy was going to spill her secret, so she killed him to keep him quiet. It had to be her. She's ruined everything. I was going to marry Jimmy Paxton, and now my life is over."

Chapter Seventeen

"You were going to marry Jimmy?" I asked, offering her another napkin.

She collapsed her head on the table, her shoulders heaving as she sobbed. "I wanted to marry him. He was the man of my dreams, and now he's dead."

I took a minute to process everything Sophie had shared, letting her release her emotions.

"You told the Professor all of this?" I asked when she finally sat up and dried her tears with a napkin.

She blew her nose and tried to compose herself. "Yeah, I was so out of it yesterday, I felt like I was in some kind of a weird alternate universe. I think the police thought I was in danger of self-harm. I wasn't, but they had me do a psych eval, and the therapist prescribed antianxiety medication. I tried to explain that I was in shock but not out of it enough to be unaware of my surroundings. Olive did it. It had to be her."

I thought back to yesterday at Uva, and saw Thomas and Kerry's questions about Olive in a new light.

"She took down all of her posts on eBay and Craigslist," Sophie said, "but Jimmy had taken screenshots of everything. I told the police to check his phone. They'll be able to find proof there. Unless she stole his phone when she stabbed him and deleted the evidence."

I wondered if Jimmy's phone had been on him when I found his body. I hadn't noticed it at the time, but my singular mission had been to get help. It wasn't like I had lingered in the cellar, looking for potential clues.

"The good news is that it's hard to erase digital foot-prints," I said to Sophie. "Even if the photos were deleted from his phone, the police will be able to access his files and records."

"I figured. I hope they arrest her today. I don't know how I'm supposed to show up at work and act like everything is fine when I know that she killed the man I love." She sighed. "That's why I was hiding out here. I'm trying to work up the courage to go and face that horrible woman."

"Did the Professor mention anything about making an arrest?"

She shook her head. "Not to me. I came to the station with him. He asked me a bunch of questions. I told him about seeing Ed and how I was sure that Ed had messed with the lights and Jimmy's marks on the stage. But I also told him about Olive. That's when he asked me to do the psych evaluation. Afterward, he said I was free to go and that it was fine to return to work if I was up for it emotion-ally. He was nice, but I don't understand why they're not doing more. Olive should be behind bars, and instead, I'm supposed to be at the vineyard in an hour to set up for the matinee. How do I pretend like everything is normal?"

I couldn't answer that, but I was sure that the Professor must have his reasons. He was likely trying to get Jimmy's phone records and confirm Sophie's accusation about Olive illegally selling costumes.

"It's a mess. I have a feeling that today's show is going to be a disaster." She gathered her dishes. "Thanks for listening. You're right, it helped—at least a little. Jimmy is still dead. My life is still over, but it was good to talk through everything with you, because now I'm certain of the truth. Olive killed him."

"I'm glad it helped." I stood and took her plate and cup from her. "The Professor is right, though. If it's too hard for you emotionally, I'm sure that Lance will understand."

"No. I want to be there. I need to be there. I'm hoping that the police will march in and take Olive away in handcuffs. That would be sweet justice." She stopped when we got to the door. "Thanks again."

I watched her cross the plaza toward the fountain. Activity was starting to pick up. A hiking group assembled near the bubblers, complete with backpacks, water bottles, and trekking poles. Another group gathered nearby. They were the OSF backstage tour crowd; I could tell from their OSF lanyards and playbills waiting to be autographed.

Everything Sophie said made sense, and I was more convinced that she was sincere in her adoration of Jimmy. I couldn't wait to connect with Lance to hear how last night went and get his opinion on Olive.

Before I had an opportunity to sneak up to the OSF campus and see if Lance happened to be in his office, the Professor wandered into the bakeshop. "Juliet, you're just who I was hoping to see." He greeted me with a lingering hug.

"That makes two of us."

He motioned to a bench in the plaza near the travel kiosk. "Do you have a minute?"

"For you, always." I smiled. "Let me set these down. Can I get you anything?"

"Thank you for the kind offer, but your mother was up early this morning making her stuffed cream cheese French toast." He patted his trim stomach. "I'm afraid *I'm* stuffed."

I chuckled. "Fair enough, but you always have room for coffee, right?"

He massaged the red and gray stubble on his chin. "As the late great T. S. Eliot said, 'I have measured out my life with coffee spoons.'"

"Oh, I'll have to add that one to the chalkboard. Back in a flash." I set the dishes in the bins and grabbed us coffee.

He offered me his arm as we crossed the street. "First and most importantly, how is your health? I heard about the fainting incident at Uva yesterday. Your mother and I were quite worried."

"I'm better. I think it was a combination of things—too much sun and caffeine, and not enough food." I tapped the top of my lid. "This is decaf, by the way."

"And perhaps the toll of discovering Jimmy's body," he suggested with a soft smile.

"Yeah, maybe that, too," I admitted.

"I'm glad to hear that you're feeling better and on decaf. I'm sure your mother will be by soon to check on you. Forgive the dual quotes, but as I reminded her this morning, 'Present fears are less than horrible imaginings.'"

"Is that Shakespeare?"

"The one and only. I appreciate the Bard's perspective

on the intrusive thoughts that can wreak havoc in our heads." He strummed his beard in thought as we sat on a bench across from the information kiosk. "It is a mother's prerogative to worry. And it's mine, as well. Would it bother you if I offer some fatherly advice?"

"Not at all." I appreciated the father he had become to me and felt grateful for his wisdom and involvement in my life.

"I'll speak from my own experience. As you know, in the last few years, I've been scaling back my caseload and passing off more to Thomas and Kerry. This precedes my upcoming retirement, and it was also a conscious choice, a necessary choice. I had been burning the candle at both ends, so to speak. Until your mother and I deepened our friendship, my work/life balance was not something to be proud of. It's one of those cases of 'do as I say, not as I do.'" He sighed and set his coffee on the ground. "I caution my team to create firm boundaries around the work we do. Investigating darker sides of the Rogue Valley takes an emotional toll."

"I can only imagine. I feel grateful that my days are typically filled with pastries and not murder scenes."

"Yes." He closed his eyes and then measured his words. "It's true that police work is taxing and requires a commitment to self-care and balancing personal boundaries. I share this with you, though, because I believe we have similar personalities. Our greatest strengths—work ethic, loyalty, creative energy that fully immerses you in the moment. You do all of this and more, including treating your staff like family, putting your very heart and soul into every pastry that comes out of the kitchen, truly caring about your customers, and retaining the tiniest details about their lives, the list could go on and on. But my point is that these wonderful qualities can also lead to burnout, as I well know. I was doing too much. I was consumed with work, and I would hate to see you follow that path. If you can learn to carve out time for yourself at this stage of your career, I think it will serve you well. Please accept my apology if I'm being too directive. That's not my intention. I see so much of you in me, and I wish I had learned a bit more balance earlier."

My eyes welled. I leaned into his shoulder. "No apology needed. I appreciate your insight."

"You have a lot on your plate, Juliet. You have since the day you returned to Ashland. Torte, Scoops, Uva, wholesale accounts, weddings, graduations, celebrations, and now partnering with the Fair Verona Players. I'm tired just thinking of all that you do."

"I don't do it alone," I protested.

"True, but each piece takes up headspace, am I correct?"

I nodded. "Honestly, I thought I was doing a better job with my work/life balance. We've taken vacations, and with Ramiro here, I've been better about taking off Sundays and sneaking out of Torte earlier in the afternoons."

"Agreed. Your mother has mentioned how happy she is to see you pulling back a bit more. Your creativity is your driving force, which is a rarity and something to embrace. It's also keeping you from sitting with yourself, your worries, rooting yourself in the present. I know something about this. What I'm suggesting, though, especially when it comes to your health, is that our bodies can often signal us that we're doing too much before we become fully aware."

I pondered this. Was my body telling me that I needed to slow down?

The Professor didn't push me to speak. He sipped his coffee slowly. We sat in contemplative silence, taking in the sound of birds flitting between the waxy leaves on the oak trees. Pink blossoms fell like a fragrant spring snow. The gurgle of the sulfuric waters in the bubblers sounded like a massage for my ears. Carlos and I had chatted about this very thing many times in the last few months. Was my body trying to signal me that I needed to slow down?

Owning multiple restaurants in my beloved hometown was like a dream, but was it too much? Torte, Uva, Scoops, private events, catering—the list was lengthy.

I had a highly capable team, and Carlos was fully responsible for Uva. Lance was a silent partner and backer at the vineyard, but the Professor's words rang true. There were times when I felt stretched thin. Maybe that was an exaggeration. Most days, it was hard to let thoughts of the bakeshop, ice cream shop, and winery go, especially at night when I would review my ever-growing to-do list. Plus, I had limited time left with Ramiro. I didn't want to put him back on a plane to Spain with regrets.

We had discussed hiring a manager to oversee operations. Maybe it was time to really consider my capacity and what was next for our ever-growing Ashland empire.

"You're right," I said to the Professor.

"I don't want to be right. I just want you to know that you're loved."

I brushed a tear from my eye. "I'm so grateful to have you in my life, and I truly appreciate your honesty. Carlos suggested that we look at promoting Sterling and hiring someone new as a sous chef. We've also talked about adding a few more staff. I think you're right. It's probably long past due, and I don't want to burn myself out."

"Thank you for being receptive to my oversharing." He squeezed my shoulder. "I would never want you to think I'm being intrusive."

"Never." I met his gaze. His weathered face held years of wisdom. Losing my dad had made me crave a relationship like the one we had. I felt grateful that he was willing to have the hard conversations with me too.

He smiled, and the conversation shifted. "Did Thomas and Kerry give you updates on the investigation yesterday?"

"Yes, and just a few minutes ago, I had a long talk with Sophie. She told me about Olive selling costumes on resale markets for personal profit."

"Indeed, that's what she reported to us as well."

"Have you confirmed it?"

"I can tell you that we're pursuing that line of investigation."

"What about Jimmy's phone? Was it with him when he was killed?"

"No, it wasn't." He looked as if he wanted to say more but couldn't. "We are in possession of the phone, though."

"Sorry for all of the questions, but I do have one more. Have you found the key to the wine cellar?"

"Unfortunately, that hasn't turned up as of yet either." He frowned. "I suspect that the killer likely had both items in their possession. They could still have the key and phone, or there's an equal chance that they disposed of the evidence."

His phone buzzed. "I'm sorry, I must excuse myself to take this call."

"Thanks for the chat."

He gave me a long hug. "Thanks for letting me stand in for your father."

I watched him walk toward the police station. Feelings of grief and gratitude flooded my body. His wisdom and insight were unparalleled. I was lucky to have him, and I intended to take his advice. Baking was my love language. It was time to refocus on that and hire some extra help.

Chapter Eighteen

After my conversation with the Professor, I returned to Torte with a new resolve. Tonight I would talk through possibilities with Carlos, and tomorrow I would start posting ads for new staff.

"Hey, boss, Mrs. The Professor is looking for you," Andy called from behind the espresso bar as I stepped inside.

"Is she downstairs?"

"Yeah, can you take this to her? I made her a double vanilla latte with a little something special." He passed me a creamy latte. "Do you need a drink?"

"No, I'm good, but I'm happy to deliver this." I took the drink downstairs. Mom was chatting with a group of customers seated around the atomic fireplace.

I waited for her to finish her conversation. Her eyes lit up when she noticed me.

"Coffee delivery, courtesy of Andy." I held up the ceramic diner-style mug.

"Lucky me." She took the coffee and studied me with concern for a long minute. "How are you feeling this morning?"

"Much better." I peered into the kitchen and lowered my voice. "I had a very sweet chat with the Professor, and I'm going to make some changes. I think it's past time."

Mom put her free hand to her chest and smiled with relief. "I'm glad to hear that, honey. The bakeshop is thriving. Carlos is expanding everything at Uva. I think this is a perfect time for you to focus on *you*."

"Yeah, I guess I've sort of shifted away from what I love, which is baking. I mean, I do find time to be in the kitchen every day, which is good. But our chat made me realize how much time I spend thinking about all the other things—schedules, vendors, supplies, events, orders."

She nodded knowingly.

"I don't need to tell you this; you did it yourself for years."

"Oh, but not like you, Juliet." She inhaled through her nose and shook her head. "You've taken Torte to an entirely different level since you returned home."

"Mom."

"I'm serious." She gave me her best mom look. "It made sense at first. The bakeshop was a distraction and something positive for you to focus your attention on. I'm forever thankful for that. Your arrival couldn't have come at a better time for me, selfishly."

"It was meant to be," I interrupted.

"Yes, and things change and evolve." She motioned to the wood-fired pizza oven. "You've expanded Torte and opened Scoops and completely revamped Uva. The business side of things is consuming all your time. I worry that you're not able to do what you love the most—bake. Things are thriving, so this feels like the perfect time to add some new staff to be able to reduce your workload, especially because I'm not as much help these days either."

"You're always a help, Mom."

"You know what I mean. Doug and I have plans to travel, and I'm quite happy to pop in without the responsibility of the day-to-day tasks, but you're doing the lion's share of the work."

"That's as it should be." I pointed to the team, who were crumb-coating cakes and slicing pizzas.

"Spin that advice around to you." She raised her eyebrows. "And do promise me that you're also going to follow up with your doctor."

"I'll make an appointment tomorrow." I made an X over my heart. I should have been more proactive about Torte's growth and the empire I was building in Ashland. My head chef in culinary school had cautioned us that owning and managing a bakery was a very different beast from working as a pastry chef. The former meant that the vast majority of your time would be reserved for the business side of baking. The latter meant that the bulk of your days would be spent sculpting cakes and testing new recipes. I wanted a balance of both.

She gave me a thumbs-up. "Good, now it sounds like I have some baking to do."

We went into the kitchen together. Mom sipped her coffee and caught up with Bethany and Steph while I washed my hands and tied on a fresh apron.

Sterling grilled onions on the stove with his left hand, while thumbing through a recipe with his other.

"What's your day like tomorrow?" I asked, wafting the sweet aroma of caramelized onions toward my face.

"Umm, more of this." He flipped an onion slice with tongs. "Why?"

"Can we do lunch? I have a proposal I want to talk to you about."

Was it just my imagination, or did he look worried? His steel-blue eyes flickered briefly before he nodded. "Uh, yeah, actually, I have something I need to talk to you about." He glanced at Steph.

"Let's go to a late lunch at the Green Goblin," I suggested. "After the lunch rush here. Maybe two-ish?"

"That works." He turned the flame on the gas burner down and removed the pan from the heat.

"I'll make a reservation." I felt relieved knowing that I was taking a first step toward lightening my load. Sterling had proven his work ethic, cooking skills, and ability to be a team player. Hopefully the shift would be positive for both of us. I could scale back a bit, and Sterling could have even more autonomy and responsibility. Not to mention a bump in his salary.

I grabbed the next specialty order from the whiteboard and made sure no one else had started on the cake. It was my favorite kind of order—the chef's choice. The only instructions were decadent flavors and a spring design. The cake was for an eightieth birthday party and needed to serve ten people.

I knew what I wanted to bake—a triple-layer cake with chocolate, banana, and white sponges. I would cover each cake with pastry cream and fresh bananas. Then I would frost it with our French buttercream, a dark chocolate drizzle, and pretty spring buttercream flowers.

For the first layer, I whipped butter and sugar in our industrial mixer; then I added eggs, mashed bananas, vanilla, and a touch of cinnamon. I greased baking tins and cut out parchment paper circles for the base of each pan.

As I slid the banana cakes into the oven, my thoughts drifted to Sterling's response to my lunch invitation. What did he want to talk to me about? Did it have to do with Steph?

They had moved in together. Could he be thinking of proposing? She was done with school, and he had finally met her parents. Were they taking things to the next level? A Torte wedding—how amazing would that be?

Another thought came to mind.

They couldn't have broken up, could they?

I tried to keep a subtle eye on their body language and interactions as I made the batter for my chocolate and white sponges. If they were on a break, neither of them gave any indication of animosity.

To be fair, Steph wasn't the easiest person to read. She tended to keep her emotions in check and safely guarded. Sterling was equally private. He was a skilled listener. If he hadn't had a passion for food, he would have made a fabulous counselor with his ability to hold space without needing to say anything, allowing his emotions to lead. They were both wise beyond their years and a good match.

They were acting normal, bantering every once in a while, but mainly keeping their attention on the tasks at hand—Sterling at the stove and Steph at her decorating station.

I sifted cocoa powder in with the other dry ingredients—flour, salt, and baking powder—and added them to the mixer in alternation with buttermilk, beating it into a smooth batter. I then used one of my favorite tricks to punch up the chocolate flavor. I added miniature dark chocolate chips to give a nice pop of chocolate in each slice. But before I incorporated them into the batter, I dusted them with flour. This would ensure that the chips wouldn't sink to the bottom of the cake while it was baking. There's nothing worse than a soggy, chocolatey cake bottom.

I placed the chocolate cakes in the oven and got more eggs from the walk-in for my white sponge. To keep the cake light and airy, I whipped egg whites until they formed soft, glossy peaks. Then I carefully folded them into my mixture. The egg whites would give the sponge an airy texture and make for a perfect top layer. I reserved the yolks for the pastry cream.

Not all white cakes were the same. When we took custom cake orders, customers often asked for clarification about the difference between a white and a yellow cake. The answer was easy—yolks. Yellow cakes used the entire egg, resulting in a slightly denser consistency and a custardy flavor. White cakes had less fat and more sponginess. They were our go-to cake for weddings.

With each of my cakes baking, I could begin on my pastry cream. The pudding-like cream would provide a nice base for the sliced bananas between each layer of sponge. Making a pastry cream involved whisking whole milk and sugar over medium-high heat and tempering a mixture of egg yolks and flour. If the eggs were added to the hot milk too quickly, they would scramble and turn out gummy. To avoid this, I slowly added half the yolk mixture while the milk was simmering, whisking constantly. Then I added the next half and kept whisking until the pudding thickened. The final step was adding butter and vanilla.

I dipped my pinkie into the batter, admiring its silky-smooth texture. The vanilla lingered on my tongue. As a chef, it was my responsibility to taste at every stage of the baking process. It was a practice I had passed on to my team.

I poured the warm pudding into a bowl, covered the top with a piece of plastic wrap to prevent a skin from forming, and set it in the refrigerator to cool completely. Once it had chilled, I would pipe it onto the cakes.

Bethany had already made French buttercream, so I went through our natural food gels to decide on a color palate for the cake. Gels brought out the clarity and brilliance of colors without adding extra liquid to the frosting. Officially called "icing colors," gels consisted of a corn syrup and glycerin base that resulted in a much more intense color.

I opted for blues, greens, and purples. Once my cakes had cooled and the pastry cream had set, I stacked the layers and frosted a crumb coat in a sky blue buttercream.

Then I used a side sweep texturing method to create a swath of green, purple, and navy buttercream stars, shells, flowers, and dots. I finished the cake with fancy sprinkles and hand piped Happy Birthday on the top.

The party was taking place at Harvey's, a wood and brass pub just up Main Street from Torte. I decided to deliver the cake myself. A little walk would do me good, and it was always fun to get to see customers' reactions.

The moody atmosphere of Harvey's, with its stained-glass table lamps, brick walls, wooden booths, and touches of brass throughout, was fitting to celebrate an eightieth birthday. Harvey's was known for their mixology as well as for their Pacific Northwest inspired cuisine. Carlos was a huge fan of their halibut with sweet chili sauce and rosemary polenta, and I loved their chicken piccata.

"I'm here for a cake delivery," I said to the hostess when I arrived. She pointed me to the back room, where silver and purple balloons were bunched on the back of chairs. Wild lilacs served as centerpieces along with printed photos of the birthday guest of honor from her early childhood to present day. I stopped to admire a collection of family photos framed on the wall, highlighting the restaurant through the years. It was a good reminder that I was making the right choice to restructure the business and free up more time to spend with the people I loved.

"Juliet, I didn't know you were coming to the party," a voice said from the banquet table.

I turned to see Tom Rudolph studying bottles of wine with Harvey's sommelier. He looked like he was dressed for a funeral in his black suit, black shirt, and black tie.

"Not as a guest. I'm here with the cake." I lifted the box in my arms.

Tom whispered something to the sommelier and waved me toward the bar. "I'm glad to bump into you. Can I bother you for a minute?"

"Sure. Just let me get this set up," I said, nodding to a small round table near the end of the bar with a silver cake stand and gold-rimmed cake plates. I carefully unpacked the cake, centered it on the stand, and made sure that the buttercream didn't need any touch-ups. Once it was in position, I returned to the bar.

It was fortuitous to run into Tom. I wanted to ask him about where he had been the night of Jimmy's murder. Why had he vanished after asking Andy to come find me?

He swirled a glass of red in his left hand like he was rocking a baby to sleep. "Would you like a drink?"

"No, thank you. I'm still on the clock."

"Sounds like you're in the wrong profession. I've always said only take a job that allows for day drinking. Isn't that why you own a vineyard?" He held the glass to the Edison style lights hanging above the bar and tilted his head to one side to inspect the wine's legs.

I had met a handful of restaurant staff over the years who subscribed to Tom's philosophy. None of them lasted long in a professional kitchen. We adhered to strict rules about imbibing while operating heavy industrial mixers or using filet knives. The same was true for Uva. None of our staff or volunteers consumed while pouring our wines. They were welcome to linger with a glass and take in a sunset at the end of a shift or after closing, but serving was a job that required being sober and coherent.

"You might think so," I said to Tom, not wanting to get into the litany of liability issues.

Tom shrugged.

"Does your job allow for day drinking?" I wasn't entirely sure exactly what Tom did for a living other than invest in startup theater troupes.

"My job is to wine and dine clients." He tipped his glass, which was a generous pour, to say the least.

That didn't answer my question, so I tried a new tactic. "How do you know the birthday guest?"

"She's my aunt." His words slurred ever so slightly as he spoke. "My beloved and extremely wealthy aunt, who makes it her mission to have me and every other member of our family pander to her needs. Has anyone mentioned that blending family and business is a terrible idea?"

I didn't respond, since I had the opposite perspective on working with Mom and a team who had become like family to me.

"I don't recommend it," Tom said, with a snigger. "My aunt likes to task me with investing her money and then gets on her high horse about the quality of my investments. She was the one pushing to diversify her investments into the arts and wanted in on the early stages of the Fair Verona Players. She absolutely adores live theater, and yet all I've heard for the last three months is complaints about the company. Maybe I should start investing in horses. That will make her happy."

There was something off-putting in his tone.

"I promised her I would pick the perfect wine for the party. Harvey's has one of the better selections in the Rogue Valley, thankfully. The sommelier was trying to convince me that the Rogue Valley has a burgeoning viticulture scene before you arrived. I wish that were true. The valley is seriously lacking. We're nowhere near on par with Napa. Those marketing materials and glossy posters around town, touting us as the 'new Napa,' are a joke."

I couldn't tell for sure, but it sounded like he meant that as dig against Uva. We'd already established that he wasn't impressed with our wine, so he was either trying to get a reaction from me or completely oblivious.

"How are things going with the Fair Verona Players?"

"Fine. Why?" He bristled. "Why would you ask that?"

"You mentioned your aunt complaining, and then of course, with Jimmy's death, I wondered how morale is with the troupe."

"It's better than it's ever been if you ask me. Everyone

is relieved to have Jimmy gone, and his understudy was phenomenal last night."

That wasn't the reaction I expected. "Did you see anything strange the night he was killed?"

Tom sucked in his cheeks. "Like what?"

"I wondered if maybe you saw the killer. Andy mentioned that you had been in the kitchen shortly before I found Jimmy. It's a good thing you didn't go downstairs. You could have run into the killer yourself."

Tom stared at me with ice-cold eyes while guzzling his wine. "I did go down to the cellar. Why do you keep asking questions?"

"You did? I thought that my staff said you were looking for the key." I didn't want to call out Andy, and I didn't like the way Tom's eyes narrowed in anger. Had I hit a nerve?

"I was looking for the key. I needed another bottle of wine to schmooze a potential investor. The theater needs ongoing patron support in order to grow, and my role is to bring in financial backers. I couldn't impress them with a twenty- or thirty-dollar bottle of wine, could I?"

Another slight against Uva. I let it slide because I wanted to hear what else he had to say about the cellar.

"The key wasn't in the kitchen?"

Tom's response was monotone. "No. It wasn't on that hook. I warned you that leaving a key to the wine cellar out in the open was a terrible idea. You should really consider more safety protocols. In any event, since the key was missing, I took a chance that meant whoever had it was in the cellar, so I went downstairs to get a bottle myself."

I ignored his lecture. "Did you see Jimmy while you were down there?"

He shook his head. "I didn't see anyone. The cellar was locked, and there was no one around. The entire house was empty."

I nodded, but internally I was confused. How did this work in the timeframe of Jimmy's murder? Andy said that I had missed Tom by minutes. How could Tom have missed seeing Jimmy if I found his body shortly after? Either he was lying or the timeline for Jimmy's murder was wrong.

Chapter Nineteen

"You're sure you didn't see Jimmy?" I asked Tom, trying to readjust the timeline of Jimmy's murder in my head.

Tom drank the final sips of his wine. Then he reached over the bar, grabbed an open bottle, and proceeded to refill his glass. He seemed quite at home helping himself to other people's wine. "No. The basement was empty. I wanted to impress two more potential donors, so I returned outside to look for you. These are theater patrons with high expectations. They're from Napa, so I knew I needed to give them a bottle of something that would meet their standards while we dissected the performance and discussed their charitable giving."

There it was again—another blatant insult of Uva.

I considered telling Tom that calling Ashland an up-and-coming growing region wasn't a marketing strategy. The *New York Times* had recently declared the Rogue Valley the next Napa. One of the most compelling things about the wine scene was its approachability. Wine lovers could mingle with the winemakers, have a picnic amongst the grapes, and immerse themselves in an intimate experience. Dropping fifty dollars for a tasting didn't mean that the wine was inherently superior. I appreciated that Uva guests could enjoy rich, earthy varietals at a reasonable price while soaking in our world-class views.

But I wanted to get as much as possible out of Tom regarding his whereabouts the night that Jimmy was killed, so I had to keep him talking.

"Did you see anyone coming or leaving the tasting room?" I asked.

He considered the question for a moment. "The police asked me that too. The only person I saw was Ed. He said there was an issue with one of the set pieces. He couldn't get a latch to close or something. That's been the theme of this entire production. Broken props. Broken sets. Missing items. It's one of the many reasons my aunt isn't thrilled about how her investment dollars are being spent. To be honest, I'm a bit fuzzy on the details of that night. I'd had a few glasses by then. The crowd was buzzing. The energy was high. I do remember he said something about needing to get his tool kit."

"Do you know when this was?"

Tom set his glass on the bar. "You have a lot of questions, don't you? Why are you so concerned about the timeframe of Jimmy's death?"

I needed to tone it down. I took a slow breath and measured my response. "I was the one who found his body, so I guess I feel responsible somehow."

That seemed to appease him. I could also ask why he was upset about my questions, but I didn't want to push my luck.

He gave me a curt nod and picked up his glass again. "I wouldn't lose any sleep over it. Jimmy wouldn't have done that for you."

The sommelier interrupted us to check on Tom's wine preferences.

"Sorry, I shouldn't keep you. I know you have a party to get to," I said when the sommelier left. "You mentioned you wanted to ask me something?"

Tom kept one eye on the banquet room. "Yes, what's the nature of your relationship with Lance?"

"I'm not sure what you mean."

"How well do you know him?"

"Very well. He and I have been good friends for years." Lance was my best friend in fact, but I didn't think that was the answer Tom was looking for.

"They say it's not wise to go into business with friends," Tom interjected.

"We have good boundaries. Lance is a silent partner and like a brother to me."

Tom shrugged nonchalantly. "It's your bank account. As I said before, business with family is the worst. I speak from experience. It's a bad idea to pair money and family. You would be smart to take my advice on this."

I wasn't about to reveal Lance's financial history to Tom, but my body went into protective mode.

"I'm not sure I follow."

"I'm not sure I made a wise choice in backing the Fair Verona Players. I'm considering pulling my aunt's financial donation."

"Really, why?" I wondered if Lance had heard about this.

"Mismanagement, lack of vision, lack of cohesion with the cast and crew." He gulped more wine. "My aunt and I have been discussing other areas where her investments might see a greater return."

But that contradicted what he'd said earlier in our conversation about the cast and crew being relieved to have Jimmy gone.

"I thought it was the least I could do to warn you, business owner to business owner. You seem like you have a good head on your shoulders, and I would hate to see you get burned with a bad investment, like I have."

He had quickly slipped into patronizing me, insulting my best friend and speaking to me like a child. I was done with our conversation.

"I need to get back to the bakeshop. Enjoy the birthday celebration." I stood and gathered my buttercream supplies.

Tom lifted his glass. "Good luck. Like I said, keep your eye on Lance."

I left Harvey's and went straight to OSF, walking up the steep hill on Pioneer Street. Elaborate costumes for OSF's summer lineup were on display in the front windows—hooped Elizabethan gowns hand-stitched with gold thread, darted pantaloons, and shiny velvet hats. A sandwich board in front of the Tudor Guild gift shop advertised an afternoon build-your-own bust of the Bard, complete with materials.

The bricks, the outdoor gathering space in front of the theaters, were empty except for a small group waiting for their backstage tour at the Lizzie. OSF provided patrons and the community free entertainment there before each show. Singer-songwriters, dancers, and poets would perform on the small stage for people gathered on the grassy slope and brick benches with picnic baskets and blankets.

Lance sometimes kept Sunday hours, especially during the season. The Bowmer Theater was unlocked, so I checked in with the team prepping for the evening show and went to see if I might find Lance in his office.

I breezed through the theater, passing concessions and massive windows that looked out onto the bricks. I knew the way well.

"Lance, it's Jules." I knocked on his office door.

"Come in," a voice called in return. Lance was seated behind his regal desk surrounded by playbills, awards, accolades, autographed headshots, and giant windows that gave him a bird's-eye view of the bricks. "Aren't you a sight for sore eyes? What brings you to the theater, darling?"

"Tom Rudolph." I curled my lip. "I just left him at Harvey's, and it took every ounce of control not to punch him in the face."

Lance motioned to the couch, went to the bar cart, and poured me a glass of water. "Well, well, well. It takes a lot to get our lovely Juliet fired up. You look quite vexed, darling, and I'm here for it." He offered me the water and sat next to me. "Spill the tea."

"Tom is throwing you under the bus."

Lance gasped and threw one hand over his mouth. "What? Moi?"

I relayed our entire conversation word for word. When I finished, Lance leaned back in his chair and stared at the ceiling. "This is an intriguing twist, isn't it?" He reached for a fine-tip Sharpie and doodled on a playbill.

"I don't get it. Honestly, I have no idea what the man even does, and why is he suddenly throwing shade at you? Do you think he did it?"

"Killed Jimmy?" Lance dropped the pen, stood, and paced in front of the wall of his accolades. "It's possible, but I don't see it. The man is a lush. He's a semi-functional drunk. Is that even a thing?"

I shook my head.

"No, strike that. The only thing I've seen Tom do around set is guzzle expensive wine and gossip."

"What does he do?" I asked. "He mentioned running the family business, which sounds like investing his aunt's money, but, like, what's his job?"

"You're correct that he manages his aunt's estate." Lance stopped to straighten a signed headshot from an actor who had gotten their start at OSF and recently won an Oscar. "You're right that his investment money isn't even his. It's his aunt's. He likes to allow people to believe otherwise. As for what his official role is, I haven't the foggiest idea."

"Okay, but isn't money a huge motivation?" I shifted on the couch. "He mentioned the Fair Verona Players being a bad investment."

"That's pure rubbish." He brushed his hands like he was trying to wipe away the suggestion. "We've sold out every show and added Sunday matinees, which sold out within minutes. I have every major OSF donor knocking on my door to hand over cash."

"None of it makes sense. And if Tom did kill Jimmy, I can't piece together the money connection. You would think that he would have done anything to keep Jimmy happy after his amazing opening performance, because word of mouth alone was going to sell out seats."

"On that, I agree." Lance strummed his fingers on his chin. "I can only surmise that Tom is projecting his financial woes on me. Why? I have no idea, but rest assured, the

Fair Verona Players are in the black. Deep in the black. If Tom thinks otherwise, he's completely delusional."

"Every time I think I've landed on a reasonable theory about who killed Jimmy, I learn something new that upends everything."

"Don't stress, Juliet. We're close. I can feel it, and I do think you uncovered a critical piece of information from our drunken investor."

"What's that?"

"Confirmation from another person that Ed was at the scene of the crime right before you found Jimmy. What was he really doing at the tasting room? Why would he leave his tools in the house? That doesn't make sense. They should be backstage. In fact, that's a requirement. There's more to his story."

"Speaking of that, we never talked about Sophie's theory that Ed is the person behind the accidents during rehearsals. What do you think about that?"

Lance tapped a prop sword hanging on the far wall with his finger. "That is a question, isn't it? I can't say for sure, although Ed is responsible for overseeing trapdoors, props, and so forth onstage. Could we chalk up the strange occurrences on set to coincidence? Yes, without a doubt. Could Ed have tampered with blocking tape, intentionally swapped a prop gun or sword for the real thing? Also yes."

"How do we find out whether the accidents were really accidents?"

"I'll ask around—subtly, of course—about Tom's finances, and in the meantime, I think *you* should have a chat with Ed."

"Why would Ed talk to me?" I bit my bottom lip, not liking where this was going.

"I'll tell him to come see you on my behalf." Lance flashed a wide grin.

"Won't that be obvious?"

"Oh, ye of little faith." Lance scowled. "I'll send him to pick up a pastry order tomorrow. You can take it from there, I trust?"

"I'll try, but I don't know him at all." How was I going to subtly bring up murder without raising Ed's suspicions? "I doubt that he's suddenly going to confess his deep dark secrets to me."

"What does our dear Helen say? 'Never underestimate the power of pastry.'" He clapped twice. "Excellent. That's settled, then. Shall we plan to reconnect tomorrow evening? Happy hour at Puck's?"

"Sure." I stood up too fast. The familiar feeling of spinning assaulted my body. I sucked air through my nose and forced my feet to stay planted on the floor. "Don't send Ed to the bakeshop in the afternoon. I'm taking Sterling to a late lunch tomorrow at the Green Goblin to talk about potentially expanding his role. I think it's time for me to scale back, hand over some responsibilities, and hire more staff."

"Smart move." Lance nodded with approval. "It's about time, and I am one hundred percent in support of that decision." He rubbed his hands together and gave me a devilish grin. "That also means more time for sleuthing."

I rolled my eyes. A bad idea.

The room rocked from side to side.

I steadied myself on the arm of the couch.

"The theater is dark tomorrow, so I'll ask him to pick up a box of pastries for our staff meeting," Lance said.

He opened the door for me. "Until tomorrow, then. Be careful, Juliet. Jimmy's killer could be unhinged. We don't want to poke the beast."

"You too." I left him and headed for the Shakespeare stairs that paralleled Lithia Park. It might have been a mistake to take a shortcut, because Richard Lord was lingering on the porch at his decrepit Merry Windsor Hotel.

"Capshaw, are you here to snoop again?" his throaty voice boomed.

He stood with a toothpick between his teeth and a snarl on his lips. As usual, he was wearing outlandish checkered golf shorts. The flowered Hawaiian shirt was a new touch, however.

Richard's idea of artisanal baking was toasting Pop-Tarts or unwrapping mass-produced muffins. The Merry Windsor was in desperate need of repair, but Richard spent his profits on his golf outfits and his behemoth yellow Hummer.

Recently Richard signed on to be a contestant on a dating reality show—*Make a Millionaire Match*. It was a dating show for the wealthy. I wasn't exactly sure how Richard had convinced the producers that he was a millionaire, and I couldn't imagine the unlucky, unsuspecting women he would be matched with. Then again, I'm a believer in love. Far be it from me to stand in the way of Richard finding his soulmate.

Filming wouldn't start for another month, but it was all he would talk about to anyone who would listen. He'd gotten a face lift, Botox, spray tan, hair plugs, and an entirely new wardrobe. He'd hired a professional photographer for headshots who followed him around the plaza for an entire week. It was like Richard had his own personal paparazzo as he posed in cowboy attire in front of the Lithia bubblers, making sure to comment about his upcoming stardom and the need for professional headshots to anyone passing by.

Maybe that explained the new shirt. Richard must be gearing up for his debut television appearance.

"You caught me red-handed, Richard." I held out my palm.

He shook a pudgy finger at my face. "Don't take an attitude with me, young lady. I'll have you know that there are going to be producers and photographers for *Make a Millionaire Match* at the Windsor for the next few weeks. They're shooting B-roll for my show. I doubt you're familiar with the industry terms, since you're not a Hollywood insider like me, but B-roll of me running around Ashland will be cut in between clips of the show, and I'm not going to let you try to get airtime."

"Trust me, that's the last thing I would want." It took every ounce of internal control not to laugh at Richard trying to mansplain B-roll. "You're in no danger from me. The spotlight is all yours."

He muttered something under his breath I couldn't make out. "I know about your agenda, Capshaw. Consider this your warning. Stay away from my property and stay away from the camera crews, or else . . ."

"Or else what?" I wasn't going to put up with his intimidation tactics. "The last time I checked, there's no law against walking on the sidewalk."

"Nice try." He broke the toothpick in half and threw it off the porch onto the pavement. "You might fool everyone else in town with your fake kindness, but you don't

fool me. I know you have your sights set on fame and fortune, and I'm here to tell you that you're not taking mine."

"I wouldn't dream of it, Richard. I genuinely hope you
find love on the show. I'm convinced your future wife is
out there waiting to meet you." I gave him a half wave and
continued walking. There was only one way to deal with
Richard Lord—kill him with kindness.

Chapter Twenty

As I'd promised, I gathered Mom, the Professor, and Carlos later that evening for a long conversation about how to restructure my workload.

Ramiro played the role of waiter, bringing plates of fresh lemon and spring pea pasta salad, grilled asparagus, and herbed focaccia outside to the deck nestled in by the towering redwood trees. Grizzly Peak was drenched in peach sunlight. Shimmery hummingbirds flittered between the feeders hanging along the deck, sipping sweet nectar. Carlos opened a bottle of crisp riesling, and Ramiro (clad in black with a white apron tied around his waist) filled our water glasses.

"Can I get you anything else?" he asked, pretending to check our orders on a pad of paper. "Chef has a special dessert for you that I'll bring out in a moment. My shift is ending soon, but you'll be in good hands with Chef." He swept a lanky arm toward Carlos.

"Bravo." The Professor clapped. "This is a feast fit for a king."

"And such exceptional service," Mom added with a wink.

"Enjoy." Ramiro turned to go back inside, tucking the notepad under his arm.

"Excuse me, waiter, there is one more thing I need to discuss before your shift ends." The Professor held up his index finger to get Ramiro's attention. Then he reached into his jacket and removed two twenty-dollar bills. "Your tip."

Ramiro turned around. His face cracked into a wide smile when he spotted the money. "No, no. A tip is not necessary."

"Ah, but I insist." The Professor waved the bills.

"No, it was just for fun that I played waiter tonight," Ramiro protested, his cheeks flushing with color. "I'm going to pizza with friends now."

"And it's customary for grandparents to pay for that pizza," the Professor retorted, reaching for his wallet again. "Come to think of it, you probably need a bit more to cover dinner for your friends."

"Don't forget about dessert." Mom nudged the Professor. "They'll need ice cream at Scoops after pizza."

"You're correct, my dear. Pizza without ice cream is like leaving *Romeo and Juliet* before the final act. It leaves you satisfied yet longing for that sweet final touch," the Professor agreed, pulling out more cash.

Ramiro looked at me with his mouth hanging open. I nodded, encouraging him to take the money. Mom and the Professor had both shared on numerous occasions how much they enjoyed getting to spoil Ramiro, and I certainly wasn't going to dissuade them.

He kissed them both. "Thank you."

"Have a wonderful time," the Professor said, beaming

with pride. "And if I might suggest, order the cheesy garlic bread as a starter. It's absolutely divine."

Ramiro left, and we dug into our dinner.

Carlos filled the Professor's wineglass. "You are too kind to him."

"They say that becoming a grandparent is a second chance. That you have an opportunity to put into practice what you learned—the good and bad—with parenting. But for me, since I never had children of my own, Juliet is the daughter I never had, and Ramiro is the grandson I always wished for." He looked at Mom, who reached out her hand in a show of support. He laced his fingers through hers and continued. "It's nearly impossible for me to articulate how grateful I am to have you all as my family. I didn't dare to dream that I would be this lucky, so I hope you'll let me indulge in my role as a doting grandfather."

Carlos raised his glass. "Salud por eso."

I held my glass of sparkling water and clinked it with Mom's glass.

"We know we're biased, but he is seriously the most amazing young man on the planet," she gushed. "What are we all going to do when he flies home to Spain?"

"Follow him there," I suggested.

"That might be the only solution," the Professor said, raising his glass in agreement.

I took a bite of the cold pasta salad packed with peas, spicy garbanzo beans, rotisserie chicken, and veggies. The lemon dressing gave it a tangy zest. "Speaking of family and support, I want to thank all of you for keeping an eye on me and also discuss plans for doing some restructuring at Torte."

"We are understaffed and overdue for extra hands in the kitchen," Carlos replied, brushing a pine needle off the table.

"I couldn't agree more." Mom set her fork down. "Sterling is the obvious choice for managing the kitchen, but if he agrees to a promotion, you're definitely thinking of hiring a replacement sous chef, right?"

"Yeah," I said through a mouthful of pasta.

We tossed around the idea of promoting Sterling to kitchen manager, hiring another sous chef, and looking for some additional part-time help, particularly over the summer months. For the next hour, we enjoyed our meal as the sun set over the sepia-toned hills. We lingered over decaf coffee and a plum almond tart, sketching out roles and budgets. I could practically feel the tension falling off my body. This was exactly what I needed—what the bakeshop needed.

The next morning at Torte, I wrote up a job description along with salary ranges for each of the new positions. I wanted to speak with Sterling first. Once I had a sense of whether he was interested in taking on a bigger role, then I would post the job offerings. I wasn't worried about finding help. With SOU in town and high school students looking for summer income, I had a feeling that we would have a line out the door for interviews.

I'd almost forgotten about Ed when Rosa came downstairs to refill a tray of black sesame chocolate and lemon Earl Grey cookies.

"Jules, there's a man upstairs looking for you. He said his name is Ed."

"That's right. Thank you. I'll grab his order and take it up for him." Lance hadn't specified what kind of pastries he wanted, so I put together a box of one of everything we had in stock.

Ed was hanging by the door, scanning the bakeshop like he was casing the place.

"I believe these are for you," I said, handing him the box.

"Yeah, Lance wanted them for morale. I don't know that jelly donuts are going to help, but I guess it's a nice gesture." His tool bag was looped over one shoulder, weighing down his left side.

"Is morale low?"

"Yeah, painfully low."

"Can I get you a latte or an Americano?"

He checked his watch and hesitated for a minute. "I guess I could be talked into a coffee. Our meeting is in thirty minutes and I'd never turn down a latte."

"Great. Grab a table, and I'll be right with you."

This was becoming a habit. Soon I was going to need to start carving out hours for our investigation services at the bakeshop. Ed picked a table outside. I brought him a cherry blossom latte and a slice of tomato and caramelized onion quiche.

"You didn't need to go to any trouble." He tore his gaze away from the blue awnings of the police station across the street.

"It's the least I can do. I feel so bad about everything that's happened."

"It's not your fault." He pushed his tool bag to the side with his feet.

"No, but with owning the vineyard and being the person who found Jimmy's body, it's almost impossible to take myself out of the situation."

An insincere smile tugged at his mouth like he was trying to give me the impression that he agreed. But his hardened, questioning eyes told another story. "You found the body? I hadn't heard that."

"Yes." I was under the impression that everyone knew that by now, so his question took me off guard.

His posture stiffened. "When?"

"I don't know for sure. It wasn't long after the end of the show. I was needed in the cellar, and when I went down to open it, that's when I found Jimmy."

"Huh." Ed nodded his head, but his skepticism lingered in between us like an unspoken secret.

Why didn't he believe that I'd found the body? And why did it matter?

"I heard that you were in the tasting room then, too."

Ed flinched. He stabbed the quiche with his fork and slowly lifted a bite to his lips like he was buying time. "Where did you hear that?"

"I don't remember. Someone mentioned that they saw you, but honestly, everyone seems to have been there. I'm still shocked that Jimmy was killed. It seems risky to have killed him with so many people around, don't you think?"

"Not for the killer." Ed whipped his head in the direction of the police station again. "They probably had enough and killed him in a fit of rage. They weren't worried about being seen. They just wanted to silence him for good."

Was he speaking from personal experience?

"Were you there?" I pressed, hoping that Ed would confirm what I'd heard from other people.

"I don't know if I was there when he was killed,

but yeah, I came to the house after the show to get some tools. During the run of the show, a board came loose that I needed to nail down before one of the cast or crew tripped." He shot a brief look at his tools. "This production has been a headache. We've had a string of bad luck. Broken set pieces, the wrong props. I know this is a new company and we're bare-bones in terms of staff, but I haven't been sleeping well because I've been worried that someone is going to end up hurt."

That didn't sound like the sentiment of a killer.

"Why was your tool bag in here?" I asked, unable to disguise my shock over that part of his statement. "Don't you keep your tools backstage?"

A brief look of panic flashed on his face. He recovered by taking another bite of the quiche. "Usually, but one of the cast borrowed my tool kit before the show. I saw it in their dressing room earlier."

"Really?" I wondered if he had told the Professor the same story. What possible reason would a cast member have for taking a tool kit into a dressing room?

"It was Bertie," he replied without emotion.

Was that supposed to answer my question?

"Bertie borrowed your tool kit?"

"Not in the cellar. In the tasting room," he corrected me. "She said she would bring it right back, but then she forgot about it in the whirlwind of opening a show, and when I asked her about it, she said I could find it in the second dressing room upstairs."

"Did you?" His story wasn't adding up. He kept contradicting himself, which raised my internal alarm bells.

"Nope. It wasn't there." He folded his arms across his chest.

"So is it missing, too?"

"No, I got it back. It was on the stage shortly after I went to find it. She must have beaten me to it."

That meant that Bertie had been in the house, too.

Was there anyone who wasn't on-site when Jimmy was killed?

Ed grabbed his coffee cup with both hands. He struggled to keep it steady as he lifted it to his lips. Then he put it back on the table without taking a drink. "Look, I can't do this anymore."

"Do what?"

His entire demeanor changed. Instead of being closed off, he suddenly seemed jittery and on edge. His foot bounced on the pavement, shaking the table. "Lie."

"Lie?" I was confused. "You mean about your tool kit?"

"Yeah. I mean about everything. I'm a terrible liar." He let out a heavy sigh. "Look, it was me, okay? I was in the cellar. I took your key." Ed thumped his chest.

I gulped and scooted my chair away from the table, trying to expand the physical space between us. Not that I thought Ed would try to hurt me in broad daylight in the middle of the plaza, but I wasn't going to take any chances.

He reached into his pocket.

My heart thudded.

Was he reaching for a weapon? A gun?

The plaza was bustling with activity. I made eye contact with Janet, who was setting out galvanized tubs of fiery red tulips at A Rose by Any Other Name. Farther down the sidewalk, a staff member at the outdoor store near my old apartment hung posters advertising a kayak training workshop.

I felt better knowing that my friends and fellow business owners had seen me with Ed.

But what did his confession mean about the accidents onstage? All of the mishaps that had gone wrong on the set—could Ed have been the cause? As set director, he would have had access to the prop guns, to everything. He easily could have placed Jimmy's marks on the wrong spot in hopes that the actor would take a deadly tumble off-stage, just like Sophie suggested. Had Lance and I gotten it wrong? Maybe we should have paid more attention to our early intuition when Carlos had mentioned seeing Ed run toward the vines.

"You don't have to look at me like that." Ed tossed the cellar key on the table. "I'm not going to hurt you. I'm trying to apologize."

I stared at the key like it might explode. "I don't understand."

"It was me. I broke into the cellar." He shifted on the bench, pounding his chest again as he spoke, like he was trying to implicate himself. "Technically, I guess it's not breaking in, since I used the key, but you get what I'm saying."

"Not really." I couldn't believe he was admitting this to me.

"When I went to find my tool bag, the kitchen was empty. Tom had told me about the key earlier. He mentioned that it wasn't a smart business decision to leave a key to a wine cellar containing an expensive collection out in the open."

That was what Tom had said to me, although I wasn't sure why he had chosen to share that information with Ed.

"I seized the opportunity." He threw out his hands. "I knew that everyone was outside and that I had a quick window, so I snatched the key and ran downstairs."

My forehead felt hot and clammy. Was he about to confess?

"I unlocked the cellar and grabbed a few bottles of your expensive wine." He reached down to his tool bag and took out a tape measure, which he proceeded to idly coil and uncoil. His words were hesitant and faltering, as if each one was a burden. "I know it's terrible to tell you right here to your face that I stole from you, but I can't keep it in any longer. I'm not proud of what I did, and I promise I'll return the wine to you."

"You took wine from the cellar?" I was trying to process what I was missing.

"Yeah, I know it's bad, and I guess I should admit that technically it was more than a few bottles. It was a couple of cases, but I needed the money, and I didn't think it was going to hurt anyone." He pulled the tape measure tight, releasing it suddenly with a sharp snap. "I was going to take more, but I heard people upstairs, and I had to get out of there quick."

"Was it Jimmy?"

"No, I swear I never saw Jimmy." His eyes remained fixed on the tape measure, tracing the markings as if trying to measure the size of his guilt. "I took the wine, and I ran back to the stage to try and hide it before anyone realized what I was up to. I'm really sorry. I know it's a long shot, but I hope that you'll find a way to forgive me and accept my apology. I'll return the wine. It's still hidden backstage."

Ed appeared genuinely remorseful. The tape measure

slipped from his fingers, landing on the table with a clink as the metal hook tapped the edge. He picked it up and returned it to his tool bag.

The truth was, I didn't really care about the wine, but I wasn't sure I trusted anything he was telling me. If he admitted to stealing wine and being in the cellar, there was a good chance that he was lying about Jimmy too.

That could mean that he had seen more than he was letting on, or it could mean that I was sitting across the table from a killer.

Chapter Twenty-one

"Gigging in this valley is tough. I've been living paycheck to paycheck, trying to work side jobs when I can," Ed said, his gaze flickering, unable to meet my eyes. "When Tom told me about the key, I don't know what got into me. I'd like to say that it's the stress of this production and dealing with Jimmy's ego, but that's no excuse. I am sorry."

"Why did Tom tell you about the key to begin with?"

Ed looked up in surprise. "I don't know. It came up in conversation, I guess. He was drinking a bottle of private reserve and told me that there was more of it in the basement if I was interested."

How thoughtful of Tom to offer our special collection to Ed. I wondered who else he'd told about the wine cellar.

Across the street at the police station, a cadet in training watered the window boxes and filled the dish they left out for passing dogs. "Have you told the police about being in the cellar? This could be critical information in determining exactly when Jimmy was killed."

He scuffed his feet on the ground, sending a pinecone rolling out onto the street. "Not yet, but I will. I know I need to come clean. For you, for me, for them. I'm not proud of my behavior, and I can promise you that it won't happen again. What can I do to make it up to you? Do you need someone to do dishes? Or I could bus tables."

"I appreciate your honesty. The most important thing you can do for me is to go share this with the police right now." I motioned to the blue awnings across the street.

"That's fair." Ed sounded like speaking with the police was the last thing he wanted to do, but he gathered the pastry box, slung his tool bag on his shoulder, and stood. "I'll do that now. I know it probably sounds like lip service, but I am sorry for taking the wine. And thank you for being kind about this."

I waited to make sure that he followed through on his promise before taking his dishes inside and heading downstairs. Was he consumed with guilt, or was taking wine from the cellar a convenient excuse to explain why he was seen right before I found Jimmy's body?

I was also stuck on why Tom told Ed about the key. What was his motivation? Had he set Ed up to break into the cellar?

But why?

None of it made sense.

The kitchen was humming with activity. Bethany prepped brownie boxes at her station. She used carbon steel brownie trays to ensure that each square was identical. She dusted the first batch with a mixture of powdered sugar, cocoa powder, and warming spices.

"Those smell divine," I said, stopping to appraise her work.

"These are my spiced dark chocolate. Next up is chocolate orange with an orange cream cheese frosting, and then a nutty caramel blondie, and finally a salted pretzel." She tapped the edge of the sifter. "What do you think sounds better for the fifth option—tropical coconut or grasshopper?"

"Can I vote both?"

"That's what Steph and Marty said." She scowled and jutted out her neck, making her freckles pop. "You're no help."

"I don't think you'll get many complaints if customers get a bonus brownie." Our philosophy at Torte had always been to overdeliver. Rosa would tuck a bonus cookie in with a pastry order. Andy and Sequoia offered customers complimentary "flubs" if they made a drink wrong or weren't happy with their latte art. We circulated the dining room daily with tasting samples and shared anything left in the pastry case at the end of the day.

"Fair point. Grasshopper and tropical for the win. It's going to be brownie boom for our weekly box subscribers." Bethany gave me an air high five.

I tried to concentrate on lunch preparations, but my thoughts kept returning to the wine cellar. Whoever killed Jimmy had limited time to sneak downstairs, stab him, and vanish without being seen.

But that begged the question—were they seen?

The most likely answer was yes. I reviewed each of the suspects' whereabouts. Ed admitted that he'd been in the cellar. Tom had been in the kitchen shortly before asking for the key, and Sophie had confessed that she and Jimmy were supposed to meet after the show. That left Olive and Bertie. I needed to find out where they both were. Ed claimed that Bertie took his tool bag, but I wasn't going to take his word for it.

For the moment, it was enough to know that three of the suspects were indeed near Jimmy before he was killed. The question was, which one of them, if any, had done it?

The afternoon breezed by. Soon it was time for my lunch with Sterling. I felt oddly nervous. "You ready?" I asked as he ladled a bowl of minestrone meatball soup.

"Yep. Let me wash my hands and grab a hoodie."

Sterling seemed nervous and jittery as we walked past A Rose by Any Other Name, where galvanized tins containing puffy pale pink peonies, sculptural purple snapdragons, and spring tulips offered a cheerful greeting. I made a mental note to stop in later and ask Janet about flowers for Ramiro's prom date.

Sterling tied his hoodie around his waist and massaged his forearm with his thumb. "Have you given any thought to a Sunday Supper?"

"No, it completely slipped my mind. We've had so much other stuff going on. Do you have any ideas?"

Our Sunday Suppers were casual affairs where we served themed dinners, family-style, around a shared table. Sometimes we added bonus entertainment like open mic poetry or live music. They were a way to bring the community together for a simple evening of a delicious meal and lively conversation. Carlos and I were both big believers in the idea that food was the great equalizer. Our mission at Torte was to be a welcoming and safe space for anyone who entered our doors, and I loved that our Sunday Suppers provided a place for people to gather and form strong bonds over a plate of Bolognese and a loaf of rustic sourdough.

Sterling stopped to listen to a busker playing guitar and

covering Ed Sheeran. "Uh, no. That's one of the things I want to talk to you about."

"Sure, go for it."

He tossed a couple of dollars into the busker's guitar case as we passed Puck's Pub. "Maybe we should wait and talk at the Goblin. I think this is going to be a bigger conversation. I have something else I need to share with you."

"Okay." I didn't like the sound of that. Neither did my stomach.

Fortunately, the Green Goblin was close. The funky restaurant sat at the far end of the block from Torte, directly across from Lithia Park. It was themed like a forest from Shakespeare's *Midsummer Night's Dream*, with ivy snaking up the walls and twisting through the dangling golden overhead lights. Wooden tables carved out of trees served as seating, and tiny goblins and fairies were tucked along the bar and in the ceiling, watching over diners with glowing little eyes.

Sterling didn't bother with small talk as the hostess seated us and took our drink order. He massaged the hummingbird tattoo on his forearm with his thumb like he was trying to work up the courage to speak.

I didn't want to stress him out, so I broke the silence first. "I have a lot to talk to you about, but I get the sense you might have something you want to discuss first."

He brushed a strand of dark hair from his eyes. "You know me too well, Jules."

"Right back at you." My mind spun with wild possibilities. Were he and Steph breaking up? Was he upset with me? With someone else on staff?

Our waiter delivered fresh mint and muddled strawberry lemonades and took our order. When they were gone, I waited for Sterling to speak.

"I don't think I can help with Sunday Suppers this summer," he said, continuing to massage his tattoo.

A sense of relief washed through me. That was what he was worried about? Sunday Suppers? We could scale those back, too. It was time to reinvent Torte, and I was open to any and all ideas on the best way to do that.

"Okay, that's fine. Don't even give it a thought." I plunged the sprig of mint into my drink. "I feel like we have so much going on that it's probably best to table Sunday Suppers until the fall anyway."

"It's more than that, Jules." He shook his head and stared at the tabletop like it was the most interesting piece of art he had ever seen.

My nerves resurfaced. Was he quitting?

"I don't think I'm going to be here next month."

I gulped.

Play it cool, Jules.

Sterling lifted his head. His steel-blue eyes were glassy and wide. "I hate saying this to you. I hate having to watch your face, but I've had another offer."

I didn't want to burden him with my sadness. If he was ready to leave Torte and move on to the next evolution of his career, I would support his decision. I would hate losing him, but I couldn't hold on to him if he was ready to stretch and expand. That was the crux of life in a commercial kitchen. It was my job to mentor and nurture my young staff. It was also my job to encourage them to leave the nest and fly away when they were ready.

I just hadn't expected it to be this hard.

Tears threatened. I forced them back by blinking and clutching the ice-cold lemonade.

"There's been an opportunity that's come up," Sterling continued in a soft voice. "Do you know Whaleshead Resort on the coast?"

I nodded. Whaleshead was a sweet seaside community of family-owned cabins nestled cliffside in Brookings, Oregon. The resort wasn't fancy, but the cabins were well stocked. Many had decks with hot tubs that offered stunning views of the rugged coastline and the tidepools below.

"The owner of the restaurant reached out to me. Their head chef is leaving next month. They want me to come to do a one-month trial . . ." He trailed off and let out a long sigh. "I don't know, Jules. I'm torn. I love Torte, and I love working with you and Carlos and the entire team, but this is also a huge opportunity for me. It would be my first head-chef position."

"That is huge," I agreed, forcing a smile—actually if I was being honest, it wasn't forced. I was genuinely happy for him, though losing him at Torte was like a punch to the gut.

"I don't know how I feel about living in Brookings. It's small and on the coast. The good thing is that if I take the position, Whaleshead will provide housing for me, so that's a pretty sweet deal. You know what rent is like in the Rogue Valley. It's hard to turn down free housing." He cleared his throat and continued. "You're not going to like this part, but they're talking to Steph, too. They are interested in having her join me as the head pastry chef. It's really tempting, but there are equal pros and cons. Am I ready to run a kitchen on my own? It would be my menu and me in charge of everything. They've got a line cook, but otherwise everything is up to me. Same for Steph. She'll be responsible for dessert, bread, any breakfast pastries. It's a big change. What if we bomb? And then there's also the piece about me and Steph feeling bad about leaving you in a lurch after everything you've done for us."

I held my hand out to cut him off. "Stop right there. You wouldn't be leaving me in a lurch. Two weeks' notice is standard in the industry, and if you aren't starting until next month, that gives me time to hire new staff, so please don't let that factor into your pro and con list. You don't owe me, or Torte, or anyone anything. This is *your* future and *your* career. You need to do what's best for you."

He started to stay more, but I stopped him.

"Wait, let me finish. This is an important life lesson. I mean it, you don't owe me anything. My job was to train you. You've been an invaluable asset to Torte and have become like family to me, but that shouldn't in any way, shape, or form mean that you're tethered to the bakeshop or Ashland forever."

His eyes misted. "Thanks, Jules. That means a lot."

"It's the way this business works. I want you and our entire staff to continue to push yourself and pursue your own dreams. Trust me, I'm going to sob a little—well, probably a lot—but I'm also going to be the first in line to make reservations and come visit you at Whaleshead. I hope that you know that you always have a friend in me and can call whenever you need support, whether that's in the kitchen or in your personal life. I also want you to know you are more than ready for this. Steph, too. You're both among the best chefs I've worked with. And that's not an exaggeration. You're already doing it. Now you just need to do it on your own."

"Why do you have to be so great?" Sterling sighed and shook his head. "It would be easier to take the job if I hated Torte. Could you be a horrible boss for a couple of weeks?"

"Sure. I'll channel my inner Richard Lord for you if that would help." I intentionally contorted my face as I winked, hoping to lighten the mood.

Sterling laughed. "What do you think, though? Is it crazy? What if we hate it? I appreciate your confidence, but what if we're not ready?"

"What if this is what you're meant to do next?" I countered. "What if this leads you to open your own restaurant? What if it gives you an entirely new experience in a different kitchen? What if the very best happens because you take a chance on *you*?"

"Steph said the same thing. It's not that I'm not open to new adventures, it's just scary, and I feel safe and comfortable with what I'm doing here."

I pressed my lips together. "Then it's probably time for you to go."

He leaned against the high-back chair. "Do you think?"

"I do. I wish I could lie and tell you otherwise, but we only grow by pushing ourselves. You know that. You've lived that."

"It's just hard to think about actually doing it."

"I felt the same when I left for culinary school and again when I took the job on the ship. I even felt terrified when I decided to come home, but each new experience has shaped me."

"Jules, you're so wise and way too good of a boss. This is making me feel worse."

"It shouldn't." I held his gaze. "Listen, I wanted to have lunch with you because I was going to talk to you about taking on a new role at Torte, but I feel like the universe is giving you a strong nudge that it's time for a new direction."

He sat up straighter. "What kind of a role?"

"Carlos and I have decided that it's time to bring in a kitchen manager and scale back a bit. We're also going to hire some additional part-time staff."

"That's smart. You're constantly running on fumes, Jules."

"I know."

"Can I take a minute to consider it?"

"Yes, but as much as I'd love to have you in the new role, I think that Whaleshead is an amazing opportunity for you and probably an important next step in your career, even more so than a promotion at Torte." I couldn't believe I was talking him out of taking the job, but I knew at my core it was the right thing to do.

"How so?" He swirled the ice in his glass and took a small taste. Like a true chef, he let the aroma of the lemonade hit his nose first, then he closed his eyes briefly while letting the liquid linger on his tongue. I'd seen Carlos do the same move at least a hundred times.

"Running a full restaurant like Whaleshead is going to give you a vastly different experience than what you've had here. It might help you decide whether you want to open your own restaurant, or it might lead you to determine that working as a head chef is the path for you. You won't know that until you've tried something new. As much as I'd love to keep you at Torte and have you stay in Ashland forever, I understand that it's my collective experiences that have shaped who I am as a pastry chef. I want that for you, and I promise that you'll always have a spot in my kitchen. If you do this for a month and hate it, you can always come back."

"Really?" His eyes widened with relief. "Are you being serious? Because that would be amazing. But are you sure? That's a lot to ask."

I held up my pinkie. "I pinkie promise. You forever have a home at Torte or any business I own."

"Yeah, but if you go to all the work of hiring replacements for me and potentially Steph, I will feel terrible about coming back."

"No way. Are you kidding me? You know better than anyone how many projects we have in the works. If it's not a match and you want to come back, we'll make a new role just for you and Steph, too."

"Thanks, Jules. You really are the best." Sterling reached across the table and squeezed my hand.

I squeezed his back, not wanting to let go.

Our lunch arrived, and we spent the remaining time talking about his ideas for refreshing the Whaleshead menu. His enthusiasm was contagious. There was no question in my mind. This was the right choice for Sterling and another reminder that things at Torte were shifting. It was going to be hard to watch him go, but I was confident in our connection and sure that even if our paths diverged, we would stay in touch.

Chapter Twenty-two

Sterling's news forced me into action. I didn't spend the remaining afternoon hours spiraling through potential suspects. Instead, I placed ads for extra part-time help and began sketching out job descriptions for three positions—a kitchen manager, cake designer, and sous chef. I wanted Mom's and Carlos's input before I posted job listings, and Sterling had asked for a couple of days to make his final decision. I gladly agreed, but I was fairly confident he had already made his choice.

I tried not to sink into nostalgia as I watched Sterling, Steph, Bethany, and Marty banter easily as they went about their day.

"I've got a joke for you," Marty said, slicing baguettes for sandwiches.

"Oh no," Steph groaned, and rolled her eyes, which were dusted in purple shadow. "How bad is this going to be?"

"I'll tell you. Why are bread jokes always funny?" Marty's eyes twinkled with merriment as he looked at Steph and Bethany expectantly.

Bethany crushed mint chocolate cookies for the grass-hopper brownies. "Okay, I'll bite, why?"

Marty used one of the baguettes to do a drum roll. "Because they never grow *mold*. Get it?"

"Boo. Hiss." Sterling tossed a dish towel at him.

"I don't know," Bethany said, pounding the crunchy cookies into little pieces. "That is clever. I might have to use it in a social media post."

"You're welcome." Marty bowed with the baguette in hand.

I soaked in the moment. What I had said to Sterling was true. I wasn't worried about finding replacements for him and Steph, but I was worried about finding the *right* replacements. Chemistry with staff was critical. Everyone on our current team had unique skills to offer while at the same time providing mutual support and collaboration. One personality that didn't mesh could throw off the entire balance in the bakeshop.

We had been extremely fortunate with our previous hires, so I resolved to remain positive. The best matches would find us. They might not be Sterling or Steph, but I had to follow the same advice I'd given him. Maybe it was time for a change at Torte. Hiring new staff would breathe new, creative energy into the kitchen.

At least, that's what I was choosing to focus on for the moment.

My heart hurt at the thought of not getting to see Steph and Sterling every day. They had become an integral part of my life, and it would be strange not to hear updates about Sterling's poetry group or get the latest celebrity food gossip from Steph. Their energy permeated the entire bakeshop. Without them, Torte would have a new rhythm and vibe. But as Mom had told me often, change was the only constant. Shaking up my routines had led me to an abundance of opportunities and insights. The same would be true for this. I just had to trust the process.

Later when we were finishing closing procedures, Steph motioned me to her decorating station. Marty had already left, and Bethany was upstairs, so it was just us.

She organized flat spatulas and piping tips, tucking her hair behind her ears, and keeping her focus on her pastry tools. "I heard that Sterling told you about the offer."

"It sounds amazing," I replied with sincerity.

"You're sure you're going to survive without me? Who's going to be the voice of reason around here?" She put the tools away and moved on to carefully organizing a drawer of sprinkles. Each row of pearlized beads of sugar was sorted by color and style. "Bethany will be out of control with her puns, and Andy is going to be lost without Sterling, you know."

"I know." I nodded. Was she trying to get me to talk her out of it?

"Marty will be despondent." Steph moved a container of edible gold foil flakes to make room for crystallized purple sprinkles. "Sterling is like a nephew to him. They collaborate on every dish. They have an entire text thread dedicated to flatbread recipes. Sterling was wrecked having to tell you, but telling Marty we're leaving might break him."

"Yeah, that's the hardest part." I could tell she needed to hear herself. There was nothing else I could say or do to help. She wanted to process. She didn't need my input or suggestions. She just needed me here to listen.

"I've been here for five years, you know. All through

college. It's going to be weird not to have that stability. The thought of leaving makes me realize how much I've appreciated the structure and security of coming to Torte almost every day. You know how much I moved around as a kid. This place has been my home." Steph was deeply emotional but rarely effusive. It was one of the things I appreciated most about her. When we'd first met, I thought she was standoffish, but I learned that she showed her love and affection in different ways. Meeting her family at graduation last year had given me more insight into her background. Her parents were free spirits who traveled the country in a van, gigging at circuses and busking from town to town. They were wonderful and adored Steph, but I also understood how her vagabond childhood played into her need for routines and personal space.

Her voice trembled slightly as she continued. "I owe you a lot, Jules. I hope you know how much I appreciate you, Helen, Torte."

I couldn't hold in my tears. "I do," I said through a sniffle. "I can speak for Mom when I say we both feel the same way."

Steph closed the sprinkle drawer and blinked rapidly as if she was fighting to hold it together, but she couldn't contain the swell. Her purple and black mascara streaked down her face as she released the dam.

"It's going to be amazing. This is such a great opportunity for you and Sterling. I'm going to miss you, but this is what you're supposed to do." I reached my arm around her shoulder with a firm grip.

She used both hands to smear tears and her makeup across her face. "Why is it so hard to think about leaving if this is what we're supposed to do?"

"The hard things are always like this. At least they have been for me."

Her shoulders heaved as the tears really began to flow. "Yeah, I get that."

"You're going to be great." I squeezed her tighter. "And I'm going to be your biggest cheerleader."

"Cheerleader, ewwww." Steph scowled and stuck out her tongue.

I laughed. "There's the Steph I know and love."

"It's fine if you tell Carlos and Lance, but don't say anything to the rest of the staff yet," Steph said, mopping her face with a dish towel.

"I would never. It's your story to tell when you and Sterling make your final decision, but I think you have, yeah?"

She nodded. "Yeah."

I left it at that. Steph had plenty to process on her own, and I was due to meet Lance for happy hour.

Lance was waiting for me at Puck's Pub at a high-top table constructed out of a rustic keg barrel. He lifted his martini. "Welcome to the party, darling."

"I have to warn you I'm not feeling very festive," I said as I pulled up a bar stool and sat across from him.

"Why the long face?"

"Sterling and Steph are leaving," I blurted out, and then proceeded to tell him all of the details of my conversations with both of them.

"Oh, this is tragic for us." Lance fanned his face. "However, I appreciate the romance of it all. Young love off to launch new careers. It's so exciting for them."

"Exactly. The word that keeps coming to mind is 'bittersweet.'" My throat tightened. I swallowed the lump. Enough tears had been shed for one day.

"Cheers to that." Lance raised his glass. "It sounds like a drink or two is in order." He signaled to our waiter. "What's your poison, darling?"

"I'll have a ginger ale."

Lance lifted one eyebrow. "Ginger ale, interesting."

"No." I waved him off. "My stomach has been off a little ever since I found Jimmy."

"Fair enough. Ginger ale it shall be."

He waited for the waiter to return with my drink before launching into a discussion about Jimmy's death. "Do tell, were you able to work your pastry magic on Ed?"

I sipped the bubbly soda and filled him on Ed's confession.

"Wait." Lance held out his palm to stop me. "Ed stole wine from the cellar?"

"That's what he said. He told me that things have been tight financially and when Tom told him about the wine in the cellar, he seized the opportunity. I'm not sure what to believe. He seemed sincere and even offered to do dishes at the bakeshop."

"I find that to be the flimsiest excuse I've ever heard. A kindergartner could have been cleverer. He might as well have said that the dog ate his homework."

"I'm glad you think so, because it seemed like an odd story to me, too."

Lance plunged his olive skewer into his drink. "Like he realized that he was in the hot seat and scrambled to come up with a story—any story—quickly. No wonder the man works behind the curtain. Can you imagine him attempting improv?"

"Not if he is lying. I called Carlos earlier to have him

check the cellar, but he must be in the vineyard. He hasn't gotten back to me yet."

"True. I suppose we will be able to confirm or deny Ed's story. If no wine is missing, then we can certainly put him at the top of the list."

A band lugged equipment onto the small wooden stage in the front corner. "Even if he took the wine, it still seems suspicious to me."

"Agreed. He's the only one we know who was physically in the same space where Jimmy was murdered. That must make him a person of interest to the police, don't you think?"

"I wish we knew the exact window of time that the Professor is looking at. I've been trying to figure out how Ed could have gotten away with boxes of wine without being seen by Jimmy or the killer."

Lance snapped his fingers above his head like a lightbulb clicking on. "Because he *is* the killer."

"Maybe." I wasn't quite as confident. "What about Tom? Did you learn anything about his finances?"

"Where to start?" Lance tugged the olive free from the skewer and popped it in his mouth. "According to my sources, things are not exactly chummy with Tom and his auntie dearest."

"What does that mean?"

"As you know, his aunt is not pleased with how he's been investing her fortune and has drastically tightened her purse strings. He's on a losing streak, except for his investment with yours truly, of course. It sounds like his monthly allowances have been reduced to pennies and that she might cut him off completely. The man hasn't worked a day in his life, so losing Auntie's money could certainly give him a motive for murder."

"But why kill Jimmy? I agree with your point. What I'm having a hard time grasping is the connection between Jimmy's death and Tom's bad investments. If anything, you would think Tom would have wanted Jimmy alive. Jimmy stole the show, so why kill him? And I still don't get why he was throwing you under the bus either."

"I have a theory on that." Lance tipped the edge of his glass to get the last few sips of his martini. "Let's assume that Tom has made continuous bad business investments with his family's trust, the Fair Verona Players aside, and his aunt has realized that her fortune is being whittled away. Then let's assume that she has indeed cut him off. What if he had something going on the side with Jimmy? A nefarious dealing that he didn't want anyone to know about. Maybe that's where his funds have vanished, and the night of the murder, they had an altercation. What if Tom demanded his money back, Jimmy refused, and in the heat of the moment, as they say, Tom stabbed him in the neck?"

"It's possible." I had to speak louder over the sound of the guitarist warming up for tonight's show. Puck's hosted a variety of local bands and comics, along with poetry slams and open mic nights for aspiring singer/songwriters. "He did mention going into business with friends or family being a terrible idea. He brought it up as a warning to me. The guy loves to lecture on best business practices, which I do not enjoy, but maybe he was projecting."

"That's quite probable," Lance retorted.

"Bertie mentioned Jimmy was having financial trouble, but I haven't heard anything about him having a side hustle, have you?"

"Alas, I haven't either," Lance admitted with a shake of his head. "That doesn't mean it's not a viable theory. I think it could also explain why Tom was attempting to diminish the success of the Fair Verona Players."

"How so?" I scooted my chair closer to make room for the lead singer, who was dressed in an emerald green cloak. The band's merch advertised that they were a hobbit cover band. I had as many questions about that as I did about Jimmy's murder, but Lance kept us on task.

"If he had invested funds in a failed venture, then the Fair Verona Players became his scapegoat. It's an easy sell to claim that the company was struggling, and that's the cause of his financial worries, rather than admitting that he's been doing shady deals all along."

"It's a good theory. The only problem is how do we prove any of it?"

"That, darling, is the rub." Lance frowned as he sipped the dregs of his martini and motioned to our waiter that he was ready for the check.

"I'm sure that the Professor is researching Jimmy's financial records. Maybe he left a paper trail." I watched as the bass player set up his instrument and began tuning the strings.

"That would be a gift. I think what we need to do next is figure out exactly what Jimmy could have had up his sleeve in terms of side gigs."

"How do you suggest we do that?"

"Sophie, for starters. She tracked Jimmy's movement like an astronomer tracing the path of a constellation across the night sky. I can't remember a time she wasn't in his orbit. Anything Jimmy was involved with, Sophie would know. I think you should have a woman-to-woman chat with her."

"A woman-to-woman chat? What is this, 1950?" I teased. Although I was surprised by the amount of thought Lance had put into this theory. It wasn't as far-fetched as some of his previous suggestions. "What about Olive and Bertie? Earlier, I was mapping out where everyone was when I found the body. I don't know about either of them. I heard that they both followed Jimmy after the show, but where did they go? No one has been able to confirm where either of them was when Jimmy was killed."

"Leave that to me." Lance finished the last sip of his martini and paid for both of our drinks. "I'll see both of them at rehearsals tomorrow."

"It's a plan," I said. I wasn't sure if it was a good plan, but any plan was better than nothing at this point.

Chapter Twenty-three

Carlos and I spent most of the night talking through replacement options for Steph and Sterling and tweaking the job descriptions I had put together. We both had extensive contacts in the culinary world after years of working in professional kitchens. We decided, before listing the openings, that we would reach out to friends and former colleagues to see if they might have any recommendations. It was always nice to have a referral come from within the industry. Hopefully, the right person would stroll into Torte, and we would have a seamless transition.

I could dream, right?

The next day the reality of that transition hit hard. My upbeat perspective on losing Steph and Sterling shifted. I put on a brave face for them and the rest of the team, but I found myself fighting back tears anytime I passed either of them in the kitchen. Twice I snuck into the bathroom to sob silently with the door locked. I had a feeling my staff were curious about my puffy red eyes and the wadded-up tissues in my apron pocket.

"Jules, is everything all right?" Marty asked, brushing

melted butter on loaves of focaccia waiting to go in the oven.

"It's Jimmy's murder. I think it's finally catching up with me," I lied.

"Understandable," Marty replied with a solemn nod. "Maybe you should take the afternoon off."

"Actually, I am going to take a break." I untied my apron. "I should be back in an hour or two."

"Take your time," Marty said. "The bread will be here when you get back."

I appreciated his concern. The truth was that my "break" involved a short walk to the hospital. My doctor's office was located across the street from the Ashland Community Hospital. It had been a while since I'd had a checkup, but the last few days had prompted me to follow Mom and Carlos's advice and book an appointment.

With a name like Juliet, I've always been a hopeless romantic, but this storm of emotions felt different. I wasn't typically prone to weepy spells, but the tears wouldn't stop as I strolled along Main Street past a row of Victorian B and Bs. A mama deer ushered two baby fawns under the protective covering of a clumping of manzanita trees. Watching her nestle her young made me think about Sterling and Steph. They had grown up at Torte, and now they were getting ready to strike out on their own. I knew it was the right choice for both of them. I knew that they needed to challenge themselves and make their own mistakes, just like I had, but letting them go wasn't going to be easy.

At the doctor's office, I checked in for my appointment and leafed through a travel magazine in the lobby while I waited. The first page I turned to was a glossy feature about the Rogue Valley's wine culture. I wondered what

Tom would say about the travel writer's perspective that Ashland should be every wine lover's first stop and a region not to be missed.

When it was my turn to meet with the doctor, I told her everything that had been going on in recent weeks, including Jimmy's murder and staffing changes at Torte.

"Have you been feeling depressed, anxious, or stressed?" the doctor asked, reviewing my chart notes.

"Yeah, I think all three, which isn't normal for me."

"Juliet, it sounds like you're overworked and stressed. Discovering a murder is a traumatic experience, which could certainly cause the dizziness, but I want to run bloodwork and make sure there's not anything else going on," she said, closing the chart notes on her computer. "We'll give you a call with the results of your labs, but I suspect that you've been running on fumes for a while, and it's finally catching up with you. I recommend taking some time off if you can. Try deep breathing, meditation, a twenty-minute afternoon nap, and cutting down on caffeine. If things don't improve, it might be a good idea to speak with a therapist. I see this often in my practice. You're not alone. Consider this your body's early warning system."

"Okay." I took her concern seriously.

"As I said, let's wait and see if anything comes back in your lab work, but otherwise, you're healthy and young. I think this staffing change at your bakeshop is a good opportunity for a reset for you."

I left her office feeling worse. Not that I didn't agree with her assessment, but I was frustrated that it had taken dizzy spells and feeling out of it to make me realize I wasn't setting a good example for my young staff. The doctor was right. It was time for some self-reflection and restructuring.

More tears spilled on my walk back to Torte, but I did feel lighter knowing that I was addressing my issues and taking steps to change my behavior. The universe might have been forcing my hand with Steph and Sterling's departure, and maybe that was ultimately a good thing.

As I passed the costume shop on my walk from the doctor's office, I noticed Sophie inside. Pastel ribbons and large hoops hung in the front windows, along with sequined bodysuits and ballet slippers. A poster announcing upcoming performances of Ashland's annual aerial circus was taped to the door. The costume shop was buzzing with tourists trying on styled wigs, Elizabethan dresses and pantaloons, and intricate masks. I didn't want to pass up a chance to speak with Sophie, so brushed away my tears, rolled my shoulders back, and stepped inside.

"Are you attending the aerial circus?" I asked Sophie, approaching the cash register.

"Huh?" She handed the cashier her credit card and spun around to face me. "Oh, Jules, hey. No, I'm not going to the circus, just picking up a few things for the show. What about you? Are you getting a costume for the circus?"

"Actually, I saw you and wondered if you had a minute to take a walk through the park."

"Uh, sure." She glanced at her smartwatch and took her bag from the cashier. "I'm not due at my next meeting for about an hour."

"Great."

I waited for her to gather her items.

"Do you know anything more from the police?" she asked as we left the store and turned onto the Calle

Guanajuato, a cobblestone pathway that paralleled Ashland Creek and led to Lithia Park. Bright yellow and red umbrellas dotted the walkway where diners could eat amid the sound of the gurgling creek and birds chattering in the leafy oak trees.

"Not much. It sounds like they're still in the middle of the investigation. That's why I wanted to talk, though. You knew Jimmy well and hung out with him a lot. Do you think that there's any chance he could have been running an underground business?"

"Like what?"

"I don't know. I've heard a couple of things about how maybe he was doing deals on the side." We walked past the back side of Puck's Pub. The enclosed deck was already packed with an early lunch crowd. I could smell the shepherd's pie and grilled sausages.

"Deals?" Sophie stopped in midstride and gaped at me. "You mean like drugs? Are you saying that the police think he was a dealer?"

"No. Honestly, I don't know what." I waved to the Puck's bartender delivering drinks to tables outside. "I've just heard that he might have been involved in other activities aside from acting."

Sophie's eyes were huge. "Not Jimmy. No way. Never. He was fully invested in the production. That and getting his big break in Hollywood. He didn't have time for anything else. He was constantly running lines, watching YouTube videos, anything to improve his craft."

"Did you see him with Tom Rudolph much?" I asked, continuing to walk. If I stood near Puck's much longer, I wasn't sure I could resist stopping in for a quick bite.

"Tom was always around set." Sophie tucked the bag

from the costume shop under her arm and followed me. "It's kind of weird, because most investors aren't showing up for rehearsals, but, hey, it's his money. If he wants to spend an afternoon watching thirty walk-throughs of the same scene, that's his prerogative."

"He was there that often?" A colorful mural depicting Ashland's sister city in Mexico, which had been hand-painted by an artist from Guanajuato with the assistance of art students from SOU, served as a cheerful welcome to the outdoor parklet.

"Yeah, every day from the start of table reads."

I knew enough about professional theater companies to know that wasn't the norm.

"What about Olive and Bertie?" We made it to the park entrance. Deep maroon Japanese maples bloomed along the perimeter. The expansive grassy area looked like it had been painted green. The colors were so intense it almost didn't seem real. We took the path toward the lower duck pond bursting with vibrant pink rhododendrons.

"Who knows about those two? They could be working together. I know Olive is up to nothing good, and Bertie tries to pretend like she's professional, but she's a complete disaster. I don't trust her at all."

"Why?" It felt like I had received the same answer from nearly every member of the Fair Verona Players. Did none of them trust each other?

We found an empty bench and sat down. Sunlight filtered through the Japanese maples and danced off the top of the water. Ducks glided along the pristine surface like they were floating on air. Signs warning not to feed the wildlife were posted around the pond, but they rarely deterred tourists, who would toss bread and crackers to the birds at will, ignoring requests to keep our natural spaces wild. It was a serious problem. We shared the Siskiyou Mountains with brown bears, cougars, deer, and dozens of native species. Even a simple act of offering a hunk of stale bread to ducks threw off the ecosystem.

"She lied about where she was when Jimmy was killed," Sophie said, clutching her bag to her chest like a security blanket. "I caught her lying."

My curiosity was piqued. This could be the break Lance and I had been hoping for.

"I overheard her conversation with the police yesterday," Sophie continued. "They came by to ask some additional questions, and I heard her tell them that she was at the wine table the entire night. She claimed to be chatting with guests right after the show, but that was a lie." Sophie set the bag on the bench next to her and rubbed her fingers together, encouraging the ducks to come closer.

"How do you know?"

"Because I saw her."

"Where? When?" My knee bounced with anticipation.

"Leaving Jimmy's dressing room." Sophie reached down like she was going to pet one of the ducks, which sent them flapping to the other side of the pond. "You know how I told you that Jimmy and I were supposed to meet in the cellar after the show?"

I nodded. I noticed a tourist on the far side of the pond trying to pet a duck. I wanted to warn them that it wasn't a smart idea. Birds carried a variety of diseases that were harmful to humans.

"Well, I saw Bertie sneaking out of his dressing room before I went downstairs to meet him."

"You did?" Why hadn't she mentioned this earlier? And

how did that line up with her timeline on the night of the murder? She claimed that she never made it to the cellar. What was she doing upstairs?

"I didn't think too much of it at the time. As the assistant director, Bertie is always leaving actors notes on their performance. I figured she probably had feedback for him on opening. It's usually stuff like quick thoughts on where to punch up a line or pull more inward, that kind of thing."

"Right."

"I didn't even consider it, not after his murder or anything," Sophie continued. "That is, until she lied to the police yesterday. She told them she never went inside after the show. She claimed that she was at the wine table chatting with guests and the actors, and then she left from there. But I saw her leaving Jimmy's dressing room *after* the show."

That explained part of why she hadn't shared this earlier, but not all of it. "Why were you in Jimmy's dressing room? You didn't mention that."

Her cheeks flamed a deep shade of red, a telltale sign of her discomfort. She fidgeted, twisting her fingers together like the ivy snaking up the side of the Elizabethan theater on the other side of the pond. "I'm sorry. It's embarrassing."

"But it might be important to solving Jimmy's murder."

"True." Her gaze fixated on a towering redwood tree in the distance. "It's silly. I wanted to do something special for him for opening. It's a big deal. The first show. It can set the tone for the entire run."

I nodded again, not wanting to interrupt her.

"I wrote him a sonnet." She tried to laugh off her embarrassment. "It's dumb."

"No, I think that's sweet. Who wouldn't want a love note?"

She tugged her eyes away from the tree. "You're being kind. If you saw the note, you might say otherwise."

"Why?"

"Um, it's just so, so—" She ran her tongue over her lips and sucked in her cheeks. "Let's just say it was a little over the top."

"How?"

"I left lipstick marks on the envelope and sprayed it with my perfume." She blew out a breath and dragged her teeth over her bottom lip. "I'm not a lovesick teenager—at least I didn't think I was—but Jimmy cast a spell over me. I made him a playlist and heart-shaped chocolate brownies, too. It's so stupid. Like that was suddenly going to be the thing that would make him fall for me."

"Listen, my name is Juliet Montague Capshaw, so you don't need to explain anything about star-crossed love to me."

This made Sophie laugh for real. "That's a lot of pressure in a name."

"Trust me, that's why I go by Jules."

She smiled.

"And I will add that in my business, chocolate and love are a perfect pairing, so baking him brownies seems like it was worth a shot."

"I wish he would have had a chance to eat them." She hung her head. "My plan was to slip into his dressing room and leave them for him and then go meet him in the cellar."

"That's when you saw Bertie. Was this before or after you left the note and treats?"

"Before. I came upstairs just as she was closing his dressing room door."

"Didn't she see you?" That didn't add up, and I needed to remind myself to stay neutral. Sophie could be lying.

"No, I ducked into another room and waited for her to leave. I didn't want her to see me with a love note and a box of brownies. That would have been mortifying. She already hated that I liked Jimmy. She kept warning me about him and told me I should steer clear of him at all costs."

"Did you see anything else?"

"Like what?" She scrunched her nose, as if not understanding my question.

"Notes for other actors, perhaps? You mentioned that's part of her role. Maybe she had a legitimate reason for being upstairs if she was leaving feedback for each of the cast members."

"She wasn't." Sophie shook her adamantly. "That's why I'm kicking myself for brushing over such an important detail. She was sneaking out of his dressing room, that much I'm sure of. She backed out of the door and stared down the hallway. I'm convinced that she didn't want to be seen."

"I wonder what she was doing up there," I thought out loud.

"Me too. Do you think she could have killed Jimmy? It makes sense, doesn't it? What other possible reason could she have had for sneaking around like that?"

"Maybe, although it didn't happen in his dressing room," I said, not wanting to jump to conclusions. "I found him in the cellar. There's no way that she could have dragged the body down two flights of stairs without being seen and leaving a trail of blood."

Sophie wasn't going to let it go. "What if she drugged him first? She could have drugged him in his dressing room."

"Did you go into his dressing room after you saw her?"

"Yeah. I waited for a couple of minutes and then went in and left the stuff for him."

"How could she have drugged him if he wasn't there?"

"Good point." She softly pounded a fist on the bench, like she was trying to work out a theory internally. "What if she killed him in the cellar first and then ran upstairs to get something out of his room? Maybe he had dirt on her or evidence that she needed."

That theory had a lot more potential in my mind. "Did you share this with the police?"

"Yes, after I overheard Bertie being interviewed by the police, I went straight to them. I couldn't believe Bertie was so blatant in her lies. I told the woman detective all of this."

"Good. That's really good." I figured she was referring to Detective Kerry. I was confident that Kerry would follow up on the new lead. Maybe we were finally on the right track.

Chapter Twenty-four

My conversation with Sophie left me rattled. Had I made a huge mistake by not paying enough attention to Bertie? Why had she warned Sophie to stay away from Jimmy? Was she watching out for the Fair Verona Players' youngest staff member, or could there be another reason?

What motive could Bertie have for wanting Jimmy dead?

She was ambitious and eager to carve her own mark on the theater world. If she saw Jimmy's behavior as a threat to her future, would that be a strong enough reason to kill him? Her frustration with him had been palpable since the first day I'd seen them interact, but frustration and murder were two very different beasts.

The one pro of my conversation with Sophie was that it had snapped me out of my melancholy about Sterling and Steph's imminent departure. My thoughts were completely consumed with Jimmy's murder again, for better or worse.

The remainder of the day at the bakeshop was uneventful. That was until shortly after closing. Everyone was going through cleaning procedures when Sterling cleared his throat and looked at me. "Hey, can we have a quick team meetup?"

My stomach dropped, but I plastered on a smile and nodded. "Of course."

We waited for Andy and Sequoia to join us from upstairs.

"Why the solemn vibe?" Andy asked, reading the room immediately.

Sterling launched right in. I had a feeling it was like ripping off a Band-Aid. If he waited any longer, he might not have the courage to say what needed to be said.

"Steph and I have some news."

"OMG, OMG, OMG. It's happening." Bethany clapped as she bounced on her tiptoes. "A Torte wedding. Can I help design the cake? Please? Pretty, pretty please?" She beamed with delight.

Steph's face turned ashen.

Sterling appeared equally pale. "Sorry, Bethany. I haven't popped the question. At least not yet."

"Don't go all traditional on me." Steph punched him in the shoulder. "I haven't popped the question yet either."

"Fair enough." He caught her eye and winked. "Anyway, sorry, but no, that's not the news."

Bethany forced a smile, but I could tell she was disappointed.

Sterling inhaled deeply like he was trying to work up the courage to continue. "Look, you all know how much we love this place. Torte will always be home to me."

"Uh-oh," Marty interrupted, clearing his throat and looking at me. "I don't like the sound of this."

"It's not bad news," Sterling replied, holding one hand

out to try and pacify everyone. "It's more like bittersweet news."

"Do I need to sit down for this?" Andy asked with trepidation.

"I got offered the position of head chef at Whaleshead Resort," Sterling said, as quickly as possible. "After some serious deliberation, I've decided to take the job. At least for a trial one-month run."

"That's awesome, man." Andy clapped Sterling on the back. "Torte won't be the same without you, but you have to chase your dreams. That's what Jules always tells us, right?" He glanced at me for confirmation.

I nodded, trying to center on the positive. It was awesome for them, if still painful for me.

The rest of the team followed Andy's lead and congratulated Sterling.

"You are going to leave an indelible mark on the food world," Marty said, like a proud parent, wrapping Sterling in a big hug. "I can't wait to make a reservation at Chez Sterling."

"Agreed." Bethany bobbed her head and brushed tears from her dimpled cheeks. "I'm going to miss you so much. Steph, how are you going to handle having Sterling at the coast? Lots of weekend getaways?"

Steph winced. "Yeah, about that."

"Oh no, not you, too?" Bethany backed away as if she could escape hearing what would come next.

"They offered me the pastry chef position." Steph stared at her black Converses, while twisting a strand of her violet hair around her finger. The spotlight was never her happy place, especially in an emotionally charged moment like this.

"That's awesome and terrible." Bethany placed both hands on her cheeks. "I mean, it's, like, seriously awesome, but like Andy said, how is Torte going to survive without you two?"

"It's not that dire," I assured her. "Trust me. Selfishly I want them both to stay forever, but this is an incredible step in both of your careers," I said to Sterling and Steph. "We are all going to miss you desperately, but I'm already planning a Torte road trip to the beach for the opening weekend of the restaurant, and while it will never be the same without you, Mom, Carlos, and I are committed to finding replacements who are a good fit." I addressed the rest of the team. "On that note, I'm going to want your input and involvement in the hiring process."

Everyone took some time to let the news sink in. Even though I knew it was coming, hearing it spoken out loud made it real.

This was happening. Torte was changing. Sterling and Steph were moving on, and after the team and I adjusted to our new reality, we would have to do the same.

My phone buzzed.

I excused myself to answer the call.

"Juliet, I need you now," Lance whispered.

"Where are you, and why are you whispering?"

"Uva," Lance said in a hushed voice. "I can't talk, but I need you out here—stat."

"Again?" Had Sophie camped out in the cellar after our conversation? If she wasn't the killer, I could easily see her setting up a shrine for Jimmy in the basement. "Is Carlos there?"

"I think he's in the tasting room. This has nothing to do with him and everything to do with murder. Hurry."

He hung up before I could say anything more.

I returned to our impromptu staff meeting. Sterling and Steph were showing everyone photos of Whaleshead and their initial ideas for an opening menu. I decided it was best to let the team have this time to connect and process.

They would probably do that better without me for the moment. I wanted Sterling and Steph, along with everyone else, to be able to talk freely without having to imagine what the bakeshop was going to look like without them around. And, I'd already had time to process the news. It would be good for the team to have space to let it sink in.

"I have to run over to Uva," I said to everyone. "I'll take the delivery van. Hang out as long as you want. I know this is a big change, but I'm so thrilled for Sterling and Steph, and like Marty said, we're going to have a Torte road trip for the grand opening. Let's reconvene tomorrow morning to talk next steps. For tonight, make more coffee and raid the pastry case."

As I gathered my things, Marty was already looking at cabin rentals at Whaleshead and Andy was riffing on potential coastal coffee blends. I felt relieved that everyone knew, and I didn't have to carry that secret any longer. Hearing the team's excitement gave me a new burst of energy. The beach wasn't far. We would stay in touch. It wouldn't be the same, but it would be something.

The winding road to the winery was dotted with family farms, grazing sheep, and pear orchards. I knew it was futile to try and figure out what prompted Lance's urgent call, but I couldn't help but wonder why he was at Uva and what he might have discovered that made him insist on me joining him immediately. Lance's timing was, as always, impeccable.

The sun was starting to sink below Pilot Rock as I turned off onto the gravel road that led to the tasting room. A prop plane circled in the distance, floating over a swath of densely forested mountains that stretched as far as I could see.

Lance flagged me down with both arms at the entrance to the long driveway.

I pulled the van over to the side and rolled down the window. "What's going on?"

"Come with me, there's no time to waste." He tapped his naked wrist.

I followed him as he sprinted toward the barn and hurried onto the stage. He didn't say a word as he took the side steps two at a time, pressed a finger to his lips, and motioned to the curtain.

I had no idea what to expect when we rounded the stage.

Backstage was dusky. Early evening light filtered through the scaffolding.

Were we walking into a trap?

Where was Carlos? Where was the rest of the cast and crew?

I started to speak, but Lance shook his head and shushed me again.

"This way." His voice was barely audible.

He slunk along the base of the scaffolding and stopped in front of the back exit. The stage had been constructed with stairs there for the actors to use as pass-throughs to get around to the other side or sneak up to the tasting room without being seen.

"Look." He pointed one long finger at the bottom of the stairs, where a pile of discarded costumes lay on the ground. A mangled mess of glitter, tulle, and hot-pink and neon sequins was scattered everywhere.

"What is this?" I whispered.

"The costumes," he mouthed.

"What about them?" I gestured with my arms to try and show him I didn't understand the significance.

"Minutes before you arrived, I caught Olive trying to make a getaway."

"With the costumes from the show?" That didn't make sense.

He nodded like he couldn't believe I hadn't caught on yet.

"Why are we whispering?"

"Because she's hiding somewhere nearby, and we need to catch her before she escapes. The killer is within our grasp, Juliet." He fanned his face. "Can you feel the tension? I can barely breathe. We're on the cusp of bringing a villain to swift justice."

Chapter Twenty-five

"Lance, why did you call me? We need to call the police." I didn't bother trying to keep my voice down. This was too much, even for Lance.

"They're already here, darling." He pressed a finger to his lips.

"What?" I checked the other side of the stage and the seats. There was no sign of the Professor, Thomas, or Kerry.

Now I was really confused.

He used his fingers like a flight attendant directing passengers to their seats to point all around us. "They're spread throughout the vineyard."

"Why did you call me, then?"

"I didn't want you to miss out on the action, darling." He sounded incredulous that I would even ask. "What a terrible friend I would be to leave you out just as things are getting good."

"Wait, the Professor is here?" I stood on my toes to try and see through a sliver of the open curtain.

"Yes, along with Thomas, Kerry, and two or three other squad cars."

"Where are they?" I hadn't seen any police activity on the drive to the vineyard.

He twisted his hand in the direction of the vines. "They parked at the orchard down below so as to avoid tipping Olive off that they have her surrounded."

"Where's Carlos?"

"He's positioned at the tasting room."

It had taken me a minute to process what he had said. "*Olive* killed Jimmy?"

Lance continued to speak in hushed tones. "It seems that way. The Professor found an unsent email on Jimmy's phone confirming that Olive threatened him. Jimmy wanted a cut of Olive's profits. That gives her a clear motive for killing him. The Professor has been looking into her side gig of selling off valuable costumes and set pieces to other theater companies and on the black market, for lack of a better phrase."

"'The black market' for costumes seems pretty over-the-top," I agreed.

"She made quite the profit, according to the Professor." Lance sounded strangely impressed. "He checked her bank records, and she's pulled in nearly five figures just last month."

"What?" As far as I had heard, the Fair Verona Players were operating on a fairly lean budget.

As if reading my mind, Lance answered my question for me. "It wasn't just us. She's been doing this with every production she's been hired for in the last year. Jimmy caught on and warned her that he was going to inform me and the entire cast and crew if she didn't pay up. It's your classic blackmail operation. She must have decided she wasn't going to share her profits and she had to kill him before he had a chance to send the email."

I couldn't believe it. Olive?

Nor could I believe that we were in the midst of a police operation.

"Should we get out of here?" I suggested, moving away from him.

"Never. Banish the thought. This is about to get good." Lance rubbed his hands together and then yanked me toward him. "Plant your feet and prepare for fireworks."

"I don't understand. Are you saying that you caught Olive? Did she get away? That's when you called me?"

"I would never have 'let her get away,' as you put it. I demanded that she stop. She refused my command. Can you imagine? I didn't realize in that moment that she was the killer. But when she took off at a breakneck pace like she couldn't wait to be rid of me, suddenly everything clicked—the missing costumes, her behavior, her interactions with Jimmy. I placed the call to Doug, and they arrived in record time." He sounded impressed. "I must apologize for not looping you in immediately. There was a bit of a frenzy. Now we're playing the waiting game. We're watching our prey, waiting to pounce."

I shuddered. "We should leave that part to the authorities."

"Semantics."

"Carlos knows about this?" There is no way Carlos would have suggested that Lance and I insert ourselves into the investigation.

"Yes. Well, not technically speaking." Lance smoothed his shirt and brushed an imaginary fleck of dust from his hand. "I wouldn't say we discussed the part about calling you, but we'll keep that as our little secret, won't we?"

I couldn't make out his facial expressions in the fading light, but I could only imagine the impish look he must be giving me.

"Olive, it's Olive," I said out loud. "I was convinced a few hours ago that Bertie did it. I hope that they're able to catch her."

"I believe you misspoke. Don't you mean *we're* able to catch her?"

I rolled my eyes. Where was everyone? It was odd that the only sounds I could hear were the cries of red-tailed hawks circling the vineyard and the evening breeze blowing in through the trees.

I had no sense of whether Olive was a threat. "Does she have a weapon? Is she dangerous?"

Lance shrugged. "Not when I saw her, but I have no idea what that woman is capable of. If she was willing to end Jimmy's life over a few thousand dollars, I wouldn't put anything past her."

I gulped down a swell of fear rising in my throat.

"You know what is odd?" Lance tapped a long, bony finger to his chin. "I would have put my money on Tom."

"Tom, really?"

"As promised, I investigated his financial situation further, and he most certainly is in way over his head. I was able to confirm from a reliable source that he indeed has overborrowed and overspent his trust."

"All clear! All clear." Shouts from the police interrupted our conversation. "That's an all clear, everyone."

Lance jumped off the stage and offered me his hand as a commotion broke out in front of the barn.

"Suspect is in custody, all clear," another police officer repeated.

Lights flooded the vineyard.

The Professor must have coordinated that with Carlos, because the strings of Edison-style bulbs, pathway lights, and the deck lighting illuminated at once, casting a soft glow on the grounds. We watched as Thomas emerged from the bottom section of the grapevines with Olive in handcuffs.

Adrenaline pulsed through my body.

I hadn't realized quite how stiff I'd been holding the muscles in my neck and arms.

Was this really happening?

Olive had killed Jimmy, and the police had caught her.

"Well, that's a shame," Lance said with a long sigh, helping me off the stage. "It's anticlimactic, don't you agree? I was hoping for something a bit more . . . stageworthy, shall we say."

"At least they're arresting Jimmy's killer." I let go of his hands as my feet touched the ground, but my body still felt like it was floating.

"I suppose, but I was holding out for fireworks, or at the very least a sword fight."

I knew this was his way of trying to lighten the mood.

"I wasn't aware that the Ashland police wielded swords," I teased, relieved for the break in tension.

The situation could have gone south quickly. I was thankful for the Professor, Thomas, Kerry, and the entire police squad for their prompt and professional response.

It took a while for them to finish their sweep of the vineyard and bring Olive up to a waiting squad car.

Darkness ushered in a band of stars and a chill to the

air. Living in the mountains meant that once the moon replaced the sun, the temperature plummeted. I shivered.

Lance wrapped a protective arm around my shoulder. "I'd say we should go inside for a nightcap and a chat with that devilishly handsome husband of yours, but I am under strict orders by Doug not to move a muscle until he informs me that it's safe to do so."

"I can't believe you're following orders."

"Moi?" He saluted with two fingers. "I'm ever the model soldier."

"Okay, now you've gone too far." I chuckled.

The Professor released Lance from his dutiful post a few minutes later. "Juliet, I wasn't aware you were onsite."

"It's a long story." I raised my eyebrows toward Lance.

Lance jumped in. "It appears you've arrested Olive. Is it safe to say that the case is officially closed?"

"As for the case of missing costumes, props, and set pieces from the company, yes." The Professor hesitated. "Regarding the murder investigation, I'm not convinced."

Lance let out an audible gasp. "You don't think Olive killed Jimmy?"

"Time will tell. Her behavior this evening is certainly of interest, as is her side *business*, shall we say? We're bringing her into the station for further questioning now, but I'm not prepared to close the case yet."

He excused himself to consult with his team. Lance and I stood in silence for a minute. If the Professor didn't think that Olive was responsible, could that mean that Jimmy's killer was still at large?

Chapter Twenty-six

Once the police told us we were free to leave, Lance and I walked to the tasting room to find Carlos.

"Julieta, Kerry said you were here. How? Why?" His naturally tanned cheeks were etched with concern as he rushed to greet me with a kiss.

"It's my fault." Lance held up a hand in surrender. "I called her."

Carlos scowled. "This could have been very dangerous, Lance."

"Agreed." Lance nodded solemnly. "I acted on a whim, not realizing the severity of the situation. I've already apologized to your lovely wife for putting her in harm's way."

I wasn't sure I had been in much danger, other than potentially catching a case of the shivers.

"You know, I'm an adult woman, gentlemen." I narrowed my eyes at them.

They laughed.

"Sí, this I know for sure," Carlos said with a playful smile. "I would say this to anyone. There is no need to involve more people in the police stakeout."

He raised a valid point.

"They said she has been stealing from you?" Carlos changed the subject, releasing his grasp on me and motioning to the collection of chairs in front of the stone fireplace. "Why don't we sit for a minute?"

I shot him a look of gratitude. Even wearing my tennis shoes, my feet were aching from a long day.

"Yes." Lance answered his question. "It appears that Olive has had quite the operation going. Although Doug seemed to hint just now that they're not convinced that she killed Jimmy."

"Is this true?" Carlos looked at me.

I nodded. "That's what the Professor said."

Lance folded one leg over the other. "Might I beg you for a glass of vino?"

"You're a part owner in the vineyard." I punched him in the arm. "You don't have to ask."

"It's my meticulous manners. I can't help myself." He raised his eyebrows.

"Let me get it." Carlos was already on his feet and halfway behind the bar. He poured a glass of merlot for Lance, delivered it, and in one fluid motion was back behind the bar again.

"Many thanks." Lance tipped his head to Carlos.

"Then why did they need to arrest her here just because you figured out her relationship with Jimmy and caught her stealing costumes?" Carlos asked as he wiped the counter, which was already sparkling. I recognized the nervous habit. On the *Amour of the Seas*, he would clean whenever things got stressful. Out of all the coping mechanisms someone could have, I certainly didn't mind his need to keep things neat and in order when faced with stress.

I had to resist the urge in this moment to pop into the kitchen and put together a platter of hand pies or frosted brownies to calm my own nerves.

"That is the question, isn't it?" Lance asked.

"It is very odd," Carlos agreed. He placed a rubber stopper in the bottle of merlot and then used a pump to vacuum out the air. This would slow the oxidation process and preserve the wine longer.

We spent the next hour or so relaxing and reviewing everything we knew about the case.

I glanced at the clock and realized that it was long past my bedtime.

"It's getting late," I said, suddenly feeling like I couldn't keep my body upright much longer. I wasn't sure if it was the adrenaline wearing off or the roller coaster of an emotional day, but nothing sounded better than my bed.

"Yes, I should let you both go." Lance picked up my cue.

Carlos tossed the towel in the sink, turned off the lights, and locked the tasting room. The only light we had to guide us outside came from the solar lanterns lining the path. We started to part ways, but Lance pointed to the gravel drive, where headlights were coming in our direction.

"The police must have forgotten something," Lance said.

So much for my cozy bed.

We waited for the lights to come closer and the person to pull in front of the tasting room. It was hard to see clearly in the dim light, but I didn't recognize the car. It wasn't the Professor's, or Thomas and Kerry's. Nor was it a squad car.

"It's Tom," Lance said. "What is he doing here at this hour?"

"Maybe news has traveled through town about Olive's arrest," Carlos suggested.

It was true that gossip spread quickly in our little hamlet, but I couldn't imagine that many people were out this late, aside from the college bar crowd.

"Perhaps Olive called him?" Lance made his hands into circles and placed them over his eyes like binoculars to try to get a better look.

"You mean like her one phone call from jail?" I asked. "But then why would he come to the winery?"

"There's one way to find out." Lance approached Tom's car.

Tom must have had no idea that we were standing nearby because as he stepped out of the car and spotted Lance, he let out a small scream, jumped backward, and dropped something on the ground. "Are you trying to scare me to death?" Tom yelled, waving a finger at Lance like he was scolding him. "What are you doing, sneaking up on me in the dark? What are you doing here?"

"I could ask you the same question. Especially given that I am a partial owner of the vineyard," Lance countered. "I'm curious what brings you to our humble winery under the cloak of darkness."

Tom glanced at his feet but didn't respond.

What had he dropped?

Lance pounced before Tom had time to react.

"Well, well, well. What have we here?" Lance dangled something in his right hand. It caught the light of one of the solar lanterns, revealing a familiar key. "Jules, Carlos, I think you might want to come closer and have a look at this."

Tom froze with one hand clutching the car door, like he was ready at any moment to make an escape.

"Is that the key to the wine cellar?" I asked with confusion. Ed had returned the key to me earlier.

"I do believe you're correct, Juliet. Tom, do you care to enlighten us as to how you happen to be in possession of this?" Lance swung the key between his index finger and thumb, practically taunting Tom.

Tom sputtered and shot his eyes in every direction, as if trying to figure out if there was any other way out. There wasn't. Not unless he got in his car and backed away.

"What are you doing with a key to the Uva wine cellar?" Lance asked.

Tom slowly put one leg into the driver's seat, while maintaining eye contact with Lance. "I found it and wanted to make sure it was returned promptly."

Lance glanced at his wrist. "At ten thirty at night? Exactly how did you intend to get inside the tasting room?"

Was he paying attention to Tom's movements?

Not much got by Lance. He might come across as flippant at times, but that was part of his theater persona. I knew he had a steely interior and uncanny ability to read people's emotions, which probably came from his years on the stage.

"I was going to slide it under the door. I wasn't going to break in." Tom inched the rest of his body closer to the car.

I could tell that he was planning to speed away the second he had a chance.

Carlos must have realized the same thing, because he began creeping toward the other side of the car. What was he going to do? Jump in the passenger seat?

"But Ed gave me the key back. How do you have it?" I asked, hoping to distract Tom.

"I took the key from Ed before he returned it and made a copy at the hardware store for you," Tom replied in a patronizing tone. "You should be thanking me. I took it upon myself to do you a favor and make sure you had a backup key. You're running such a loose operation."

"We're all adults here," Lance said to Tom. "Don't patronize us with obvious lies. We know the truth. You murdered Jimmy."

Tom's entire body flinched, like he'd been punched.

Lance didn't stop. "We know about the trust, Tom. We know that you've squandered your aunt's fortune and you're deep in the red. We know that Jimmy found out and was going to announce your struggles to the world, wasn't he? Or did he demand money from you? You had to kill to keep him quiet. How did it go down? Was it a battle, or did you lure him to the cellar and lie in wait to strike the deadly blow?"

"No." Tom recoiled more, hunching his shoulders, and shrinking into himself. "I don't know what you're talking about."

"Oh, I think you do, so let me repeat my question. Why did you kill him?"

Carlos had made it around to the other side of the car without Tom noticing, but he didn't stop at the passenger door—he kept moving toward the trunk. He wasn't considering blocking Tom's escape path with his body, was he? Because if he was, that plan was a solid no in my book. It wasn't our responsibility to stop Tom, and I wasn't about to let Carlos risk his life, even if it meant letting Tom go.

We could call Thomas or Kerry. They would be able to apprehend Tom before he made it back to the plaza.

"I can't believe you were fooled by him. He was ruining the show. For an esteemed director, it's juvenile that you tolerated his behavior. The Fair Verona Players is my ticket out of debt, and I wasn't going to let some actor with a hugely inflated ego ruin that for me."

"How would Jimmy's ego impact your finances?" Lance asked.

I was glad he was keeping Tom talking. My phone was in my jacket pocket. I rubbed my hands together, pretending to be cold and then slowly put them into my pockets. Hopefully Tom would simply think I was trying to warm up. If I could maneuver my screen with my fingers there was a chance I could place an emergency call without him being any the wiser.

"You should know that better than anyone," Tom said with disgust. "I can't believe you allowed Jimmy to tank the company before we'd had a chance to bring in more investment dollars."

"What are you talking about?" Lance caught Carlos's eye.

Carlos stood behind the vehicle and appeared to be fumbling for his phone as well. I was grateful for the patch of stars above us, shedding hazy light on the roof of the car.

Odds were good that one of us would have luck.

"While you've been playing darling to the media and fawning over the cast, I've been doing what I was brought on to do—grow the company. Find bigger investors to build this into something lasting. Something that one day might dwarf OSF," Tom lashed out. The rage in his voice was as thick as our Sunday morning pancake batter.

"That's never been my plan," Lance responded, with a casual confidence I didn't feel. "The Fair Verona Players is a joyful project. It's enhancing my creativity and adding additional value to the region, but no part of my vision includes growing to anywhere near the size of OSF."

"It should have been," Tom spat. "Do you realize how much money is in the Rogue Valley? I was about to make the Fair Verona Players a household name. I had big plans to expand—partnerships with other vineyards, brand deals, private wine labels, interest with companies in the Valley to do private parties and performances. But Jimmy's ludicrous behavior was going to ruin that. He should have kept his mouth shut except for reading his lines."

"Help me understand—how would you personally profit and be in a position to pay off your debts with this influx of investment capital?" Lance asked. "Funds would go into the company, yes?"

Tom didn't reply.

"Ah, so you intended to pocket a large portion of said cash, I assume?" Lance was eviscerating Tom with every word. "Jimmy realized this, didn't he? How much did he demand in exchange for his silence?"

Again, Tom had no retort.

He jumped into the car and slammed the door shut before Lance could stop him.

"Carlos, move!" I yelled. Tom had already killed once. I had no doubt that he would mow Carlos down if Carlos didn't get out of the way.

Tom blared the horn.

Lance and I both startled and backed away.

Carlos held his position, placing both hands on the trunk as Tom turned the key in the engine.

What was he thinking? This wasn't normal behavior for him.

"Carlos, please, move," I pleaded. Tom wasn't worth it.

"I've got this, mi querida." He firmed his stance.

Tom revved the engine in a warning.

Carlos kept his stance.

I couldn't believe this was happening.

"It's not worth it, Carlos," Lance shouted. "Let him go. He won't get far."

Tom clicked the car into reverse and rolled down the window. "I don't want to hurt you, but I'm getting out of here one way or another. This is your chance to move."

My knees buckled.

My heart thudded against my chest.

"Carlos, he's not bluffing," I yelled.

"No, I'm not," Tom said, laying on the horn again. "This is it, move now, or I run you over."

How had we ended up in this situation, and why was Carlos playing chicken with a killer?

He'd never had a hero complex before, and this didn't seem like the best time to develop one.

With one last press of the horn, Tom began accelerating.

Carlos leapt out of the way at the last minute.

The tires squealed as Tom peeled out backward, spun the car around, and shot down the driveway, kicking up a trail of gravel and debris behind him.

I ran over to check on Carlos. "What were you thinking? You could have been killed."

He cradled his right arm, which had taken the brunt of his fall. "I'm okay, mi querida. And I was buying time for that." With his other hand he pointed to the bottom of the driveway where three police cars with flashing blue lights and wailing sirens had blocked the exit and surrounded Tom.

"Thank goodness." Lance and I helped him to his feet.

Lance clapped one arm around each of us. "A job well done, team, if I do say so myself."

Chapter Twenty-seven

The rest of the evening was a complete blur. Thomas arrested Tom and took our statements. Kerry tended to Carlos's arm. I should have gone with my first instinct, which had been not to trust Tom, but there had been so many other suspects who all seemed to have valid motives for wanting Jimmy dead.

When we finally made it home, I collapsed into bed and was asleep in minutes. I barely woke to the sound of my alarm the next morning, which was not typical for me. I felt almost hungover as I tugged on a pair of jeans and a thin hoodie with a T-shirt underneath, and tied my hair into a ponytail.

It was a relief to start the day knowing that Jimmy's killer had been arrested, but I couldn't shake the sluggish feeling, not with my first cup of coffee at Torte or a sugar-coated cardamom bun. The events of the past week had finally caught up with me.

I spent the bulk of the day talking with the team about the new roles we'd be hiring for, and chatting with a couple of former colleagues about potential replacements. I was motivated to try and get new hires in place quickly so they could shadow Steph and Sterling for a few days. As much as I wanted to wallow in losing two of my favorite staff, I had a job to do, which in some ways made the reality easier to face.

Around noon I went upstairs to check on the dining room. As I circled past tables, clearing dishes and refilling coffees, I noticed Bertie, Olive, Ed, and Sophie gathered at one of the booths.

"Can I top anyone off?" I held up the fresh pot.

"Yes, please." Sophie passed over her cup.

"I'm guessing you've heard about Tom?" I asked as I poured the aromatic brew.

"It's so sad," Sophie said, fighting back tears. "Why did he have to kill Jimmy?"

"If you ask me, it sounds like things got out of hand," Ed said, holding his cup for a refill. "I wonder if he had planned to kill Jimmy, or if things escalated once they had the confrontation in the cellar."

"Yeah, but the police mentioned money and investments." Sophie blew on her coffee. "It sounds like Tom may have planned to kill him for that reason alone. He was desperate for money and saw Jimmy as the only obstacle in his path. It's just mind-numbing to me that someone could kill another person in cold blood over something as stupid as money."

Olive unzipped an oversized purse, pulled out leather notebook, and flipped it open. "Speaking of money, I know I owe you all an apology. I've started making an itemized list of everything I sold. I'm going to work with Lance and Arlo on a repayment plan. I wish I could go back in time and make a different decision, but instead all I can do is try and make it up to you and assure you that even with my financial challenges, I never would have resorted to violence."

"That's the problem with working in the arts," Bertie said, placing her hand over her cup to signal she didn't need a top-off. "It's a real challenge to pull in a living wage. We constantly hear this message about doing it because we love the work and the craft, but the truth is we all need to pay rent and eat."

"I appreciate that," Olive replied. "It doesn't excuse what I've done, though. And, to your point, Sophie, I think Jimmy ultimately sealed his own fate. He confronted me about stealing from the company and wanted a cut. When I spoke with the detectives and confessed about what I'd done, they told me that Jimmy had a habit of blackmailing people for money. He was good at learning secrets and using them for his benefit."

"You think Jimmy was blackmailing Tom?" Sophie asked with a gasp.

"I'm sure of it." Olive shot her an apologetic smile. "I know that's not what you want to hear, and I don't think it condones Tom's behavior, but if Tom saw Jimmy as an obstacle in his path, it was because Jimmy was threatening to go public with Tom's secrets. I'm speaking from my own experience. Jimmy gave me an ultimatum. I either had to split the money I'd made with him, or he was going to tell everyone what I'd done."

That tracked to what Lance had learned about Tom's poor investments. Tom had been tight-lipped when Lance confronted him last night, but I agreed with Olive. I didn't know how, but Jimmy must have learned about Tom's predicament and attempted to use it to his advantage. It was likely what got him killed.

"What's going to happen with the Fair Verona Players now?" I asked. That hadn't come up with Lance last night, although that wasn't surprising given that we had helped apprehend Tom. If it weren't for Carlos blocking Tom's getaway in order to give the police time to arrive on the scene he might have gotten away.

When I thought about it, it didn't seem real. Had my husband really placed himself in the direct path of danger to bring Tom to justice? It made me love him even more, but I never wanted him to do something like that again.

Bertie answered first, looking directly at each member of the troupe. "The show must go on. In fact, that's just what I was saying to the group. We're having an all-hands meeting with Lance later today. The rave reviews continue to come through. We have a week to reset and regroup."

Her pep talk reminded me of Lance. I had a feeling Bertie was going to make a great director one day.

"I think we should dedicate the next performance to Jimmy," Ed suggested.

"Wow, I'm shocked to hear you of all people say that about Jimmy," Sophie said, staring at him with wide eyes. "I thought you hated him."

"Jimmy and I never were going to be the best of friends, but that doesn't mean that I wanted him dead." Ed frowned. He reached his hand out to Sophie to comfort her and then pulled it back, as if he wasn't sure how.

"I thought you killed him for a while there," Sophie said, taking a long drink of her coffee. "Come to think of it, at different points I thought each of you did it. Which reminds me, why were you in Jimmy's dressing room that night?" she asked Bertie.

Bertie thought for a minute. "When?"

"After the show. I saw you sneaking out of his dressing room shortly before he was killed."

"Oh, that." Bertie nodded in acknowledgment. "Show notes. I left them for all the cast members."

"Why were you being so secretive about it?"

"Was I?" Bertie shrugged and guzzled more coffee. "I don't know. I didn't think I was *sneaking*. I was trying to hurry back outside to patrons and didn't want to disturb the winery staff. I knew that I wasn't going to have a chance to speak with Jimmy because everyone was going to want autographs, so I figured I would leave my notes for each of the actors to review and then we would discuss the next day."

"Oh, okay. I was probably being paranoid. Once I learned that Jimmy was killed, you sneaking around in his dressing room seemed so suspicious. When I think about it now, it doesn't even make sense. How would you have killed him upstairs and dragged his body to the cellar?" Sophie's voice quivered. She laced her fingers together tightly and tried to compose herself. "I've been so desperate to figure out who killed him, I guess I probably should have taken a breath and let the authorities investigate instead of accusing all of you. It's pretty terrible to think the worst about your colleagues."

"Yeah, but in fairness to you, we all had reasons to lie," Ed added, glancing at me, his chin dipping to his chest as his shoulders sagged slightly with remorse. "I think Tom set me up. He gave me the key to the cellar. He wanted me to take the wine so that I was the one seen in the basement. He wanted me to take the fall. Once you realize that you were near the crime scene, even if you're innocent, it's hard not to freak out a little."

Olive nodded in agreement. "We're our own worst emeries."

"Hopefully we can change that moving forward," Bertie said with confidence. "We have such a good thing going with this production. It has the potential to put the Fair Verona Players on the map, and all of you are part of the show's success. We need to reward that and make sure that we compensate you accordingly. I'm going to speak with Lance about raising pay. I know that he'll be in full support of the idea. Tom was the one who insisted that his aunt's money not be earmarked for salaries. It's time to change that. It sounds like everyone is barely scraping by, and I'd rather scale back our expansion plans and focus on better equity for the cast and crew first."

"That would be another awesome way to honor Jimmy." Sophie brushed away a tear.

"Maybe we can set up a Jimmy Paxton memorial fund," Ed suggested, which made Sophie cry harder and throw her arms around him.

I left them to brainstorm and discuss what was next for the Fair Verona Players. It sounded like, despite the terrible events, the troupe was all committed to making the outdoor theater a success.

They had also inadvertently answered several questions that had been bothering me, like why Bertie had been in Jimmy's dressing room and what had motivated Olive to steal from the company.

I hoped that they could find funds to raise salaries and pay the artists what they were worth. I made a mental note to talk to Lance and Carlos about what else Uva might be able to do to support their efforts.

The artistic community in Ashland was unparalleled, and I would do anything I could to make sure that more artists could not just continue to live here but also to thrive.

Chapter Twenty-eight

Later in the day Marty pulled me aside. He took off his white chef's coat and hung it on a hook by the pizza oven. "Do you have a minute, Jules?"

"Of course."

"Could we go talk in private?" He pointed to an empty couch in the basement seating area.

My body tensed. Was he about to tell me he was leaving, too? I didn't think I could take any more news of staff departures.

Marty sat across from me. In conversations, he had the gift of making others feel heard and cherished. He studied me with concern, his face etched with lines from countless smiles. "You look pale, Jules, are you still feeling unwell?"

"I feel okay, I'm just bracing myself for what you're about to say. You're not leaving us, are you?" I chomped on my bottom lip as the question hung between us.

His trademark infectious laughter rang out like a melody reverberating through the basement. "No, you're not getting rid of me that easily."

"Whew, that is such a relief." I put my head between

my hands. Thank goodness. If Marty had told me he was leaving, that might have put me over the edge.

"Although that is what I wanted to talk to you about. Sterling and Steph leaving, that is." The overhead lights illuminated his full head of neatly combed silver hair. Marty had emerged from his own grief after losing his wife. He was attractive, kind, funny, easygoing, and an incredible baker. I could name about a dozen women his age who would have jumped at the chance to date him. I wondered if he was ready or interested in finding love again.

"Sure. Do you have an idea for replacements?" I asked, tabling the question for the moment.

"I can ask around to some of my former bakers in San Francisco if it would be helpful."

"I would love that. Carlos and I have put out asks too, but we have at least three roles to fill, and it's always nice to have someone come in off a recommendation. Of course, enticing them to move to Ashland might be tricker."

"What? Who wouldn't want to live in this beautiful place?" Marty gestured with an animated grin.

"Maybe someone who's interested in clubbing and nightlife?"

He laughed again. "Puck's Pub has been known to keep the tunes pumping until after midnight. Keeping the tunes pumping probably isn't what the kids are saying these days, but I digress. I want to talk to you about two things. The first is about my future here."

"Okay." I braced myself.

"If you'll have me, I'd like to be considered for the position of kitchen manager." Marty's eyes were filled with hope. "I know when I came, I said I was heading for retirement, but I love it here. I'd like to mentor the kitchen staff and take on a larger role, but I don't want you to feel any pressure."

"Pressure." I had to stop myself from leaping into his arms. "That would be a dream. Yes. One thousand percent yes. I didn't want to ask you because I didn't want to put *you* in an awkward position."

"Well, we're two peas in a pod, aren't we?" His cheeks creased with excitement. "We can discuss it further later once you post the position. While I have your ear, what about a goodbye bash for Sterling and Steph? I heard that we're skipping Sunday Supper this month, which is a good idea. What do you think about taking that Sunday spot and throwing a surprise bon voyage party for them? A Torte Sunday Supper just for us."

"I love it." I gave him double thumbs-up. "Great minds think alike. I was just pondering the same thing earlier this morning. I considered doing a team dinner out somewhere, but since Steph and Sterling have been such integral parts of our Sunday Suppers, that sounds like the perfect send-off."

Marty leaned to one side to see into the kitchen. "How do we pull it off without them catching on, though?"

"That's a good question."

We both paused in thought for a minute.

"What if you send them to Uva next Sunday to do service for the matinee, and while they're gone, we can pull everything together? That will give us ten days to make it happen."

"Yes, that's perfect." My mind was already spinning with possibilities. "I can work with Bethany and Rosa on desserts and decorations. I'll put together a fake custom cake order. They'll be none the wiser."

"I'll do the same with a menu." Marty's eyes twinkled with enthusiasm. "I would bet Carlos will help."

"For sure. Count on it." I didn't have to ask. I knew that Carlos would be fully in support of the idea.

"Excellent. If you focus on dessert, I'll work on a list of their favorite dishes, and we'll put a menu together." He gave me a fist bump as he stood.

I already knew what I wanted to bake—a sculpted whale cake for their new adventure at Whaleshead Resort. I filled Bethany in our plans while Steph was upstairs.

"So cute. What if I make whale macarons to go with it? I can do them in blue and gray in the shape of whales and fill them with blue raspberry and Earl Grey buttercream. We can have a whole pod of dessert whales."

"A pod of whales, yes please." I put together the fake order and got to work right away on the cake. I wanted to do a practice round to dial in the flavors and brush up on my carving technique.

To go with the ocean theme, I decided on a pineapple cake that I would layer with pineapple compote and frost with coconut buttercream. I gathered everything I needed and began by adding butter and sugar to the industrial mixer and set it to medium. Once they had creamed together, I added eggs, vanilla, and coconut extract. I incorporated that and then alternated the dry ingredients and fresh pineapple juice.

I tasted the thick and creamy batter. It had a lovely fruity sourness mixed with a vanilla sweetness. Confident that the flavors were strong and balanced, I stirred in small chunks of pineapple by hand and placed the cakes in the oven to bake. For the frosting, I used our traditional French buttercream as a base and added more coconut extract.

The pineapple compote was a simple mix of fresh diced pineapple that I simmered over low heat with sugar, honey, and vanilla beans until it formed a thick sauce.

Carving cakes requires each layer to be structurally sound. I achieved this by placing cake dowels in the center of the cakes to make sure they were level. I would carve the cake naked, meaning before it had even been crumb-coated.

Chilling the cake before carving it was the most important step. A cold cake helps firm up the butter and means that the cake won't collapse or crumble during the carving process.

I chilled the cake for two hours and then began the delicate process of unearthing the shape of a whale.

We had spent weeks in culinary school on the cake carving unit. There were many techniques I had learned along the way, plus new ones that Steph and Bethany had introduced me to. In addition to chilling, I used a sharp edge knife and exaggerated my cuts. Any minor imperfections could be masked with buttercream, so the most important thing to focus on at this stage was getting the general shape right.

My whale came together slowly, as it was also better to take smaller sections off the cake to begin with.

"That's looking so good," Bethany gushed when she saw my progress. She spoke louder for everyone to hear and gave me a subtle wink. "The client is going to be so thrilled with that. I'm going to need social media pics of this cutie before you deliver it."

I was pleased with how the cake took shape. It was

easily identifiable as a whale. I crumb-coated it with the coconut buttercream and put it in the walk-in to chill overnight. Tomorrow I would do the detail work of making my whale come to life.

By the time closing rolled around, Marty had sketched out a menu of Sterling's and Steph's favorites—Hawaiian teriyaki beef sliders with charred pineapple, vegetarian egg rolls, sweet and spicy barbecue chicken cups with green onions and cilantro, tuna rolls, and deep-fried cream cheese wontons with sweet chili sauce.

Not surprisingly, the menu naturally complemented my tropical cake.

Rosa offered to deck out the dining room in a beach theme the night of the party.

I felt satisfied knowing that Sterling and Steph deserved a night of celebration in their honor. It helped mitigate the waves of sadness.

As I was locking up for the evening, my phone rang. I recognized the number right away—it was my doctor's office.

"I'm calling to speak with Juliet Capshaw," the voice on the other end of the line said when I answered.

"This is Juliet." My muscles quivered and twitched with nerves. Was she calling with bad news?

"I have your test results. Are you someplace you can talk?"

My mouth went dry.

That didn't sound good.

I was alone in the bakeshop, though, so now was as good of a time as any to take in whatever news she had to share with me. "Yes."

"Okay, well, you mentioned that you had taken home pregnancy tests, which came back negative, is that right?"

"Yeah." My hand instinctively went to my stomach. My breath stalled. I walked a step toward the door and then turned around.

"And how long ago was that?"

"I don't know for sure, but probably a few weeks." Was she about to say what I thought—could only hope—she might say?

"Interesting." She paused. "Well, I have good news for you, your pregnancy test is positive."

"What?" I nearly dropped the phone as my heart seemed to freeze and then began to pound wildly.

"It's very positive."

Wasn't there only one kind of positive?

"It is?" I could barely think over the sound of blood rushing to my head.

"Your hCG levels are much higher than expected at this stage of a pregnancy."

That didn't sound good. I braced myself for the bad news. "What does that mean?"

"I'm going to put in an order for an early ultrasound. High levels of hCG may indicate that you're carrying multiples, but we'll need to wait for an ultrasound to confirm that one hundred percent."

"Wait, carrying multiples?" Had I heard her incorrectly?

Multiples?

"Twin pregnancies often have increased hCG levels, but the same can be true for singleton pregnancies. I'll have my office reach out tomorrow to get that scheduled, and I'm putting in a prescription for a prenatal vitamin. Do you have any questions?"

I had about a thousand questions, but all I could think about was twins. I was pregnant and potentially carrying twins.

Chapter Twenty-nine

Carlos was equally enthusiastic when I told him about the news at home. "Twins, Julieta. Twins. Double the babies. This will be so wonderful. They will be best friends."

I was still trying to adjust to the idea that I was pregnant, let alone potentially pregnant with twins.

"You must sit, immediately, mi querida." Carlos ushered me into the living room and proceeded to prop my feet up with pillows and wrap a blanket around my shoulders.

"I'm fine. I'm just pregnant." Saying it out loud didn't make it feel any more real.

"You must keep your feet up and rest, Julieta. I will make you a delicious and protein-packed dinner. Then you must get good sleep." He sat next to me and gently massaged my belly, his eyes filled with emotion. "Twins?"

I sucked in a breath and reached for his hand for support. "The doctor said she doesn't know for sure. We'll have to wait and see what the tests show."

"It is twins. I'm sure." Carlos linked his fingers through mine.

We sat together in a comfortable silence, meditating on

the profound change this was going to have on our lives. I knew that Carlos was going to be an amazing partner and dad. I had already witnessed it firsthand in his relationship with Ramiro. I was less sure about myself. What if I didn't know what to do with a baby? How was this going to impact Torte? How would a baby—or babies—shift my relationship with Carlos?

I tried not to let my anxiety take root. This was the best news, and I didn't have to do it alone. I had Carlos and Mom and the Professor and my entire Ashland family.

"You relax," he said after massaging my flat stomach again. "I'll make us dinner and then you must get good rest."

Ramiro was out to ramen and a movie with his prom date, which meant that Carlos and I had the night alone to process.

He tucked a second blanket over my feet. "First, I will make you a healthy shake. Then dinner. You do not move a muscle, sí?"

"I'm not an invalid." I appreciated his pampering, but it wasn't as if I was going to spend the next nine months on the couch.

"This is what I can do for you, my love, so please let me." He didn't blink as he beamed at me with glowing cheeks.

"Okay." I smiled wistfully. It was a lot to take in, but knowing that he would be at my side every step of the way made it easier to digest. Not that I wasn't thrilled to be pregnant. I had just convinced myself that I wasn't. To go from that to twins was a shock.

Carlos read websites about what to expect in the first trimester out loud from the kitchen. He returned shortly with a blended peanut butter and banana smoothie. "Drink this. It says you need lots of protein in these first months."

I didn't protest. The smoothie was thick and creamy with almond milk, yogurt, peanut butter, and fresh bananas.

"What about names?" Carlos called from the kitchen as he seared chicken breasts and chopped veggies.

"Too soon. Too soon," I teased. The smoothie settled my stomach and calmed my nerves. Maybe the timing was perfect. I had already made a commitment to scale back at the bakeshop. Having a baby—or two!—would force that issue. Change was coming one way or another.

By the time dinner was ready, I was famished. We enjoyed a leisurely meal together and talked through what was next. We agreed not to share the news with anyone until I was farther along and after the ultrasound had confirmed whether we were having twins or not. My eyes began to flutter shortly after I'd consumed two slices of Carlos's plum cake. I drifted off to sleep dreaming of tiny onesies, little hands, and Carlos singing sweet lullabies.

The rest of the week was relatively uneventful, thankfully so.

I finished testing the whale cake and started on one for our surprise Sunday Supper, lined up a series of interviews, and mapped out schedules for the remaining performances of *The Taming of the Shrew* at Uva. Marty and I conspired on plans for Steph and Sterling's goodbye.

By the time Sunday arrived, my jeans felt snug around my waist and my stomach was constantly rumbling, though it could have just been my imagination.

I sent Sterling and Steph to Uva at noon under the guise of helping with the matinee and sitting in on interviews for their replacements with Carlos.

"I'll start on the wontons and spring rolls," Marty said, rolling up his sleeves once they were both gone. "The buns for the sliders are already done and cooling."

"Excellent. I'll work on barbecue chicken cups and assemble the sliders," I replied, walking to the fridge for supplies.

The barbecue chicken cups would be served in puff pastry shells. I started on those first by spraying the bottom of muffin tins and cutting the buttery pastry into squares. I pressed the dough into the tins and filled them with pie weights. They would bake until they were puffy and golden.

For the filling, I shredded rotisserie chicken, added chopped green onions, cilantro, and our house-made barbecue sauce. I let that chill in the walk-in. We would fill the cups right before serving dinner.

Next, I seasoned organic ground beef with garlic, honey, ginger, and teriyaki sauce and formed the mixture into small patties. They would be grilled and then layered with thinly sliced pineapple, sautéed onions, and tomatoes.

The afternoon went by in a flash.

Rosa and Bethany pushed the tables together to create one long shared table when I went upstairs shortly after closing. We covered the table in a seafoam green cloth and decorated it with pretty shells, candles, and flowers from a Rose by Any Other Name. Marty and Andy brought up platters of Hawaiian sliders and flaky cream cheese wontons.

We hung bon voyage banners and set plush toy whales at every place setting.

Mom and the Professor arrived with Ramiro.

"This looks so festive," Mom gushed, shrugging off her lightweight coat. "Do they have any idea?"

"I hope not." I crossed my fingers. "Carlos and Lance are at Uva with them. Lance promised to text when they're on their way, so we have a heads up."

"I see someone wisely brought tissues." The Professor never missed a detail. He motioned to the boxes of tissues Bethany had placed on each end of the table.

"Yeah, I have a feeling there might be a few tears tonight," I admitted.

"Don't worry, Jules. I'm not leaving yet." Ramiro winked and wrapped his arm around me.

"That is going to require a truckload of tissues." I nudged him in the ribs. "But not so soon. We still have a few weeks with you, and I intend to follow you everywhere. How do you feel about me tagging along to prom?"

"Now, this is a full-circle moment. Juliet Montague Capshaw, you would have revolted if I'd tried to sneak into your prom." Mom gasped. "Ramiro, don't let her."

I grinned.

The Professor cleared his throat. "If I may, I think tonight's theme centers on this passage by Havelock Ellis, 'All the art of living lies in a fine mingling of letting go and holding in.'"

"Well said." I squeezed Ramiro as tight as I could. "I feel good about the holding in. The letting go, not so much."

"Indeed." The Professor let out a contented sigh. "Shall we pour a letting-go drink?"

"That sounds lovely." Mom placed her coat over her arm and moved toward the table.

My phone buzzed with a text from Lance alerting us that our guests of honor were minutes away. "Places, everyone." I flipped off the lights as we all took our seats around the shared table.

"Surprise!" we shouted in unison when Sterling and Steph strolled through the front door.

They both froze like the deer in Lithia Park.

"Bon voyage," Marty boomed.

Carlos reached for the lights, illuminating our little merry party.

"What?" Steph gaped and turned to Sterling. "Did you know about this?"

"No." Sterling shook his head, his mouth hanging open too. He pointed to his chest. "This is for us?"

"For you," I said, clutching my hands into fists to keep the tears at bay.

Rosa turned on an ocean-themed playlist. Sequoia poured drinks. Andy waved Sterling and Steph to their seats.

Steph blinked like she had something stuck in her eye. "Is this a whale cake?"

Bethany scooted her chair so close to Steph's that she was practically sitting in her lap. "Jules and I were sure that you were onto us multiple times. It's so much blue buttercream."

"I had no clue." Steph tucked her hair behind her ears and leaned closer to get a better look at our detailed work.

Marty handed Sterling the tray of sliders. "Help yourself, Chef."

Sterling threw his hand over his mouth, too overcome with emotion to speak.

"That's why I got tissues." Bethany reached past Andy to hand Sterling the box.

"This is amazing. Huge gratitude," Sterling said, once he had pulled himself together.

Mom clinked her spoon to her wineglass and stood. "I'd like to offer a toast."

I was glad she had stepped in. We hadn't coordinated a toast, and I wasn't sure I could speak without falling apart.

"When we first opened Torte's doors, it felt like a pipe dream. We joked that we would be lucky if we lasted a year. That was the prevailing advice about opening a bakery or restaurant. If you could make it a year, good—maybe you have a chance. Three years, though, that was the mark of viability. I distinctly remember Juliet sitting right over in that corner with her face covered in chocolate ganache at our three-year anniversary celebration." She pointed to the chalkboard menu. "Well, my wildest dreams have been exceeded, and that is thanks to each and every one of you seated at this table. Torte isn't a bakeshop. It's community. It's creativity. It's food. It's love. It's family. A business isn't the brick walls or the espresso machine. It's you. It's the people. And I can say unequivocally we have the *best* people."

Everyone let out a collective "aww."

"Now, I realize that tonight is bittersweet, just like Andy's dark chocolate mochas."

Andy pumped his fist. "Thanks for the shoutout, Mrs. The Professor."

Mom tipped her glass and continued. "I've come to

cherish these bittersweet moments the most, because they show our connection. How deeply we've touched and molded each other's lives. Steph's designs and Sterling's exquisite flavors and recipes will live on in these walls and in every future kitchen that is lucky enough to be graced by their presence. I cannot wait to see where this grand new adventure leads you both, and most importantly I want you to know that you always have a home and family at Torte. Cheers to you."

"Cheers." There was a mix of clapping and tears as we clinked glasses.

Lance leaned over. "Helen knows how to bring down the house."

I wiped my nose with a tissue. "Yes, she does."

The mood for the remainder of the night was more subdued than a typical Sunday Supper, but the atmosphere was festive, and I kept reminding myself that in addition to the sadness of Sterling and Steph venturing out on their own, it was also a time of celebration. Things were changing on so many levels—Torte, our family, my body.

All of it was for the better. Even the sad parts.

That was life.

Love, loss, food, family, and sharing a comforting meal around a table while raising a glass in toast to all the good things yet to come.

Sticks and Scones Recipes

Strawberry Scones

Ingredients:

2 cups all-purpose flour
¼ cup sugar, plus extra for dusting
1 tablespoon baking powder
½ teaspoon salt
½ cup (1 stick) unsalted butter, chilled and cut into small
   cubes
½ cup chopped fresh strawberries
½ cup heavy cream
1 large egg
1 teaspoon vanilla extract
2 tablespoons unsalted butter, melted

Directions:

Preheat oven to 400°F. In a large mixing bowl, whisk together the flour, ¼ cup sugar, baking powder, and salt until well combined. Add the cold cubed butter to the dry ingredients. Using a pastry cutter or your fingers, work the butter into the flour mixture until it resembles coarse crumbs. Gently fold in the chopped strawberries.

Whisk together the heavy cream, egg, and vanilla extract in a separate small bowl until smooth. Make a well in the center of the dry ingredients and pour the wet ingredients into it. Use a spatula or wooden spoon to gently mix until the dough just comes together. Place the dough on a floured surface and pat it into a circle (about 1 inch thick). Cut the circle into 8 wedges. Place the scones on a parchment-lined baking sheet. Lightly brush the tops of the scones with melted butter and sprinkle them with granulated sugar. Bake the scones for 15–18 minutes or until they are golden brown and cooked through. Serve warm.

Chocolate Tahini Cookies

Ingredients:
½ cup tahini
½ cup cocoa powder
½ cup maple syrup
1 teaspoon vanilla extract
¼ cup ground flaxseeds
1 cup almond flour
¼ teaspoon sea salt
½ teaspoon baking soda
½ cup dark chocolate chips
Sesame seeds, for coating

Directions:
Preheat oven to 350°F. Combine the tahini, cocoa powder, maple syrup, and vanilla in a mixing bowl and whisk until smooth and creamy. Add the ground flaxseeds, almond flour, sea salt, and baking soda to the mixture and stir until a thick batter forms. Fold the chocolate chips in by hand. Form the batter into 1-inch balls and then roll them in sesame seeds. Place the cookies on a parchment-lined baking sheet about 2 inches apart and flatten them with your hand. Bake for 10 minutes and allow cookies to cool slightly on a cooling rack before serving.

Huevos Rotos (Spanish Broken Eggs)

Ingredients:
Olive oil
4 Yukon Gold potatoes, peeled and diced into small cubes
2 cloves garlic, minced
1 teaspoon mixed dried herbs (Carlos uses thyme and rosemary)
Salt and pepper (to taste)
4 Spanish sausages
4 large eggs
Smoked paprika
Fresh herbs (Carlos uses chives and parsley)

Directions:
Add a couple of teaspoons of olive oil to a large skillet. Warm the pan over medium heat and add the diced potatoes. Let them cook until crisp on one side. Flip them over and cook until golden brown on all sides, about 2–3 minutes

per side. Add the garlic, herbs, salt, and pepper and cook for another minute.

Use the same skillet to cook the sausages until they're browned and cooked through, about 5–6 minutes. Remove them from the skillet and set aside. Using the same skillet again, add a little more olive oil and crack the eggs. Cook them on medium heat until they're sunny-side up, about 2 minutes.

To serve, divide the crispy potatoes among serving plates. Slice sausages and place on each portion and then carefully place an egg over the top. To finish, sprinkle the eggs with smoked paprika and chopped fresh herbs.

Pineapple Cake with Coconut Buttercream

Ingredients:
For the cake:
1 cup unsalted butter, at room temperature
1½ cups granulated sugar
4 large eggs, at room temperature
1 teaspoon vanilla extract
1 teaspoon coconut extract
2½ cups all-purpose flour
2 teaspoons baking powder
½ teaspoon salt
1 cup fresh pineapple juice
1 cup fresh pineapple chunks

For the Coconut Buttercream:
1 cup unsalted butter, at room temperature
4 cups powdered sugar
2–3 teaspoons coconut extract

For the Pineapple Compote:
2 cups fresh pineapple, diced
¼ cup granulated sugar
2 tablespoons honey
1 vanilla bean, split lengthwise

Directions:
Preheat oven to 350°F. In a mixer, cream the butter and sugar together at medium speed until light and fluffy. Add the eggs, one at a time. Then mix in the vanilla and coconut extracts. In a separate bowl, sift together the flour, baking powder, and salt. Alternate adding the dry ingredients and the fresh pineapple juice to the butter mixture. Mix until just combined. Gently fold in the diced pineapple chunks. Divide the batter evenly into two greased 9-inch round cake pans. Bake for 25–30 minutes or until a skewer intserted into the center of the cake comes out clean.

Allow the cakes to cool.

While the cakes are cooling, prepare the buttercream by beating the butter in a mixer until creamy. Gradually add the powdered sugar, 1 cup at a time, mixing well after each addition. Add the coconut extract and continue to beat until smooth and fluffy.

For the pineapple compote, combine the diced pineapple, sugar, and honey in a saucepan. Scrape the seeds from the vanilla bean into the mixture. Simmer over low heat, stirring until the mixture thickens into a sauce-like consistency. Remove the compote from the heat and let it cool. Once the cakes are completely cooled, assemble them by spreading a layer of coconut buttercream and then compote between the two cake layers. Use the remaining buttercream to frost the top and sides of the cake.

Barbecue Chicken Cups

Ingredients:
1 package of puff pastry, thawed
Baking spray
2 cups shredded rotisserie chicken
½ cup chopped green onions
¼ cup chopped cilantro
½ cup barbecue sauce (store-bought or homemade)

Directions:
Preheat oven to 400°F. Grease a muffin tray with baking spray. Roll out puff pastry on a floured surface and then cut it into 12 squares. Press the squares into the muffin tins, making sure the dough comes up the sides. Prick the bottom of each pastry with a fork. Place a piece of parchment paper or aluminum foil over each pastry cup and fill them with pie weights or dried beans. Bake the pastry cups for 10–12 minutes, or until they are lightly golden and puffy but not baked through. Remove the pie weights

and parchment and set the partially baked cups aside. Do not remove the pastries from the tin.

Combine the shredded rotisserie chicken, chopped green onions, chopped cilantro, and barbecue sauce in a large mixing bowl. Stir until everything is combined. Divide the chicken filling among the partially baked puff pastry cups. Bake for an additional 8–10 minutes until the filling is hot and the cups are dark golden brown. Remove from tin and serve warm.

Cherry Blossom Latte

Andy's latest coffee creation blends bold espresso roast with floral notes of the cherry blossoms and a touch of sweetness. As Marty said, it just may have you dreaming about a trip to Tokyo.

Ingredients:
2 shots of freshly brewed espresso
1 tablespoon vanilla syrup
½ teaspoon cherry blossom water
1 teaspoon brown sugar
½ cup oat milk
Cocoa powder, for dusting
Cherry blossom, for garnish (optional)

Directions:
In a mug, combine the espresso shots with the vanilla syrup, cherry blossom water, and brown sugar. Stir well.

Heat the oat milk in a small saucepan. Pour the hot milk over the espresso mixture and stir to combine. Top with a dusting of cocoa powder and, if it's in season, a dainty cherry blossom.

READ ON FOR A LOOK AHEAD TO
KILLING ME SOUFFLE —
THE NEXT BAKESHOP MYSTERY
FROM ELLIE ALEXANDER
AND ST. MARTIN'S PAPERBACKS!

Chapter One

They say that moving on is part of life. I knew that to be true, but it didn't mean it was easy. I had carved out a sweet and wonderful world in my hometown of Ashland, Oregon, where my days were filled with baking, laughter, family, and friends. But my little hamlet was changing, and I was changing right along with it.

I breathed in the dewy morning air as I turned onto Siskiyou Boulevard and was greeted by neat rows of antique lampposts highlighting my path. Banners for upcoming performances of *Much Ado About Nothing* and *Jane Eyre* at the Oregon Shakespeare Festival fluttered in the light breeze. I passed bungalows and historic Victorian houses with organic gardens fenced in an attempt to keep the deer from grazing on wild summer roses and leafy bunches of kale and arugula. It was a losing battle. Deer outnumbered people by an ever-growing ratio. It wasn't uncommon to watch a mother doe guide her spotted, spindly-legged babies through crosswalks or bump into herds nestled under flowering Japanese maples in Lithia Park.

Our corner of Southern Oregon might not be densely populated, but what we lacked in numbers, we made up for in creativity. Our community was thriving with artists of every type—musicians, actors, writers, dancers, painters, and some might even say bakers. In my mind, there was no question my team at our family bakeshop, Torte, were artists. What my staff could create out of layers of chocolate sponge and buttercream never ceased to amaze me.

The only problem was two of my most talented team members were departing for greener, or perhaps in this case, wetter pastures. My sous chef, Sterling, and lead cake designer, Stephanie, had been offered an incredible opportunity to manage an ailing restaurant at Whaleshead Resort in a small beach town on the stunning Oregon Coast. When they approached me about the possibility of taking the job, I encouraged them to go. Not because I wanted to lose them but because, as a professionally trained pastry chef, I knew this was the nature of our business. Much like grains of sand shifting with the tide and wind, staff often drifted from one establishment to another, picking up new skill sets and experiences and leaving behind their own flavorful footprints. Many other chefs had trained and mentored me in my journey to finding my way back to Ashland. I had made it my mission to do the same for my young staff, and now it was time for them to spread their wings and venture out into the great big restaurant world.

I was truly excited for Sterling and Steph, but I had to admit that lately, I had a propensity to break out into tears whenever I thought about how empty Torte felt without them. Of course, in all honestly, I had a tendency to break out in tears pretty much all the time at the moment—blame it on the pregnancy hormones. In a classic twist from the universe, I had learned I was pregnant with twins at the same time Sterling and Steph announced they were leaving. I suppose that's the way things are meant to ebb and flow, much like the spontaneous waterfalls that tumbled down into tiny rivers, cutting through the old-growth forests. People come. People go. Some leaving lasting imprints on our hearts and our lives.

I inhaled deeply, centering myself in the thought as I forced a hard swallow and arrived at the bakeshop. Torte sat on the corner of the plaza like a happy beacon for pastry lovers with its red and blue striped awning and large, inviting windows. The sound of the Lithia Bubblers gurgling in the center of the plaza made me smile. Later in the day tourists would crowd the infamous fountain to taste the sulfuric healing waters. Usually, they quickly regretted taking a big swig of the natural spring water, which was infused with the less-than-palatable flavor of rotten eggs.

The thought made my lips pucker. I tried to keep my breakfast down while fumbling through my pockets for the keys. I wasn't surprised by the morning sickness and roller coaster of emotions, but I hadn't expected pregnancy to leave my brain so empty. My organizational skills seemed to be shrinking as my belly expanded.

While I dug through every pocket in my bag, I admired the bakeshop's front window display. Rosa and Steph had outdone themselves once again. Colorful paper flower bunting was strung across the bright awnings. Pastel cake stands displaying an array of tiered cakes and cupcakes decorated with pale yellow, pink, and green buttercream flowers invited customers in, and whimsical battery-powered flower tea lights flickered like little fireflies.

The plaza was calm at this early hour except for a trail runner, lit up like a Christmas tree with a headlamp and reflective gear. He waved as he jogged toward Lithia Park. The day held the promise of plenty of sunshine, but my day began with the stars. Bakers' hours aren't particularly conducive to late-night partying, not that clubbing was my scene. Although, during my years running the pastry kitchen on a boutique cruise ship, the *Amour of the Seas*, my husband, Carlos, and I spent plenty of nights salsa dancing under the moonlight while cutting through calm, black waters.

When I finally retrieved the keys, I unlocked the front door and flipped on the lights. Inside, the bakeshop was equally still. I loved the quiet of being the first person to warm the ovens and start yeast rising. Torte was naturally cheery with red and teal walls, corrugated metal siding, a long espresso and pastry counter, cozy booth seating in front of the windows, and an assortment of two- and four-person tables arranged throughout the dining space. Our large chalkboard menu took up a quarter of the far fall. We offered a rotating Shakespeare quote, a tradition started by my parents, and a place for our youngest guests and burgeoning artists to connect with their inner Picasso. Today's quote read: "Summer's lease hath all too short a date."

For the moment, summer's lease felt long, but maybe that was because my ankles liked to swell at night, I had multiple new staff members to train, and I needed to pack for our weekend getaway to Whaleshead Resort. Sterling and Steph had invited us to help them celebrate the grand re-opening of SeaBreeze Bistro, and there was no chance I would miss it. I couldn't wait to see how they transformed the restaurant and the menu.

SeaBreeze had been through a variety of chefs and managers, none of whom could find a way to revive the failing venture. Whaleshead housed a collection of cabins perched atop a craggy hillside with sweeping views of the Pacific Ocean and the rocky prominences that made Southern Oregon's beaches uniquely gorgeous. Most cabins were family-owned and well-loved. The resort had a casual vibe. It was a place where friends gathered for weekend hikes through the mossy conifer forests, bonfires on the beaches, and misty walks on the shoreline searching for treasures washing ashore. Given the soggy nature of the coastal region and the fact that the area attracted hikers and backpackers, there wasn't anything fancy about the property.

SeaBreeze Bistro was hoping—or betting—Steph and Sterling could bring some fresh, young energy and new menu ideas to the restaurant. It was a huge undertaking for even the most seasoned chef. I had faith they were up to the task, though. I'd been consulting with them and was extremely impressed with their vision. They'd been logging eighteen-hour days prepping for this weekend's re-launch. In addition to giving the menu a "glow-up"—Steph's phrase, not mine—they'd gutted the dining room, giving it a fresh coat of paint and deep cleaning, and re-arranged the seating. I was tired just thinking about it.

For the moment, I needed to focus on our menu, specifically our daily specials. I did a quick walkthrough of the dining room and headed downstairs. A few years ago, we had expanded into the basement space, doubling the size of our kitchen and allowing for a bonus cozy seating area perfect for rainy afternoons curled up with a book and a cappuccino. In the process of renovations we had also unearthed a wood-fired oven, which had quickly become the centerpiece of our baking.

I brewed a pot of decaf and turned on the bread ovens. Then, I lit a bundle of cured applewood in the fireplace. While my coffee brewed, I warmed water, added sugar, and started the yeast rising. Soon, the kitchen smelled of woodsmoke, and the nutty decaf blend my head barista, Andy, had roasted especially for me. I'm not typically a decaf drinker, but pregnancy meant I had to curtail some of my caffeine consumption. He had taken me on as his "pity project," trying out a variety of decaffeinated roasts, like my current brew, aptly named Othello's Tragedy.

Andy had begun roasting on his grandmother's kitchen stove as a passion project a few years ago. He had fallen in love with the process and decided to take a break from his collegiate studies to learn everything he could about the craft. His talent was unparalleled and his beans were so popular that coffee lovers traveled to Ashland just for his roasts. We featured his custom blends at Torte and sold bags of whole beans. Demand was so high Andy was considering upgrading his equipment.

I poured a cup of the rich blend with notes of almonds, cherries, and dark chocolate and stirred in a splash of heavy cream. The coffee was layered and nuanced with a bright, fruity finish. It reminded me of biting into a chocolate-covered cherry, which gave me inspiration for a dessert. Bing cherries were in season, so I would make a layered chocolate sponge with a Bing cherry compote and chocolate whipped cream and top it with dark chocolate shavings and fresh, plump cherries.

To start I beat egg whites and vinegar in our electric mixer until they firmed into soft peaks. Then, I gradually added in sugar. Next, I sifted flour, cocoa powder, instant coffee, cornstarch, baking powder, and salt into another bowl. I whipped the egg yolks with warm water, vanilla, and oil and incorporated it with the dry ingredients. The final step was to carefully fold the egg whites into the batter to create a light and airy sponge.

By the time I had slid the tins into the oven to bake, the back door jingled, and Andy strolled in with a wide grin and a box of new coffee blends. "Morning, boss. I've got the gold here and some new decaf samples for you to try." His cheeks, sprinkled with freckles, were tanned from the summer sun.

I adjusted my ponytail and held my mug in a toast. "I'll never turn down a chance to taste any of your creations, but this one might be my favorite yet."

He scrunched his boyish face into a scowl and adjusted the box, propping it in his left arm so he could shake his finger at me. "Listen, up, Jules Capshaw, you say that every time I give you a new roast. *Literally* every time."

"And that's a bad thing?" I countered, placing my lips on the mug and intentionally savoring my next sip like it was the best thing I had ever tasted, because it was.

"It's terrible. You always tell us about how your culinary instructors and mentor chefs pushed you out of your comfort zone and gave you feedback to make your baking stronger and better. You're constantly inflating my coffee ego, and I'm worried it's going to go to my head." He flicked a strand of auburn hair from his eye and tipped his head to the side. Andy was tall and muscular from his time spent playing football at Southern Oregon University.

"First of all, that will never happen because you're one of the most humble and grounded people I know, and second of all, I'm sorry, but you've never made a bad roast. I swear to the coffee Gods and Goddesses that should you produce a blend that bombs, I will tell you." I made an "X" over my heart to prove my point.

"Fine. Whatever." He pretended to glower, but his cheeks tinged with a hint of pink at my compliment. "How's the decaf serving you? Are you enjoying Othello's Tragedy, or are you ready for something even more mouthwatering?"

"Ooohhh. What are the new roasts?" I tried to peer into the box, which was neatly packed with brown paper coffee bags, each with tasting notes marked with a black Sharpie and finished with little coffee doodles.

"Not so fast." Andy yanked the box closer to his body. "You'll have to wait and see. I've got some drink specials in mind, but I wanted to see what you're baking first." He paused and stared at the island with concern. "Unless my eyes are deceiving me, that appears to be the remnants of cherries; well, I hope it's cherries because otherwise, it looks like a murder scene."

I rested my coffee on the island and showed him my cherry-stained fingers (one of the cons of working with the juicy, tart fruit). "Guilty as charged. I'm baking a chocolate cherry torte, thanks to your delicious decaf."

"That's sick." Andy patted the box. "Great minds think alike. I had a killer idea for a summer latte this morning that should pair perfectly with your torte. Give me a few minutes to get the espresso machine fired up, and I'll be back with something for you to try."

"Great." I grinned. "I'll be ready for it because decaf doesn't count, right? I can drink it all day long."

He frowned, tugging his eyebrows together. "Uh, I don't

know about that. But I am very happy with this Swiss Water Process. It removes the nasty chemicals, so in theory, I guess you could drink it all day, but I'm pretty sure there's a limit even for decaf."

I loved that he was looking out for me. "I'm kidding."

He scowled and studied my face like he was trying to decide whether I was or wasn't kidding. "Anyway, I want to remind you that you just swore an oath you'd give me honest feedback, so I'm going to hold you to it."

I nodded as solemnly as possible while fighting back a smile. "Understood."

He went upstairs. I began mixing our sweet bread dough for cinnamon rolls and morning buns and then began assembling everything I needed for our cookie base. We made large batches of basic cookie dough each day and then added different ingredients. Today, I would stick with the cherry theme and do a cherry, vanilla, and white chocolate cookie, along with some standard favorites—double chocolate chunk, oatmeal raisin, walnut and orange spice, and classic peanut butter.

The rest of the team began trickling in. Marty, our bread baker, arrived first, followed by Bethany, Rosa, and Sequoia.

"Good morning, Jules. What a gorgeous day we're in for," Marty boomed. He was in his sixties, with white hair and a matching beard. His energy mirrored that of someone half his age. His easy-going and jovial spirit brightened the kitchen and everyone's mood. Marty had become Torte's surrogate grandfather, sharing his wisdom on scouring designs into sourdough and how to manage life's unexpected turns.

"It's going to be a scorcher," I replied with a nod as

I formed cookie balls with an ice-cream scoop and set them on parchment-lined baking sheets.

"You're going to have weather shock when you leave for the coast. I texted Sterling last night, and he said it's overcast and drizzling at Whaleshead, so be sure to pack your rain jacket." Marty washed his hands and tied on our signature fire-engine-red Torte aprons.

I loved hearing that the two former colleagues were staying in touch. Not that I was surprised. Marty and Sterling had formed a deep bond over their shared foodie obsessions and grief. Marty lost his wife a few years before he moved to Ashland, and Sterling's mom died young. Loss connected them, and the kitchen healed some of their most tender tears, as it had for me. Having lost my dad when I was in high school, I had come to learn that grief lived on inside of me, morphing and changing like a rising bread dough. Trauma had a way of transforming in the kitchen, and one of the ways I came to connect with my father was by letting him live on in what I was baking. That was the gift of food—the simple smell of his signature lemon bars would transport me back in time when we were in the kitchen together, his hands dripping with lemon juice and him offering me a mini whisk to help him bake. That was my vision for our twins. Food was Carlos' and my love language, and I wanted it to be theirs, too.

"Yeah, I heard it's supposed to be drizzly," I said to Marty, returning my thoughts to our upcoming trip. "I love that you and Sterling are texting."

"He's like a grandson to me. I couldn't be prouder of those two." Marty's smile faded. "I have to admit I'm worried about the restaurant opening."

"Why?" I scooped another ball of cookie dough.

"They're having some issues with their new manager, Erik." Marty grabbed the sourdough starter. He nurtured the starter like it was a baby animal, constantly adjusting its feeding schedule and checking its temperature. "Do you know him?"

I shook my head. "I chatted with him briefly when he hired them. He called for recommendations, and during our conversation, he mentioned the restaurant has been through three different chefs in the last year. Not a good sign, but he seemed to think the problem was with the chef's grandiose visions. The past few chefs have tried to make SeaBreeze Bistro into a fine dining establishment. That doesn't work for the beach crowd looking for comfort food and family-friendly options. He was very clear about wanting young blood, so to speak, and chefs who could re-imagine the restaurant."

"That's what I heard as well." Marty scooped flour into the industrial mixer for our rustic ciabatta. "According to Sterling, there's a lot of drama among all of the staff and even some of the guests at the resort. Erik is very demanding, and it sounds downright awful—not to Sterling and Steph, at least not yet—but to the rest of the staff. Sterling was quite upset and is worried that there's going to be backlash during opening weekend."

"Backlash? What kind of backlash?" I didn't like the sound of that. I knew that my young protégés had plenty to worry about when building a brand-new menu and giving the restaurant a facelift.

"He didn't elaborate, but he said Erik has a violent streak." Marty's eyes lost their usual merriment as he attached the dough hook to the mixer. "I'm concerned about them. I hope they're not in over their heads, and I wonder if Erik's behavior explains why the restaurant has gone through so many chefs as of late."

"Yeah, that doesn't sound good," I agreed.

"It's good you, Carlos, your mom, and Doug will be there." Marty assessed the bubble activity in the starter which we kept on the counter in order to maintain a temperature of seventy to eighty degrees. "I'm sure they'll appreciate the support. I told him that Bethany and I already had plans to go out the following week. We'll bombard them with Torte support."

Andy came downstairs with a tray of cherry lattes made with his newest roast using pineapple and brown sugar as a base. "Honest feedback only, please. This is a decaf cherry latte with a touch of rose water, almond, and dark chocolate. I think the fruity roast pulls the flavors together nicely, but hit me with your thoughts." He passed around samples.

Bethany, our cake designer and brownie baker extraordinaire, took a first big sip. "No notes. No notes." She beamed at Andy with her wide eyes and dimpled cheeks.

She and Andy had been dating, or maybe hanging out was a better description. I knew they both enjoyed each other's company, and I knew she had a massive crush on him, but I couldn't tell whether they were content with where things were or ready to get more serious. I didn't care either way, I just wanted my staff to be happy.

That went for my current and past staff. As the morning wore on, I couldn't stop thinking about Steph and

Sterling. Hopefully, things would settle down and smooth out once everyone got through the stress of opening weekend. And if worse came to worst (which, for their sakes, I hoped it didn't), they always had a place at Torte.

Chapter Two

The rest of the day was a whirlwind of activities. Replacing Sterling and Steph, who were invaluable team members, was a daunting task, but as they say, the pastries must "bake on," to borrow a page from my best friend Lance. He was the athletic director at OSF, as locals refer to the Shakespeare Fest, and a partner in our shared winery, Uva. When I had lamented to him about Steph and Sterling's impending departure, he had tapped the side of my cheek and offered me a pragmatic smile. "Chin up, darling. There are dozens of young pastry ingenues waiting in the wings for their chance to step into the spotlight and shine. Mark my words, you'll have a line around the block with budding, eager-eyed chefs begging for an opportunity to take the pastry stage the moment you list the jobs."

He was right. As soon as we posted the open roles, résumés flooded into the bakeshop. It helped that Southern Oregon University was located on the south end of town, and there were plenty of college students hungry for work and experience. Plus, the benefits of free meals during shifts and deep discounts on food and coffee were an added perk.

We had sorted through the stack of applications and landed on four new candidates. In many ways, the timing was good. My goal was to scale back once the twins arrived. Expanding our team and having ample time to train them over the summer and into the fall should put me in good shape to take extra leave and delegate some of my responsibilities.

Bethany was eager to take on more projects. She agreed to step into the role of pastry manager. She would oversee our baking efforts and to my surprise, Marty approached me about managing the kitchen. He had a breadth of experience and a centered energy that made him perfect for the job. I just hadn't expected he would be interested. When he first came to the Rogue Valley after his wife's death, he had planned on retiring but was lured back into the kitchen by the siren call of sourdough. We were all the better for it, and I was thrilled that he was willing to take the lead. Bethany and Marty would make a good team and have been with us long enough to know the bakeshop's quirks, like how the industrial mixer needed a simple hip bump to get it unstuck or why it was imperative to keep a close eye on flatbreads in the wood-fired oven, so they didn't char to a crisp.

I was feeling more solid about our plan. Marty would train our sous chefs, Bethany would supervise the new decorators and bakers, Andy and Sequoia would continue running the espresso bar, and Rosa would oversee the dining room and operations.

Our new staff had varied skill sets, and as hard as it was to swallow the reality that Sterling and Steph were gone, having fresh energy and ideas would likely breathe new life into the bakeshop. I was choosing to embrace the change. What other choice did I have?

We were closing Torte early for an initial meet-and-greet. While Carlos and I were on the coast, our new staff members would spend the weekend shadowing our seasoned employees. When I wasn't running trays of salami and roasted red pepper flatbread or slices of my chocolate cherry torte upstairs, I spent the bulk of the day preparing employment kits, schedules, and paperwork. I wanted everyone to feel welcome and have a clear idea of where to find recipes and supplies and who to ask for help.

By the time we locked the doors for the evening, I had four packets, Torte aprons, and bags of Taming of the Brew, our summer roast waiting for our arrivals. There was a buzz of nervous anticipation in the kitchen as everyone gathered around the island. Andy prepared iced coffees, and Marty had arranged a selection of small bites—herbed cheese bread, cold pasta salad with mozzarella, basil, and heirloom tomatoes, and crostini with roasted chicken, honey, and brie.

"Have you seen my special brownies yet, Jules?" Bethany asked, tugging off her apron and running her fingers through her springy curls. We originally met at Ashland's annual Chocolate Fest, where Bethany debuted her Unbeatable Brownies. Mom and I were so enamored with her baking talent and her infectious optimism that we approached her with an offer for a small percentage of ownership in the bakeshop and an opportunity to expand her brownie empire. It had been a dreamy match. In addition to baking daily brownies, she was an expert cake designer and moonlighted as a photographer—managing our social media with her beautifully stylized food pics and clever posts.

"No, I've been so busy getting everything ready. What surprises do you have in store for our new crew?" I asked, peering over her shoulder to get a better look at the island.

"Check these out." Bethany reached for a platter of brownies that she'd cut into the shape of the Torte logo—a fleur-de-lis pattern with a simple torte cake stand in the center. She had hand-piped the outline of the logo in red and blue buttercream and wrote: *Welcome Team Torte* in an elegant cursive scroll.

"These are so sweet," I said, suddenly feeling ravenous for a brownie. I'm not always great at remembering to eat—not intentionally. I love food, obviously, but during work hours, I usually have dozens of irons in the fire. Pregnancy had put an end to long stretches between meals. Carlos teased me that I was turning into a grazer. Not more than thirty minutes went by before I was desperate for a snack, and chocolate was my weak point.

"Do you want one now?" Bethany asked, handing me the plate and brushing crumbs from her T-shirt, which read: DON'T GO BACON MY HEART.

"I can wait," I lied.

She lifted the platter to display her scrumptious sweet bites. "You should probably test them to make sure they're okay."

"Am I that transparent?" I stared at the platter longingly.

"Um, well, you're looking at my brownies like you're a bookish heroine in one of my romances who's just been swept off her feet by a dashingly handsome man. Why can't the man of my dreams ogle at me with dewy eyes like that?" She pushed the plate closer.

"Hey," Andy interrupted. "Who's this man of your dreams?"

"Only about a hundred of my book crushes," Bethany shot back, tossing her hair over her shoulder and gave me a sly wink before turning her attention back to him. "If you want to keep up, you might want to read a love story or two."

"I thought that coffee was the way to your heart," he said, sounding worried and glancing at Bethany with his wide, eager blue eyes for confirmation.

"Coffee's good, sure. But, you know, give me a burly guy with a book in his hands, and I turn to pure mush." She waited for me to take a brownie and then nonchalantly put the platter back on the island. I could tell she was taking pleasure in making him sweat.

"I like to read . . . I . . . I . . . read," Andy sputtered. "Check my backpack. I'm reading about Costa Rica's history with coffee right now." He waved his arms in defense of himself. "It's a historical look at the political, economic, and social impacts of coffee on the culture. Costa Rica is on the top of my bucket list. I'm dying to go visit the coffee farms and meet with growers. The country produces some of the best coffees in the world—coffees I want to emulate here, but I'm also learning so much about sustainability and how mass producers and climate change are putting the coffee farms at risk."

"I think you're too young for a bucket list, Andrew." Marty clapped him on the back. "Now, an old guy like me, that's another story. My bucket list is practically a tome at this point."

Andy chuckled.

Bethany took out her phone and moved the plates of

food around to get a shot for social. "Coffee history is great and all, but reading a little romance never hurts." She caught my eye and wiggled her eyebrows in mischievous delight.

"Okay, give me a list. I'll do it," Andy challenged, motioning with his hands again. "Hit up with your romance recs—bring it."

"Maybe we should start a baking book club," Rosa suggested, a small smile tugging at the sides of her apple-shaped cheeks. Her dark eyes twinkled with a touch of joy. I knew she took as much pleasure in the friendly banter amongst our staff. Her naturally calming aura made her someone everyone sought out for advice. "We could match a book and a pastry every month. I think people might really enjoy that."

"Oh my God, I love that idea!" Bethany squealed. "I have the perfect book to kick it off, too. It's called *Batter of the Heart*." She scrolled through her phone to find the cover to show us. "It's a meet-cute between a young baker who is determined to save her grandmother's bakery. She clashes with a snobby pastry chef who has plans to open a French patisserie in town. But their rivalry turns into an unlikely partnership when they're forced to spend late nights in the kitchen baking for charity. Their midnight pastry sessions spark a romance and some serious heat in the kitchen. It's spicy, but not too spicy. I won't give away any more of the plot, but we could totally bake some of the recipes from the book. You're brilliant, Rosa. We have to do this, right?" Her gaze landed on me for approval.

"I absolutely love it. Mom and I have talked for years about hosting a book club, so I'm a solid yes. And just a reminder for everyone." I paused and looked around the kitchen. "You don't need my permission. You're all taking on more, which I'm so grateful for, and I'm serious about scaling back." My hand instinctively went to my stomach as I thought about how very different the future was going to look. "I want everyone to feel empowered in their roles. If you have an idea like this and the capacity to make it happen, go for it."

"So, what I'm hearing is I should book a ticket for Costa Rica?" Andy gave me a lopsided grin.

"*That* we might need to discuss more, but it's not off the table," I replied with a crooked wink. I've never had a good poker face or mastered the ability to wink. What I didn't tell Andy was Carlos and I had already been discussing the possibility of making an excursion to the coffee-growing region. One of Carlos's sous chefs from the *Amour of the Seas* recently moved back to her hometown just outside of San Jose to take over her family's coffee plantation. She invited us to come stay, tour the farm, and potentially partner on some future blends. I didn't want to get Andy's hopes up until we firmed up our plans, but his bucket list might just have an item crossed off it soon.

The conversation shifted as a knock sounded on the basement door. Marty went to let in our new staff, and within minutes, the nervous energy shifted to happy chatter and lots of hugs. I wasn't surprised, but it was lovely to see everyone connect and the instant sense of camaraderie. If day one was any indication, things were going to go smoothly.

I was excited to watch our team start to mesh and confident that our new staff members were in good hands when it came to learning the ropes at Torte. Knowing that brought me ease. Now, I could concentrate on my trip to the coast and supporting Sterling and Steph as they stepped into their next chapter.